BETRAYAL

INFIDELITY - BOOK 1

ALEATHA ROMIG

NEW YORK TIMES AND USA TODAY BESTSELLING AUTHOR
OF THE CONSEQUENCES SERIES

BETRAYAL

Book 1 of the INFIDELITY series

Published by Romig Works, LLC

2015 Edition

ISBN 13: 978-0-9863080-5-5
ISBN 10: 0986308056

Cover art: Kellie Dennis at Book Cover by Design (www.bookcoverbydesign.co.uk)
Editing: Lisa Aurello
Formatting: Angela McLaurin at Fictional Formats

This is a work of fiction. Names, characters, places, and incidents either are the product of the author's imagination or are used fictitiously, and any resemblance to any actual persons, living or dead, events, or locales is entirely coincidental.

This book is available in electronic form from most online retailers

2015 Edition License

DISCLAIMER

———•○•———

The Infidelity series contains adult content and is intended for mature audiences. While the use of overly descriptive language is infrequent, the subject matter is targeted at readers over the age of eighteen.

Infidelity is a five-book series. The series is a dark romance. Each individual book will end in a way that will hopefully make you want more.

The Infidelity series does not advocate or glorify cheating. This series is about the inner struggle of compromising your beliefs for your heart. It is about cheating on yourself, not someone else.

I hope you enjoy the epic tale of INFIDELITY!

ACKNOWLEDGMENTS

To every one of you who has purchased my books and given me the even more valuable commodity of your time, thank you! You have allowed me to share the make-believe people who wake me at night and talk to me during the day. To each one of you, I'm grateful.

I hope you enjoy the new world of Infidelity!

To my agent, Danielle Egan-Miller, my publicist, Danielle Sanchez with Inkslinger, my editor Lisa Aurello, my formatter Angela McLaurin, and my cover artist Kelly Dennis, thank you for your patience and constant encouragement and support. If it were not for each of you, the world of Nox and Charli wouldn't have come to life.

To my wonderful family, Mr. Jeff and our children, thank you for indulging my passion. I love you more than life itself.

To my author friends, I learn from you every day. Your support and encouragement is a daily blessing. This community is amazing and I'm honored to be a part of it.

To the wonderful bloggers who found me either through Tony, Victoria, or Nox, I thank each of you for every mention. I know that if it were not for you, no one would know my name.

I hope you all enjoy!

BETRAYAL

—•◦•—

Is it really cheating if you're doing it to yourself?

PROLOGUE

Present

THE GIANT OAK trees parted, giving way to the flood of sunlight. If it weren't for my sunglasses and the tinted windows, the saturation would be blinding. The effect was undoubtedly the intention of the designers and architects when they mapped out the plantation centuries ago. The shadowed lane—quiet, secluded, and draped in Spanish moss—was a prelude to the crescendo of Georgia blue sky spotlighting the splendor of the manor. Each inch up the cobblestone drive tightened the muscles in my neck and back, reminding me of the appropriate posture for a Montague.

No matter how many times I told myself that I was no longer the child trapped within the iron gates or that I was a competent woman who'd recently graduated summa cum laude, the little girl's voice inside of me repeated the mantra I've known since the beginning of time: some things never change. The closer we got to the giant house, the more I tensed, my years of separation slipping away as my confidence threatened to dissolve.

The original structure had burnt in the late 1800's. According to family lore, though it was considered stately in its heyday, by current standards the original home would barely suffice for a guesthouse. The current Montague Manor was now one of the most admired mansions in the Deep South. Where others saw beauty, I saw a prison and loss of innocence.

1

Willing my jaw to unclench, I reminded myself again that this was only a visit—temporary at that. It had been almost four years since I'd graced Montague Manor with my presence, and if it hadn't been for my mother's invitation—correction, summons—I wouldn't be here now.

"Miss Collins?"

Lost in my own thoughts and memories, I'd missed the stopping of the car and the opening of the door. Turning toward the sound of my name, I saw, framed in sunlight with his hand extended, my stepfather's driver, Brantley Peterson. The older gentleman had worked for my family for as long as I could remember. Though I barely recalled a time before my mother married Alton, I knew from stories that Brantley had been here then too. He'd worked for my father just as his father had worked for my grandfather, Charles Montague II.

"Miss Alexandria?" he said. "Your parents are waiting."

Taking a deep breath, I moved my legs outside the car, purposely avoiding his offer of help. "Just *Alex*, Brantley."

"Not forever, miss. In no time you'll have 'counselor' in front of your name." A hint of a smile emerged. The rarely visible emotion threatened to crack the façade of his aloof veneer as his cheeks rose and the deep-set wrinkles brought on by age multiplied near his gray eyes. "Your mother is very proud. She tells everyone how you were accepted to both Yale and Columbia to study law."

Rubbing my moist palms against my jeans, I looked up—and up—at the pristine walls, spotless windows, and large stately porches. In another place, another time, I would have thanked Brantley for his compliment. I may have even confessed that I was also proud of my accomplishments, but more than that, I would admit to being pleased to hear that my mother still spoke about me, acknowledged that I was her daughter.

The relentless Georgia sun upon my skin and humid air within my lungs confirmed that this wasn't another place or time. The years of Montague training suppressed any advancement I'd since made in becoming Alex Collins, a real individual with thoughts, feelings, and dreams. In merely the time it took to pick me up at the Savannah airport and drive me into the past,

I was once again, Miss Alexandria Charles Montague Collins, the flawless proper lady, pretentious to the help, and people pleaser—the well-bred Southern belle who wore the mask of perfection because no one wanted to see the truth underneath.

It didn't matter that this was the twenty-first century—not to the bluebloods. This was and would always be the world where appearances were essential. The secrets that darkened the corridors and doorways were forever left unspoken.

The movement of the curtain on the second floor caught my eye. It was so fast that I could have easily missed it. I may have, were it not for the interior location of the window: it was my old bedroom—a place I loathed more than any other.

With his stoic poise returned, Brantley asked, "Shall I take your bags to your room?"

I swallowed. "Not yet. I haven't decided if I'm staying."

"But, miss, your mother—"

I lifted my hand dismissively—something I would never have done in California. "Brantley, I'll let you know my plans once I know them. In the meantime, keep the car in the drive and leave my bags in the trunk."

Nodding, he murmured, "Yes, miss. I'll be here."

He always was.

Did that make him part of the problem or solution?

Biting the inside of my cheek, I gracefully made my way up the cement path.

Why did I come back?

CHAPTER 1

———●○●———

Six weeks earlier

"DON'T LOOK SO guilty. We deserve this!" Chelsea's hazel eyes sparkled from the glow of the setting sun. We were standing at one of the many railings along the resort edge, overlooking the Pacific Ocean.

Inhaling the salt air, I nodded. "We do. We've worked hard. I-I guess, I've never…"

"Let me help you," she said with a smirk. "You've never let yourself have fun." With more seriousness, she added, "Your grandparents left you that trust fund. Tell me, when have you *ever* used the money for anything other than education and essentials?"

I shrugged. "I'm sure if you asked my attorneys, I haven't always made the best financial decisions regarding either of those."

"To hell with them."

That was part of what I loved about Chelsea. No matter the situation, she said exactly what she thought. Granted, sometimes it was too much information, but nonetheless, you knew exactly what you were dealing with.

"Besides," she went on, "in two years the money will be all yours. You won't have to answer to some stuffed-shirt lawyer."

"Hey!"

"You know what I mean. And in *three* years you'll be someone else's lawyer. Then you can tell whomever what they can and can't do with their own money."

I scrunched my nose. "I don't know for sure, but I don't think civil law is for me. It seems boring. I want something more exciting."

My best friend's arms dramatically spread toward the horizon. "I can see it now. Some high-profile case and there you are, on the steps of a big courthouse somewhere." She spun toward me. "I know! That one on the T.V. show—*Law and Order*. It's in New York." She nudged her shoulder against mine. "The perfect place for a Columbia graduate."

I didn't want to think about law school, not yet. I'd just graduated from Stanford and the four years I'd spent in California were undoubtedly the best of my life. I loved everything about the West Coast, from the beautiful campus nestled in the Palo Alto valley to the winding beautiful coastal highway. The idea of heading back east made me physically ill.

"Stop that," Chelsea said with her hand on my arm. "Stop thinking about it. You know applying to East Coast schools made the most sense."

"I know. But I would've loved to have stayed here."

"Just like Professor Wilkerson told you, you've made your mark here. Summa cum laude. California knows you. Now it's time to make your mark back east. In three years you'll be the most sought-after attorney from coast to coast. Every big firm will want you."

"Chels, I really don't want to think about any of it. Not this week. This week is for us." I grabbed her hand and squeezed. "I don't want to think about being without you next year. I want us to have the time of our lives."

"You know I'd love to pick up and move with you. But when it comes to right now—I couldn't agree more. For this one week, let's forget about everything. Let's be the opposite of ourselves."

Let's be each other?

I stopped myself from saying the thought aloud. Instead, I looked out over the gorgeous view. The setting sun was casting shadows over the cliffs in the distance, as rolling white-capped waves crashed against the rocks and shore. This was one of the scenes I'd miss on the East Coast. There may be an ocean, but never on the beaches of Georgia had I ever seen waves or felt the refreshing breeze as I did here.

"I'm in. As a matter of fact," I whispered with a grin, "no more Alex or Alexandria. For the next week I'm Charli."

Chelsea's eyes narrowed.

"It's short for Charles, one of my middle names." I lowered my voice, but before the pounding surf and murmuring voices around us could dominate, I added, "I think Alex needs a break."

Locking our elbows, Chelsea sighed. "Girl, that's the best thing I've heard since we've met. If you ask me, Alex has needed a break for a long time!"

As we made our way to our suite, I contemplated the possibilities of leaving Alex behind, if for only a week.

Can I do that?

I could. I'd done it before.

I'd put away the pretentious snob I'd been raised to be when I left Alexandria Charles Montague Collins in Savannah. The minute I'd stepped off the airplane in California and made my way to my freshman orientation, I'd vowed that Alexandria had been left behind and I became Alex.

She was a clean slate, with no demons on her back or skeletons in her closet. I had the rare opportunity to reinvent myself into someone I liked to be, and I did.

Alex was everything I'd wanted to be growing up: a hard worker, a good student, and someone who refused to stay trapped in the cage created by the Montague name. After my mother shared a secret with me right before I left Savannah, I had the confidence to do what she was never able to do.

For that one evening, with her husband Alton out of town on business, I had a real mom. It's a night I'll never forget. She even looked different. Instead of her normal designer clothes, when she came to my room she wore shorts and a t-shirt. I hadn't known she owned regular clothes. With her hair pulled back in a ponytail and little to no makeup, she knocked on my bedroom door. The knock had been so faint that over the sound of my music, I almost didn't hear it.

For a change, the sound didn't alarm me. I knew Alton was away and I knew I'd be gone before he returned. When I peered around the door, I almost gasped. Adelaide Montague Collins Fitzgerald looked like she could have been my sister instead of my mother. With her large blue eyes, she looked at me with a mixture of love and regret. Though everything within my eighteen-year-old self wanted to tell her to leave, I couldn't.

There was something final about that night. Though neither of us came out and said it, I think she understood I didn't plan to return. I sometimes wonder just how much she knew.

Instead of saying anything, I opened the door and welcomed her into the chaos. My bed was covered in suitcases. The drawers to my dressers were in all stages of openness while my closet doors were spread wide. Not once did she use the tone I'd come to expect and admonish the disarray. Instead, she gracefully sat on the edge of my bed and asked if she could help.

Though years of secrets and regrets momentarily swirled about us, as I listened to her sincerity they disappeared. For one evening we were more than mother and daughter. We were friends. Time passed as we packed, laughed, and cried. She told me that she was proud that I was going to Stanford. It wasn't only that I'd been accepted—which was an accomplishment—but she was also proud that I was moving away. She confessed that her parents didn't want her to move away. After all, she was the last Montague. Even though she wasn't a male, continuing the bloodline was her responsibility. The way my grandparents saw it, her only purpose in higher education was to find a man worthy of fulfilling that role of husband. Of course that meant a man who understood the heritage.

That night, in my room, she did what she always did and spoke favorably of my father. She said he was a good man, a revered businessman, and a man of whom my grandfather approved. It wasn't until I was in high school that I realized she never mentioned the word *love*. Not in relation to her affection for my father or for Alton. The only time she mentioned love was to remind me that my father, Russell Collins, loved me.

For the first time I could recall, she admitted to wanting a different life. She confessed that when she was my age she wanted to leave Georgia and find a life away from Montague Manor. Holding tightly to my hands, with tears in her blue eyes, she told me to do what she couldn't. She told me to go and discover life beyond Savannah.

My entire life, I'd been told that even though the Montague assets were now handled under the name of my stepfather, Alton Fitzgerald, and my name was Collins, one day I would be expected to take my rightful place. It was what my grandmother, grandfather, and mother had told me since I was old enough to remember—I was the heir to a prestigious name. Since my father was killed in a car crash while out of town when I was only three, I couldn't remember him ever telling me about my future.

On a late August afternoon, when I stepped off the airplane in San Francisco, I chose to do what my mother never could: discover life—not Alexandria's, but Alex's. The blue sky was my encouragement. For the first time in my life, it seemed as though the clouds that loomed around Montague Manor couldn't reach me. On the West Coast I could breathe.

As if being reborn at nearly nineteen years old, I put Alexandria behind me and became Alex Collins. Since my tuition was paid by my trust fund, neither the name Montague nor Fitzgerald was associated with the new me. I suppose if someone dug into the fine print my past could be found, but no one needed to do that. My grandparents' law firm handled all my monetary needs. Even now, ascending the heights of the Del Mar Club and Spa in the glass elevator, it was only the law firm of Hamilton and Porter who knew my whereabouts. They'd been the ones to wire me the money for our excursion, not my mother or her husband.

For four years I was able to live a life free of anyone's expectations but my own. I created the perfect persona with real personal edges. I put away the ghosts from the past and discovered what life had to offer. Though Alex was different than Alexandria, I sometimes wondered if either one was really me.

Who am I?

Maybe for one week, I could live without the pressures of my old or new life. Maybe I could experience life as others did—as Chelsea did—completely untethered from the monsters of my past or the aspirations of my future. Alexandria Charles Montague Collins had a perfect façade to maintain. Alex Collins had a future and a career to build. For one week, Charli—no last name—wanted to see what life could be like without a past or a future.

"LOOK… NO, DON'T," Chelsea whispered as she covered her lips with the edge of a fashion magazine. Her sunglass-covered eyes scanned the deck around the large pool.

"How can I look and not look?" I asked playfully between sips of my strawberry-mango slushy.

"Do you see those guys over there?"

"You told me not to look," I reminded her. Yet I had seen them. It was hard—no impossible—not to look. The patrons of the exclusive resort were beautiful. After all, the resort catered to the wealthy, and those people spent a lot of money to maintain their perfection.

"Just take a quick look."

As I turned my head, I caught the stare of a man about our age. He was tan and blond and looking our direction, not even pretending to be looking elsewhere. With his sunglasses down, he peered over the frames, lifted his brows, and smiled. His closed-lip grin was both cocky and confident. My first instinct was to look down at my Kindle, but as pink filled my cheeks I remembered my mission. This was my week to *live*, to do what Alex wouldn't and Alexandria couldn't.

Lowering my sunglasses, I returned his grin.

"Oh shit," I whispered. "He's coming over here."

Nearly dropping her magazine, Chelsea sat taller in her lounge chair. "I said look, not invite him over."

I didn't have time to reply before Mr. Tanned Surfer Dude and his equally attractive friend were at the foot of our chaise lounges.

"Hey, we haven't seen you two around here before," Mr. Surfer Dude said.

"We got in last night," Chelsea replied.

Guy number two extended his hand. "Hi, I'm Shaun and this is my nosy friend, Max."

"I'm Chelsea and this…" She looked my way. "…is Charli."

Max lifted his brow. "You don't look like any Charlie I've ever met."

"It's Charli with an *i*."

He sat on the end of my chair. "Well, Charli with an *i*, would you like a drink or something?"

I turned toward my half-filled glass of slushy. "I'm good, thank you. Besides, it's not even noon. Isn't that a little early for drinks?"

Shaun laughed. "We're on vacation, and if you haven't heard, it's always five o'clock somewhere."

Chelsea swung her legs off the chair and offered her hand to Shaun. "I have heard that, and I'd love a drink."

I tried to maintain my smile as Max settled onto Chelsea's recently vacated seat. I loved Chelsea, but playing the field, and playing men for drinks and whatever else, was her specialty. Why hadn't I realized that bringing her to an exclusive resort would be like taking a child to a candy store?

"We are having a nice time. Thanks for asking," Max said with a grin.

"Oh, I'm sorry. I was just thinking about my friend. As you can see, she has a hard time making new friends."

He cocked his head to the side, his tanned torso absorbing the sunshine, and his long legs stretched out on the lounge chair. "I bet you don't have any trouble making friends either."

"I guess that only leaves one of us."

His hand flew to his chest. "You wound me! First you don't listen to a word I'm saying, and then you send me back to second grade."

"Second grade?"

"You know, when I *did* have trouble making friends."

I shook my head. "I doubt you ever had trouble. The thing is that this week is supposed to be about my friend and me. We'll be going different directions soon. I thought she might, I don't know, hang around with me for more than breakfast."

"Where are you going? Or is it her?"

"It's both of us. Tell me about you."

"Oh," Max said, "I get it. We're being secretive. My guess is there's a boyfriend…" He glanced at my hand. "…no ring. So it can't be a fiancé. But there's someone back wherever home is."

"Guess again."

"You're an aspiring actress, and this is the week before you do a big shoot."

I laughed. "Two strikes. One more and you're—"

"Out."

Max and I turned to the deep voice coming from beside Max's chair. With the sun shining directly behind him, the source of the baritone command was partially hidden by shadows. But as my gaze lingered, allowing my eyes to adjust, my breathing hitched. The man beside us was tall and tan, with broad shoulders that cast a shadow over both Max's and my legs. He wasn't as young as Max, but then again, he wasn't old. The longer we sat in stunned silence, the more visible the pulsating vein in his neck became. This man was obviously upset with Max.

When we didn't speak, he repeated, "You're out."

"Excuse me?" Max asked. "Who the hell are you?"

I lowered my glasses and continued to appreciate one of the most perfect specimens of man I'd ever seen. Small droplets of water hung from his short dark hair and glistened against the cobalt blue sky. More evidence of his recent swim coated his defined abs and his wet swim trunks clung to his thick thighs…

Everything about this man screamed confidence. Not the cocky kind I'd seen in Max. No, this man wasn't a college kid who specialized in picking up girls. This man dominated every situation. He was a man who knew what he wanted and took it.

Moving my gaze back upward, I sucked in a deep breath at the most stunning light blue eyes I'd ever seen. As if summoned by my gasp, those eyes moved from Max and unashamedly scanned me from my auburn hair and floppy hat to my brightly painted toes. The sear of his gaze peppered my skin with goose bumps and pebbled my nipples as it lingered on everything in between.

Noticing my visible reaction, the side of his scowl moved upward to a lopsided grin. And then he once again turned back to Max and his threatening yet protective tone returned.

"I'm her husband."

Though I should have argued, I was too intrigued to interrupt.

"That person you mentioned…" he paused for effect and then went on, "is me and I'm not somewhere else. I'm here. Leave my wife alone or I'll have you thrown out."

Words came to my mind, ones that could both confirm or negate the charade he was playing, but something in this man's demeanor held me mute on my chaise while simultaneously lifting me above the clouds. He obviously didn't need my help to be convincing. Besides, this week was supposed to be about exploring life and the real me. In that instant, I knew that I didn't want to do that with Max, but if given the opportunity to live out my fantasies, I was confident that the man eclipsing the sun would be perfect for the job.

Shaking his head and lifting his hands in surrender, Max stood. His silhouette dwarfed by that of *my husband's*. My insides tingled, wondering what else about this mystery man would outshine the retreating frat boy.

"Bye, Charli with an *i*," Max said, adding, "Maybe you should wear your rings?"

"Yes, *Charli*," the deep voice scolded, "don't tell me you've misplaced them again."

"No," I replied with a smirk, making my decision to play out this game. "I'm most certain they're right where I left them."

CHAPTER 2

—●○●—

Past

"SHALL WE GO check the room?" the mystery man asked, his deep voice sending more chills to my sun-kissed skin as he extended his hand.

Although the desire to take his hand and look for my nonexistent rings was growing, the part of me that I was trying to suppress came to the surface, and I shook my head. When I looked up to the way his gaze narrowed at my refusal, my heart clenched. "Why don't you have a seat…?" I pointed to the chair Chelsea and Max had both vacated. "…dear? I'm sure they're in the safe. I put them there last night." My witty response floated away with the rush of the nearby surf.

What is he thinking? Is he questioning me or admonishing me with those eyes?

Holding my breath, I hid behind my painted smile and shifted slightly in my chair, suddenly very aware of the coarseness of the beach towel below the thin material of my bathing suit. His silent glare continued as I caught the back of Max's blond head in my peripheral vision. I watched as Max approached a buxom blonde. Within seconds he was seated beside her in the pool bar. I shook my head slightly, thinking how he obviously wasn't plagued by second-grade insecurities.

Before I could divert my gaze, Mr. Deep Voice followed my line of sight. "If you'd rather be graced with *his* presence, I could go tell him that we

13

have an open marriage."

"What?" I asked, turning back toward him, my mouth agape.

"My only condition," he added with a grin, "is that I get to watch."

Crossing my arms over my too-exposed breasts, I said, "Excuse me? Who the hell—?"

The vein in his neck jumped to life as he leaned closer. "No. The appropriate reply to what I just did would be to thank me for saving you from that leech."

I opened my eyes wide before moving my sunglasses back up and laying my head upon the chair. "Thank you," I mimicked in my most snobbishly dismissive voice.

"You don't know the half of it."

"No, but I'm sure you'll tell me."

His shoulders stiffened. "No, Charli, with an *i*. Apparently I mistook you for someone who wouldn't want to be taken by one of the club whores. You see Mike, or Max, or whatever he's calling himself today, makes his way by seducing new arrivals. He and his friend pick out the new women who they believe will shower them with food, drinks, and whatever else. I've watched him work the pool decks and clubs off and on for a while now. You were about to be taken."

I wasn't sure if it was his condescending tone or arrogance at believing I would have *been taken*, but whatever it was, I was done. Straightening my neck, I said, "Well, sir, you've done your good deed for the day. Since I'm obviously not *smart* enough to spot a swindler, I better avoid all possible accomplices." I reached for my slushy. "You may go."

I lowered my eyes to the now melted drink and began to suck. With each slurp of cool strawberry and mango over my tongue, I waited for his shadow to move and my legs to once again be bathed in sunlight. By the time I reached the bottom of the glass, my heart was pounding in my chest, and my head was fighting a brain freeze, but the shadow hadn't disappeared. It'd gotten bigger as he inched closer.

Whipping my face toward his, I asked, "May I help you? Would you like a tip or something for your *kindness*?"

The annoyance I'd seen earlier was gone. The light eyes, now merely inches from my own, danced with amusement. I wasn't sure which emotion made me more uneasy.

"Something." The word rolled from his lips, deep and full of promise.

I let out an exasperated sigh. "What?"

"You asked if I wanted a tip *or something*. I want something. I want dinner, tonight. Eight o'clock in the presidential suite. Don't worry, Charli with an *i*, I'll take care of the tip."

"B-But—"

"Tell the doorman your name. He'll take you up the private elevator."

I stared incredulously, unsure what to say.

Is this guy for real? Or is this my fantasy? Charli's fantasy?

I lifted my chin. "What if you're no better than Max?"

One side of his full sensual lips quirked upward, diverting my gaze away from his chiseled jaw, the one covered with just enough beard growth to be abrasive to sensitive skin. My nipples hardened at the thought.

"I guarantee," he said, "I'm much better than Max."

Just then he turned and walked away, leaving me with a view of long, tanned legs, a tight ass covered with swim trunks, a trim waist, and broad shoulders. He wasn't overly muscular, but definitely fit. Though older than Max and Shaun, I couldn't gauge his age. By the sound of confidence in his tone and judging by our surroundings, he was successful. Hell, he'd told me to have dinner with him in the *presidential suite*. I knew how much our two-bedroom suite cost for a week. The presidential suite definitely required money.

As I continued to sit, I contemplated what had just happened or what would happen.

Am I even considering going to dinner with him in the presidential suite?

"Who was that?" Chelsea asked as she slid back into her chair, an icy pink drink in her hand.

I shook my head. "I don't know."

"You don't know? Weren't you talking to him?"

"Yes," I answered, unsure why I hadn't asked his name or why he hadn't offered.

"Max whispered something to Shaun, and he asked if he was your husband."

I started laughing. "Well, actually, he's not mine. He's Charli's."

"What?" she asked, turning toward me with a big smile. "Wow! Charli moves fast! I think it's the *i*. Women with names that end in i get to have all the fun."

"What happened with Shaun? Why aren't you two over there whispering sickening things to one another?"

Chelsea pursed her lips together. "He ordered our drinks and then asked for *our* room number. The creep was going to charge them to me!"

I smirked. Maybe the things Mr. Deep Voice said were true. "Oh Chelsea, tell me you didn't give it to him. I don't want him or Max showing up at our door."

"No." She laughed. "I've been the player too many times to be played. I gave him a sob story about my being here with my boyfriend. I said he was up in the room sleeping off too many drinks from last night, and if he saw the drinks on our tab I'd be in big trouble." She leaned closer. "I made him out to be a real badass. Shaun felt sorry for me and bought the drinks."

"Not sorry enough to stick around?"

"No! I think I scared him off. My imaginary boyfriend was going to kick his ass."

"Good riddance!"

"Yeah. Remember," Chelsea said, "this week is about us. I'm sorry I left you. From now on it's just us."

"Well, about that..." As I filled Chelsea in on what happened in her absence, she trembled with excitement.

"Oh my God! Alex—I mean, Charli—that stuff just doesn't happen to you. I mean, in all the time I've known you, you've never gone out on a date until you've had the prospective guy fill out a ten-page résumé."

I rolled my eyes. "That's not true."

"No. It's not, but seriously, I saw that guy over here. I couldn't see him that well because I was a little busy getting my drink paid for, but the parts I saw were hot! He's tall and buff. I'm sure he works out."

"The sun was in my eyes. I'm really not sure." I tried to sound unimpressed. "He could be hideous without the glare."

"Right. I'm sure. That's why you agreed to go to dinner with him, and not even in a public place but in the presidential suite!"

My stomach twisted. "Oh shit. That wasn't smart. I-I don't think I should go. And technically, I didn't agree. I didn't answer."

"What?"

"I don't even know his name. How can I go to the presidential suite if I don't even know who I'm going to see?"

"You said that he told you what to do... he said to say your name to the doorman."

I nodded as the twisting in my stomach moved lower. He had. He'd *told* me what to do. I hated to admit that it excited me more than scared me. I shouldn't like that. Alexandria knew that and so did Alex. That was why Alex was always careful about whom she dated. They were all *nice* men or boys, and all respected Alex as a classmate and friend. None of them would have *told* her where to be. They would have asked. That's what women were supposed to want.

Why then are my insides melting at the thought of Mr. Deep Voice?

"Who do you think he is?" Chelsea asked.

I lifted my shoulders. "I have no idea, but I think I want to find out."

She clapped her hands. "Oh! I love Alex, but I think that maybe even I could learn a thing or two from Charli."

"With an *i*," I added with a grin.

"DON'T LET ON that you're nervous," Chelsea said as she spun me around for the hundredth time.

"I'm not nervous. You're making me dizzy." With each turn, the skirt of the simple yet elegant blue dress billowed as it flowed from the halter bodice.

The high, wide sash accentuated my waist while the bodice dipped between my breasts. It showed enough cleavage to be sexy but not enough to be slutty. That was what Chelsea said. I pulled the material together hoping she was right.

"He saw you in a bikini. You're not showing any more in this dress. Besides, it still leaves something to the imagination."

As Chelsea continued to play with my long auburn hair, the style in the mirror began to grow on me. "I don't usually wear my hair up."

"And you don't usually meet perfect strangers for dinner and *dessert*," she added, allowing her voice to emphasize the last word.

I shook my head. "No dessert. Charli may be spending this week discovering life, but she's not spending it on her back."

"No one said you had to be on your back. Come on, there are a lot better positions than that!"

I playfully hit her shoulder. "You know what I mean. Alex still has standards."

"But this week *Charli* is taking over." She backed me toward the bed in my room. As I sat, Chelsea sat beside me and squeezed my hands. "I'm not saying to go against your moral code, but come on and live a little. Have some fun. Be daring."

"Be you?"

"Yeah," she said with a smile.

"I don't know if you've noticed, but I'm not exactly the daring kind."

"Do you want to know what I'd do?"

I shrugged my shoulder, and the long silver chain around my neck moved between my breasts sending a cool shiver down my spine. I was curious. After all, I knew what Alex would do. I knew what Alexandria had done. I wondered exactly what someone else, someone not haunted with a split personality, would do. Then again, Chelsea may not be the one to ask. She had always been more daring than, well, than anyone I'd ever known.

"First," she said, standing and strutting a circle before me. "I wouldn't let his deep, velvet, sexy voice make me all wet and weak in the knees."

"I didn't say that it did. And I never used the word *velvet*."

"You didn't have to. It's pretty obvious. I mean, I'd recommend going pantyless, but damn girl, the way you fidget when you talk about him, I'd be afraid the material of your dress would give you away."

I raised my chin. "I disagree." I sounded confident, but the memory of the beach towel forced me to face the fact—I was at the very least mildly turned on by this man.

"So you're willing to take off—"

"No! Tonight isn't going that far. My panties or lack thereof won't be a conversation topic."

"No one said anything about conversation topics," she added as she leaned against the far wall, crossed her arms over her chest and stared me up and down. "Face it. You're beautiful, and in that outfit you're stunning. Listen to me. I know you have shit you've never told me. It's none of my business. That shit is Alex's or maybe Alexandria's—I don't know. Tonight, be Charli. Be bold, be fun, and play out your fantasy.

"How often does some hot man walk into your life without any hold on your future? You're leaving for Columbia soon. You don't need this guy. Have fun with him. Hell, use him. Men have been doing it to women forever. This is our fun, no-regret week. You only get one of those in a lifetime."

I sat taller. "You still haven't said what you'd do."

"I'd find out as little as I could about him. The less you know, the less connected you'll be. I'd eat a little, drink a little too much, and I'd explore every position—except missionary—that I've ever known or he was willing to teach me."

I glanced over at the clock. "Well, if I'm really doing this, this shit is about to get real. I'm supposed to be there in less than an hour."

"The presidential suite isn't that far away." Chelsea reached for my hand. "Let's go to the bar and have a pre-mystery-date drink, a liquid boost of courage. My treat."

I wasn't much of a drinker, but if I was really going to go through with this, liquid courage sounded like a great idea. "*Your* treat?"

I loved Chelsea, but Stanford wasn't her college because she could afford it. Actually, she'd only attended there her freshman year by the grace of scholarships. That's when we met, paired together by fate. Some of her choices didn't sit well with the administration and her grades wouldn't allow her to keep her scholarships. After our freshman year, she transferred to a state college. Even though we didn't take classes together, we'd become too close to part ways. We found an apartment together, off campus.

I'd like to think that we've helped each other. My determination rubbed off and she worked hard. The fact that she still graduated in four years made me as proud of her as my own achievements did of me. We both accomplished our goal. Her degree just had a different school's name at the top.

While I was the studier, she was the survivor. She knew more about the game of people like Shaun because she did what she needed to do. And even though she was now a college graduate, extra money wasn't one of her luxuries.

"Well," she said with a wink. "I was going to sign the receipt. You did book this room in my name after all."

I stood. "I did. If Alex or Alexandria isn't who I am this week, I didn't want my name on the reservation. I mean, Charli with an *i* can't be listed on the reservation." I shrugged. "She doesn't have a last name."

"Oh! I know! We could be sisters! You can share my last name."

As I grabbed my small purse and took one last look at the creation in the mirror, I shrugged. "Our eyes are different colors. Yours are hazel and mine are some weird shade of brown."

Chelsea hugged my shoulder and looked at us in the mirror. With her head close to mine, she said, "Our hair could be the same color. I've changed mine so many times, I forget what it really is. And hazel is close to gold. That's the color I've always used to describe your eyes—golden."

"Okay, sisters it is. And if I'm not back by midnight—"

"Oh no. I'm not sending out the cavalry until tomorrow. Charli with an *i* has some life to discover. I'm not the type of sister to put her on a time clock. There's no magic pumpkin or glass slipper. Charli will be here all week. The stroke of midnight will have no bearing."

CHAPTER 3

———●○●———

Present

"ALEXANDRIA!"

Alex, *I silently corrected.*

My mother's greeting echoed through the enormous foyer as she stepped quickly from the sitting room. Her high heels clicking across the floor as she made her way toward me, arms open wide.

The brief pleasure I felt at seeing her evaporated as soon as Alton turned the corner only a few steps behind her. Of course he'd be on her heels. Heaven forbid that I'd have even a few seconds alone with my mother outside of his earshot.

"Mom," I murmured against her shoulder as she wrapped me in her arms.

Almost immediately, she stiffened and held me at arm's length. "Look at you. Are you ill? You look pale. I thought you were supposed to be resting before moving to New York. It's that horrid girl, isn't it? What does she have you doing?"

"Alexandria." Alton's icy tone sent a chill through the air.

Ignoring him, I kept my gaze focused on my mother. "I'm fine. I'm just tired, that's all. I've been flying most of the day."

"My dear, that's why you should have flown privately and not commercial, all those layovers are ridiculous. You should rest, but first we can eat. I had Martha hold dinner."

The idea of sitting in the dining room with my mother and Alton made any possible twinge of hunger evaporate. "Really, Mom, I'd like to settle whatever business you deemed so important it warranted my immediate trip to Savannah. Then I'd like to go."

"Go?" Her perfectly painted face scrunched as her eyes narrowed. I wasn't sure how many appointments she'd had with her plastic surgeon, but I wondered if her skin could be pulled any tighter. "Nonsense. Brantley! Brantley!"

"Yes, madam."

It was an amazing feat that all well-instructed house staff possessed. They could materialize out of thin air. One moment, they weren't there, and you were alone. The next, they're beside you. If they were truly well-trained and well-paid, they also had the ability to be blind and mute to their surroundings. The employees of Montague Manor were among the best-trained staff on the face of the earth.

"Where are Alexandria's bags? Have you taken them to her room?"

"Madam—"

"Mother, I asked Brantley to leave them in the car. I was hoping that we could conclude this family meeting and I could be back in the air. There's a flight scheduled—"

"Brantley," Alton's voice superseded our discussion. "Retrieve Miss Collin's bags and put them in her room. You may retire the car for the evening. We won't be leaving the property."

Though my neck straightened in defiance, my lips remained still, glued together by experience. Just like that, Alton had declared the future and sentenced me to prison behind the gates of Montague Manor.

Mother reached for Alton's hand and turned back to me. "Dear, have you said hello to your father?"

"No, my father is deceased. I hate to be the one to break the news to you."

Alton's glare narrowed while Adelaide did her best to make light of my comment. "Alexandria, you always did get cranky when you were tired. Now show Alton the respect he deserves."

If only I truly could, but I was quite certain that my mother wasn't speaking literally.

"Alton, hello. You can only imagine my disappointment when I learned that you wouldn't be out of town on one of those meetings of yours this weekend."

"And miss this family reunion? I wouldn't think of it."

My skin turned to ice as he reached out and patted my shoulder. Keeping his hand there, in a silent reminder of his dominance, he scanned me up and down. Slowly his beady eyes moved from my flat ballet-styled shoes, blue jeans, and top, to my hair pulled back in a ponytail. "Well, I'm glad you didn't accept your mother's offer of the private jet. I'm most certain they would've assumed you were the help. Then again, if you'd flown privately at least the entire world wouldn't have seen you gallivanting around airports like some common…"

Mother's glare stopped his assessment.

"Common *twenty-something*?" I asked through clenched teeth.

"Well, dear, you do look a little haggard. Why don't you go up to your room and clean up? We'll meet you in the dining room in fifteen minutes."

I turned around for Brantley, ready to tell him to forget Alton Fitzgerald's decree and take me back to the airport, but of course he had disappeared, evaporated into the mystical invisible plain. More than likely he was delivering my bags to my room. If I didn't hurry, some poor young woman on the staff would be unpacking before I ever made it up the stairs. I wondered what that same person would think of my vibrator. It was the first thought since I'd been picked up at the airport that put a smile on my face. Honestly, I didn't care if it was the talk of the kitchen. Montague Manor needed a good laugh.

"Mother, you know I'm in the middle of getting things set in New York. I have a lot that needs to be done before classes begin. I don't have time to spend wandering around Montague Manor."

She reached for my hand and led me toward the large staircase. "No one's asking you to wander, dear: straight up to your room and back down. It's been so long since you've been home. Don't forget to wear appropriate clothes for dinner." She squeezed my hand, like she was doing me a favor. "I may have done a little shopping. Besides, I'm sure the things in your suitcase are wrinkled." She kissed my cheek. "Just peek in the closet."

With each step up the stairs, I lost a piece of my life. When I'd entered the front gates I was Alex, a twenty-three-year-old college graduate. In less than ten minutes, I'd regressed to Alexandria Charles Montague Collins, a teenager caught in the tower of lies and deceit. If only the stairs went higher and higher. Instead of a teenager, I could go back further to a time of pure innocence.

How far back would I need to go?

I closed my eyes and inhaled the familiar scents. Even after four years, nothing had changed. The closed doors to unused rooms were like soldiers along the corridor, assuring that I did as I was told. They didn't need rifles upon their shoulders. The glass doorknobs that glistened from the crystal lighting were their weapons, locked portals to destitute lands.

Before the loss of innocence, I pretended that Montague Manor was truly a castle and I was the princess. It was the name my mother said my father called me, his princess. But the princess I imagined was more like the one from storybooks I was read as a child, trapped in a tower.

A memory hit, stilling my steps. I hadn't thought of it in years, but it was as vivid as if it were happening.

I was ten years old, and I'd embarrassed my mother by refusing to let a stylist cut my hair. It was the princess thing. I believed that if it grew long enough I could escape my room high in the sky. The second floor wasn't that high, but it was to a ten-year-old.

Every time she'd talk about having my hair trimmed I'd cry and stomp. Thinking she could lull me into it, she made reservations for us at an upscale spa. We had pedicures and manicures. However, it was as they moved me to a stylist's chair that I figured out their devious plan. I screamed at the stylist and my mother as I ran to the car.

Even now I remembered her ashen expression of disappointment and embarrassment. Per her usual response, I was sent to my room. It was all right: my hair would eventually get me to freedom.

That evening after Alton came home, I was summoned to the grand hall. When I arrived there was a chair. I didn't understand at first and asked where my mother was. He said she was resting, too upset over my behavior to leave her room. Then he told me to sit in the chair. One by one the entire Montague Manor staff materialized around me until the hall was full of eyes.

That was when I learned about the staff's ability to see and yet not see. That was my first lesson. He told me matter-of-factly that neither a Montague nor a Fitzgerald behaved in the manner I had. I reminded him I wasn't a Montague or a Fitzgerald. I was a Collins.

He said that my behavior was unacceptable in public or in private, and if I wanted to behave like a common street urchin, then I could look the part. It wasn't until he stood back and a man I recognized as one of the gardeners came forward with large shears that I understood what he was saying.

Alton wasn't the one who cut my hair, and the cut wasn't a trim. He and the rest of the staff watched as two other members of the grounds crew held me down and the other man cut. By the time he was done, my tears and fright had faded to whimpers and the room of eyes had disappeared, evaporated away. I was left alone with my stepfather in the grand hall in a chair surrounded by chunks of red hair.

"You will not tell your mother about this." It was the first time he told me that, but not the last.

I wondered how he thought she wouldn't know. After all, the entire staff had witnessed what had happened and with one glance she'd see that my once-long hair had been butchered. But my lesson in Fitzgerald / Montague living wasn't complete.

After Alton made me sweep the lengths of hair from the floor, he handed me off to Jane, both my nanny and friend. She was the one who read me my bedtime stories when I was little and tucked me into bed. As I aged, her role in the household morphed. Her responsibilities grew, but always she was there for me.

That evening, as she held me, she promised to make it better. She wouldn't let me look in the mirror, but I could feel it. It was almost my bedtime when Jane brought a woman to my room and explained that the woman would do the best she could to make my hair pretty. I was only ten, but I was certain that pretty wasn't possible.

With delicate scissors, the woman snipped and clipped. When she was done, it was the smile on Jane's face that gave me the courage to look at myself in the mirror. The cut was even and maybe even stylish, but it was short and I felt like a boy. It wasn't until Jane *tucked me in that I finally understood: my hair wasn't the only thing that was gone. So was any hope of escape.*

Jane explained that I'd thrown a temper tantrum about the salon. In my own rage I'd taken scissors to my long hair. I cut some places so short that the only way to fix it was to cut it all off. Though she told me the story with determination in her voice, I saw the sadness in her eyes and knew that she was telling me the story my mother would hear. And it was.

I straightened my neck, my long ponytail sliding across my back, and resumed my walk toward my room. The memory reminded my why I'd successfully avoided this house and room for nearly four years. Though my stomach turned, I was now an adult. I could make it for one night.

"Oh!" I exclaimed as I entered my room. It wasn't the sight of my canopy bed or flowered wallpaper that excited me. My heart leapt at the sight of the woman standing beside my bed. Her smooth, dark skin had a few wrinkles and her brown eyes were older, but they'd been my anchor. I'd assumed that after I left Savannah, her job would no longer exist, or Alton would find a way to get rid of her. "Jane! You're still here."

She wrapped me in the warmest hug I'd had since I arrived. "Child, of course I'm still here. Where did you think I'd go?"

When I was little, Jane seemed so old, but now I saw her as closer to my mother's age, actually younger. Memories spun through my mind like a carousel. It was everything: the bedroom, the house, and the grounds. It was the sense of imprisonment and the love of the woman squeezing my shoulders.

"I don't know." I squeezed her too. "You're the best surprise I've had since I arrived."

Her cheeks rose and a dimple appeared. "Look at you! You're all grown up." She tapped the top drawer of my bedside stand and let out a low whistle. "I'm glad I was the one who unpacked your things."

My cheeks filled with crimson. "I guess I am. Grown up *and* also glad it was you."

She spun me around. "And look at you! So pretty! You're going to be a big, fancy lawyer."

I nodded. "That's the plan."

"I've missed you."

"I've missed you, too." It was the sincerest statement I'd made since I returned.

She walked into the closet and came out with a pink sundress. "Your momma's been real excited about your visit. She's been shopping."

"Oh please, Jane. We all know my momma doesn't need a reason to shop."

Jane winked at me. "Did I hear that you're not Alexandria anymore?"

I nodded. "That's right. I'm Alex." Just saying the name gave me strength. "I'm Alex Collins."

"Well, look at you, all-grown-up Alex Collins. I know you don't need no nanny, but maybe for tonight, could you settle for an old friend? After your dinner, maybe I can come back up here and we can catch up. You can tell me all about California."

The black hole of Montague Manor evaporated. In a room I hated, I remembered how I'd survived. "Under one condition," I said with a grin.

"What would that be?" she asked with a wink.

"You sneak some mint chocolate chip ice cream up here and we find my old DVD of *A Knight's Tale*."

Jane walked to the bookcase and immediately pulled out the DVD. In a low voice she whispered, "I bought two pints! Now hurry up: the sooner that dinner's over, the sooner we can eat that ice cream and ogle at Heath Ledger."

"Thank you, Jane."

"Really? A pretty woman like you willing to spend the night with an old lady like me? I should be thanking you."

As she spoke I walked into the attached bathroom. All my toiletries from my suitcase were neatly arranged on the counter. When I looked into the mirror, the haunted girl who'd walked up the stairs was gone. In her place was Alex Collins. I splashed my face with water and let down my hair. It wasn't as red as it'd been when I was ten, but it was long and flowed over my shoulders with waves that spilled down my back. After a few swipes with the brush I said, "Okay, I'm ready to get this dog and pony show going."

Jane's smile monopolized her entire face. It was a phrase she'd used for most of my youth. She'd remind me that the Montague way of life was nothing more than show, a display for the outside world. Whenever I'd be forced to attend a public function or do something I didn't want to do, she'd make me feel better by reminding me that it was all *a dog and pony show*. It helped. I could do whatever I was supposed to do as long as I remembered who I really was. She'd tell me that pretty on the outside wasn't as important as pretty on the inside. And she'd always remind me of how beautiful she thought I was.

Her smile dimmed. "You forgot to put on that dress your momma bought."

"No," I said with the confidence I'd almost forgotten I possessed. "I didn't forget. Alexandria doesn't live here anymore."

"You're even more beautiful than I remember."

"Thank you, Jane. So are you."

CHAPTER 4

Present

THE MURMURED CONVERSATION between Alton and my mother turned to silence as I stepped into the dining room. I watched with satisfaction as red crept from the starched collar of Alton's shirt like a tide, making its way up his thick neck to the tips of his ears. Time had changed his once blonde hair to white. I fought back my smile as something about the contrast of the reddening of his skin and the white of his hair amused me. With the vein in his forehead popping to attention and his jaw clenched, he pushed back his chair. As he was about to stand, my mother reached for his hand and turned toward me. The eerie calmness of her voice threatened to transport me back in time.

Then I saw the glass of red liquid, a cabernet wine, and I gave myself permission to smile. As a child I never realized the depth of my mother's self-medication. White wine during the day and red at night: Montague Manor didn't need clocks. We could tell the time by the color of the drink in my mother's glass. Occasionally, other names were used: mimosa or sangria. It was all the same. Adelaide Fitzgerald lived her life in a blissful state of serenity because without it, she would have had to face the gruesome reality. She wasn't strong enough to do that ten years ago. She sure as hell wasn't strong enough today.

But I was.

"Alexandria, dear..." Her words never slurred. "Didn't you find the dresses I bought for you?"

"I did. Thank you." The programmed words weren't totally insincere. The dress Jane showed me was lovely—for a teenager. "It's late and I had a few text messages to answer. I know how you like to eat at precisely seven. Seeing that you held dinner for me, I didn't want to make you wait any longer."

The text part wasn't a lie either. I just hadn't responded to them yet. I wasn't sure how I wanted to answer Chelsea. I'd messaged her to let her know I'd landed. It was in response to *How are you holding up?* that rendered me at a loss for words. Since I was someone with a degree in English, words should be my forte.

"Well, it is just us tonight," she reasoned. "Tomorrow will be different."

The fork I'd just lifted grew heavy. My hand landed upon the tablecloth with an exasperated sigh. "Tomorrow? Mother, I can't stay. I have things that need to be done. I have a life."

"You're staying until after our meeting on Monday," Alton replied.

"What meeting?"

Mother pressed her lips into a disapproving straight line toward her husband. "Let's not get into all of that. We have the whole weekend before we need to worry about that."

"That *what?*" I asked again.

A young woman entered from the kitchen with a pitcher of water. Her presence left my question floating unanswered in the air.

"Water, miss?" she asked.

"Yes. I'll also have a glass of cabernet."

Her eyes widened and she turned toward Alton. Ever so slightly he nodded.

Asshole. If they planned to keep me trapped in this house for three full days, it would take more than mint chocolate chip ice cream to get me through.

"Leave the bottle," I said as she poured my glass.

The back of my throat clenched as I sipped the thick liquid. Unquestionably, the wine from the Montague wine cellar was more expensive than what I purchased at the grocery. I savored the dry cedar-wood flavor.

When I had control over my trust fund, I would consider spending more money on my wine. The taste I'd just enjoyed reminded me that it would be money well spent. As I inhaled the fine aroma, a recent memory came back and filled me with warmth.

I'd rather be drinking wine in Del Mar with him than sitting in this stuffy dining room.

"I'm not sure I approve of the way you've changed while away at school." Alton's words were as dry as the wine.

Lifting my brows, I tilted my head. "I'm not sure I approve of the way things have stayed the same here."

"Please," my mother began. "Alexandria, I'm delighted to have you home, if only for a few days. Can you please make an attempt to get along…" She took a long drink from her glass and eyed the bottle. "…for me?"

Alton poured her another glass. I sighed and began to eat my salad. It wasn't until the main course was served that I remembered our earlier discussion.

"What is happening tomorrow night?"

My mother's eyes came back to life. "Well, since it's been so long since you've been home, and we need to celebrate your graduation, I've invited a few friends over."

My stomach sank. So much for coming in and getting out of Savannah unnoticed. "A few friends?" I asked.

"Yes. It would've been bigger, but this was all done on short notice and as you know, many of our friends vacation this time of year."

"Most of the people I know work this time of year."

"Really, Alexandria?" Alton questioned. "How has your job been? Last I heard you were at an expensive spa in Southern California."

I turned his direction. "Why would you know that? Are you having me followed?"

"No." The word spewed forth as if the idea was preposterous. "Your mother is still listed on your trust. It's Ralph's job to keep us informed."

"No," I corrected. "It isn't. If that's the way Mr. Hamilton does his business, perhaps I'll move the trust elsewhere."

"If you'd read the trust, you'd understand the legalities."

"I received the trust when I was nine years old. But you're right. If I'm stuck here for three days, I'll make a trip to Hamilton and Preston and take a look at it."

"Because an *English major* will understand," Alton said, obviously demeaning my choice of study.

"More so than a child."

"Please," my mother implored. "As I said, can we talk about all of this later? Tomorrow, Alexandria, I have plans for us."

I exhaled. "What plans do we have?" It was clear my time wasn't my own.

"I thought it would be nice for us to go to the spa."

I closed my eyes, fighting the memory I'd had as I walked to my room. Careful to avoid Alton's glare, I plastered my best Montague smile on my face and said, "That sounds lovely, Mother. What time should I be ready?"

"I made our appointment for ten. Then we can go to the tearoom for lunch…"

I smiled dutifully as she went on and on about the changes that had occurred in Savannah since I'd moved. With Alton's occasional glare in my peripheral vision, I knew the truth. Nothing ever changed—not in Montague Manor and not in Savannah.

"DINNER FROM HELL IS OVER." I hit send. *"I CAN'T LEAVE UNTIL MONDAY EVENING."* I hit send again.

My phone buzzed with Chelsea's reply. *"CAN'T?"*

"I TOLD YOU. THIS PLACE IS A PRISON." I hit send.

Chelsea: "I TOLD YOU THAT YOU SHOULD HAVE TAKEN ME WITH YOU. I KICK ASS AT JAIL BREAKS!"

I laughed. Damn, I missed her. I couldn't believe we'd really be separated when I moved to New York. I only had two weeks before I needed to move. Of course, that meant that Chelsea needed a new roommate or she needed to move too when our lease was up. There was no way she could afford our apartment on her own.

"I'LL KEEP THAT INFO UNDER WRAPS!" I replied.

Every time I asked her what she was going to do, she'd tell me to take her with me to New York. She'd interviewed for a few jobs in and around San Francisco, but I was seriously beginning to think she planned to move to New York. I wanted that, but I didn't. The apartment I'd found on the Upper West Side was small with only one bedroom and cost as much as the place we had in Palo Alto.

Chelsea: "SERIOUSLY, WHAT DOES YOUR MOM WANT?"

Me: "I STILL DON'T KNOW. SOME MEETING ON MONDAY THAT SHE DOESN'T WANT TO DISCUSS. I KNOW IT'S TOO EARLY FOR IT TO GO TO ME COMPLETELY, BUT I'M THINKING IT HAS TO DO WITH THE TRUST FUND."

Chelsea: "DO YOU THINK THEY'LL SIGN IT OVER TO YOU?"

Me: "I DON'T KNOW. MAYBE THERE WAS SOME CLAUSE ABOUT GRADUATING COLLEGE THAT I DIDN'T KNOW ABOUT."

The faint knock at the door made me jump. I looked at the clock and my pulse increased. It was after nine-thirty.

"Alex, don't let the ice cream melt."

I took a deep breath. Jane. I'd forgotten about our ice cream and movie night.

Me: "I'LL KEEP YOU POSTED. TALK TO YOU LATER!"

Chelsea: "LATERS!"

Somehow I thought that salutation would be better coming from a hot billionaire than my best friend.

"I'm coming," I called as I crawled off my bed and moved toward the door.

The locking mechanism clicked when I turned the key. The old house still had skeleton keys for each room. It was how the unused rooms could be locked from the outside. The obvious problem with skeleton keys was that most every one of them was the same. It didn't take a jailer's ring to open any of the doors. All you needed was one key, unless the key was in place on the other side.

I opened the door to Jane's smiling face. Tucked in the crook of her elbow was a basket with two visible pints of ice cream, spoons, and napkins. My grin grew.

"I don't think I've eaten ice cream directly out of the carton since I was here," I said as I let her in. Turning the key and locking the door from the inside was habit that didn't even register.

"Then what have you been doing?" She narrowed her eyes. "That's why you're so skinny and me..." She pointed to her behind. "...I got cushion!"

I flopped down on the bed. "Oh, I have cushion. It's just not in the rear."

"Yes, you do! When did that happen?"

I laughed. "Sometime during my freshman year. I woke up one day and boom! There they were."

As Jane began emptying her basket, I noticed she was no longer wearing her normal slacks and blouse, but comfortable yoga pants. "Hey," I said, "I haven't had a chance to change. How about you get our movie going while I go put something better on than jeans that have been in three states today?"

"I've got it. Don't worry about the ice cream." She tried to stick a spoon into hers. "It's still hard as a rock. Some things in this old house don't work like they used to, but that walk-in freezer... it's a dinosaur... a frozen one!"

"Ice age!" I exclaimed as I pulled an old pair of running shorts from my dresser. When I stepped into the bathroom, I noticed the shower. Peeking my head back out into the bedroom, I saw Jane's *cushion* as she leaned down to put the DVD in the DVR. "Jane, I'm going to take a quick shower and rinse off today's crud."

She looked my way. "Hurry, child. Don't forget the ice cream."

"Oh, I won't."

About ten minutes later with my long hair in a towel wearing shorts and an oversized t-shirt, I opened the bathroom door. From the bathroom all I heard was the opening music to our show playing over and over. But as I stepped out, I heard Jane shutting and locking my door again.

"Did you forget something?"

Her rosy expression was gone. "No."

"What is it?"

She walked toward me and grabbed my hand. Giving it a squeeze, she said, "Nothing at all. Let's not spoil our reunion."

"Jane?"

"You had a visitor."

My heart fell to my stomach as my knees grew weak.

"See. That look there is why you don't need to know any more."

I knew whom she meant. "What did he say?"

"Said he wants you to stop upsetting Mrs. Fitzgerald."

I sighed. "God, I hate it here!"

Jane patted my arm. "I said you would probably be awhile. You were indisposed. I offered to give you the message and may have mentioned that we were planning an all-nighter—a movie marathon."

Swallowing, I nodded weakly. "Jane, tell me again."

"What, baby girl?"

"What you used to tell me."

"You're as beautiful on the inside as you are on the out." Her cheeks rose. "And, baby, with those knockers—sorry, *cushions*—you're gorgeous on the outside. Don't let anyone or anything ever make you forget that."

She took a step toward the ice cream and stopped. Turning back to me she added, "And you ain't no baby no more, Miss Alex Collins. You're a beautiful, successful adult."

"Thank you, Jane."

"Now, let's eat some ice cream, or we'll be drinking mint chocolate chip milk."

"Yuck!"

CHAPTER 5

─●─○─●─

Six weeks earlier

CHELSEA NUDGED HER elbow into my side. "It's time."

"M-Maybe." I hesitated. "Maybe this isn't a good idea."

She smiled her most encouraging smile. "Stop it. I know you can do this."

She was my biggest cheerleader. Through everything—tests, papers, late night studying, and even the occasional boyfriend—Chelsea was always there, telling me I could do it. She was truly the sister I'd never had. I sometimes wondered what it would have been like to have a sister growing up, someone to talk to—about anything. But then, I'd remember what she would have had to live through, and I wouldn't wish that on anyone.

"I'm still not sure what I'm doing."

She waved to the bartender and leaned closer. "You know those bracelets people used to wear? The ones that said WWJD—what would Jesus do?"

"Yes?" I answered suspiciously, certain that she didn't mean for that to be her advice.

"Well, pretend you're wearing one that says WWCD. Whenever Alex starts to respond or react, stop and think, what would Chelsea do?" She winked. "*Charli* would do, and then do that."

"I'm not going to sleep—"

"Of course you're not going to sleep. You'll be awake the whole time. Just be sure to come back and tell me everything!"

I shook my head. "What if—?"

"Stop. Stop overthinking this. It's dinner. That's all. We're on our *me* vacation. Have fun. Next week boring Alex can be back in your head. Let Charli have some fun."

"Boring?"

Chelsea pressed her lips together and scrunched her nose. "I didn't say that aloud, did I?"

Standing, I looked down at Chelsea's high-heeled sandals and smoothed the material of my blue dress. Shrugging I said, "Maybe I'm just getting better at mental telepathy."

"Good. That'll make it easier to know what to do." She touched her temples with the tips of her fingers. "I'll be in your head all night."

My heart beat faster with each step toward the doorman's desk.

What if my mystery man didn't think I'd follow through? What if he didn't tell the doorman? I'd look like a complete idiot—that's what would happen.

By the time I reached the counter, the palms of my hands were moist. Instead of thinking of what-ifs, I tried to concentrate on the click of my shoes against the marble floor and channel my best friend.

"May I help you?" asked the tall man with the same color jacket as all of the resort employees.

Squaring my shoulders and securing the mask of my upbringing, I replied, "Yes, I was told to tell you that my name is Charli."

His dark eyes sparkled. "Yes, Miss Charli. I'm Fredrick, and we've been awaiting your arrival."

I swallowed my apprehension. After all, this was good. Now more than Chelsea knew my whereabouts. Fredrick did too. He picked up the telephone and after a few moments said, "Yes sir, I'm escorting Miss Charli to your suite." Next he turned toward me. "Please follow me. I'll take you to the private elevator."

Slipping back into the person raised to believe that staff needed no more than to do their job, I simply nodded. It wasn't as if I still believed the Kool-Aid my grandmother had fed me, but at that moment my mind was too much awhirl with the possibility of what I might find at the end of the elevator ride. Nervousness and excitement vied with fear and anticipation.

Fredrick led me down a quiet hallway, the only sound that of my heels echoing off the paneled walls. Even though I worked to calm my breathing, as he pushed the button for the elevator, I may have jumped with the *ding* as the doors opened. This elevator wasn't as large as the ones used by the other guests nor was it glass. Instead, it was lined with the same rich paneling from the hall, and where as the others had panels of multiple buttons, here there were only two. Fredrick pushed PS.

I had the almost unstoppable urge to ask Fredrick about the man I was meeting for dinner. I wanted to ask his name, but my pride wouldn't allow it. After all, who got all dressed up and met someone in the presidential suite if they didn't know whom they were meeting?

Me.

As I realized the answer to my own question, I lifted the corner of my lips. I was really doing this—well, Charli was.

The doors opened, not to a hallway, but to a foyer, large and light. I couldn't help but look around as I stepped onto the white tile. In the center of the room was a large round table with an enormous arrangement of fresh flowers. The sweet aroma saturated the glass room. Through the skylight I noticed the darkening sky. Then my attention went to one of the glass walls. Through it was a spectacular view of the setting sun over the ocean.

"Miss Charli," a woman's voice brought my attention back to present. I turned toward the petite, older woman. Since she wasn't wearing the resort's signature navy jacket, I didn't think she worked for the resort.

"Yes, hello," I offered with as much confidence as I could muster.

Her cheeks rose as her brow lengthened. I still didn't know who she was, but I got the distinct impression that she was assessing whether or not I should be allowed any farther into the suite.

"I was told to come here for dinner," I said, afraid that the words emerged as more of a question than a statement.

"Of course." Her expression relaxed. "I believe your arrival is anticipated on the patio. It's such a lovely night. It was requested that dinner be served outside. Let me show you the way."

I breathed a sigh of relief as I returned her smile. Though I'd hoped that someone would mention the name of the man awaiting my arrival, no one did. It was as if everyone knew not to say it in front of me.

I'd tried to recall exactly what he'd looked and sounded like earlier that day. But with each passing hour, the recollections became embellished in my mind. I recalled the sun behind his head now as a radiating glow. His voice, deep and stirring, rolled like thunder in my memory, fluttering my tummy while melting my insides. His chest wasn't just muscular, it was sculpted, and I no longer just remembered the sight of his dark hair and slight facial stubble. Now my skin tingled at the thought of its touch—so real, as if I'd felt it against the most sensitive of my parts.

When I stepped past the woman and exited the glass doors, my breathing hitched.

I hadn't embellished, not really. With the orange glow of the setting sun sending prisms dancing off the waves below, the man casually leaning against the rail was everything I'd imagined and more. Despite the ocean breeze, his casual stance, the way one hand lingered in the pocket of his pants while the other held tightly to a tall fluted glass of light-colored liquid, filled me with warmth.

I was glad that Chelsea had talked me into wearing a dress *and* that I'd insisted on wearing panties. As he righted himself, the light gray suit coat he wore moved effortlessly, accentuating his shoulders and forming a V to his trim waist. If I'd thought he was handsome in his swim trunks, he was even better in a silk suit. The white shirt he wore was unbuttoned at the neck and his strong jaw was covered with just a hint of stubble. Whoever this man was, he wore the combination of casual and class with ease.

I remained still as his grin grew and he scanned me from the top of my head to the tips of my toes. Just like earlier at the pool, the gaze of his light blue eyes burned my skin, sending a rush of heat and leaving goose bumps in its wake. I found myself lost in the paleness of his eyes. Like pools of liquid, I imagined drowning in their depths, and then they settled on mine.

"Welcome, Charli with an *i*. I'm very glad you accepted my invitation." Flutters like butterfly wings filled my tummy as I searched the horizon for clouds of an impending storm. There were none. It was him. His voice *did* roll like the low rumble of thunder.

I continued to remind myself to do as Chelsea would do. With all the issues that girl had in her life, lack of confidence was never one of them. As he closed the distance between us, I stood as tall and resolute as I could, diligently fighting the urge to look away.

When we were merely inches apart, I replied, "It wouldn't be very nice of me to refuse my *husband*." My cheeks flushed at the sound of my own words. Although I hadn't meant them the way they sounded, I saw in his microexpression that he heard the alternative meaning.

"That's good to know," he said with a grin.

Damn, maybe I am channeling Chelsea.

I closed my lips to stop the explanation from spilling out while trying to maintain my air of composure. Looking past his handsome face, I nodded toward the ocean, as the sun sunk closer to the horizon.

"This is an absolutely stunning view."

"Yes, Charli. I couldn't agree more."

I turned back to him, but his eyes weren't on the setting sun. They were on me.

"I wondered if you could be as beautiful as you were this morning, wearing more than you had at the pool." He cocked his head to the side. "I no longer need to wonder."

Blood filled my cheeks, but before I could respond, the woman who'd met me at the elevator came out onto the patio pushing a cart. When I turned her direction, she was taking the cart toward a small table with two chairs. It was off to the side, in an area with a glass partition that blocked the sea's breeze. The small table was covered in white linen and in the center was a flickering flame within a glass globe.

"Would you like to have a seat?" he asked, reaching for my elbow and leading me toward the table.

I almost jumped at the touch of his warm skin against mine. Electricity like I'd never felt surged through my veins, setting off detonations at each synapse. My eyes snapped to his, and for just a moment, I believed he felt the same thing, but just as quickly, his expression returned to its casual, confident demeanor.

"Yes," I said, trying also to ignore the chemistry that threatened to knock me off my feet. "Thank you. You didn't need to go to all this trouble."

He laughed. "It wasn't me. It was all Mrs. Witt. She was happy when she learned that I wasn't dining alone."

My knees bent as he helped me with my chair. I turned toward Mrs. Witt. "Thank you. It's lovely."

"I can't take credit for the cooking. It all came from the dining room. However, I did choose the menu," she said confidently. "I do hope you enjoy seafood."

"I do."

My mystery man began to pour a light-colored wine into my glass. It was then I noticed the bucket with ice beside the table and the private pool on the other side of the partition.

"It's a chardonnay." He lowered his voice. "I know we're in California, but I'm partial to this label. It's from the Burgundy region of France. Just don't tell anyone I'm not supporting local wineries."

"I promise," I said, leaning forward. "Your secret is safe with me."

I saw his gaze lower toward my breasts. But instead of calling him out or covering myself, I remembered my invisible bracelet and sat tall, leaving the V of my dress in full view. I'd never been a fan of my breasts. For most of my teenage years they didn't exist. And then one day, my B-cups overflowed. I truly don't know what happened—genetics or hormones. Whatever it was, my B's became D's. I didn't know what to do with them and complained that they made me look heavy. Again, it was Chelsea who told me to embrace them. She promised that the doors my education and intelligence didn't open would be flung open by my girls standing proudly at attention on my chest.

I lifted the glass and took a sip of the wine. The flavor was crisper than other chardonnays I'd had. "I like it," I exclaimed. "It's crisp, not as sweet as others."

His pale eyes relaxed. "I knew *my wife* would have a discerning palate, or is it your tongue?"

While I struggled with the appropriate response, Mrs. Witt came back, filling the silence and leaving me with my mystery man's suggestive smile. She placed a tray of cheese, olives, and crackers on the table and just as quickly disappeared, leaving us alone.

"Thank you, again," I said, "for saving me from Max."

"So that's what he's calling himself this week."

I motioned around the patio. "Is this what you do? You save women from the resort leeches and lure them to your lair?"

"My lair? Am I Batman?"

"Are you? I don't know."

He smirked. "If only I could make a living at doing just that, but alas, no. You're my first rescue."

I stopped my reach for a piece of cheese and looked back up at him. "Your first?"

"My first *rescue*," he clarified. "Hardly my *first*."

"Why?"

He lifted his glass toward me in a toast. After I lifted mine, he said, "To you, Charli with an *i*, and to learning more about you."

After our glasses clinked and we both took a sip, I asked the question that I'd been dying to know ever since our morning encounter. "You seem to have a clear advantage. You know my name, but I've yet to learn yours."

"Do I?"

"Do you what?"

"Do I have an advantage?" He leaned closer. "Do I know your name? You see, I had the resort's reservations scoured. I wanted to send a gift to your room and confirm our dinner, yet Charli was nowhere to be found."

I took a deep breath. "Well, I'm here with my sister. I guess my name isn't on the reservation."

"Your sister?"

"Yes, and you? If I were to have the reservations scoured?"

The sun had now fully set, falling below the water and the darkening sky was beginning to fill with stars, especially over the water.

"Would you believe, Batman?" When I didn't respond, he said, "Bruce Wayne?"

Though I pursed my lips, I felt the twinkle in my eyes.

"Since I suppose you could have the reservations scoured, you'd have the advantage of being able to zero in on this suite."

Why hadn't I thought of that?

"But I'll save you the trouble." He lifted his right hand over the table. As I reached to take it, he turned mine and lightly brushed his lips over my knuckles filling me again with warmth. "Let me introduce myself. Charli, I'm Nox."

"Knox?" I repeated his name, more like a question. "Like Fort Knox?"

"In some ways, but without the K. I do however have a thing for locks and security."

Retrieving my hand and allowing his name to roll through the corridors of my mind, a smile graced my lips. His name was perfect—unique and powerful—like the man seated across from me.

He went on, "Tell me something about you. How did your parents come up with the name Charli. Surely they knew what a beautiful *girl* they'd had."

I shrugged. "If you're asking if they wanted a boy, I can answer unequivocally yes. However, Charli is short for Charles, my grandfather's name."

Nox grinned. "Well, the name Charli is as lovely as you."

Mrs. Witt returned with salads and our conversation waned. It wasn't awkward silence, but comforting in a way. We knew very little about one another, but what little we knew surrounded us like the glass partition, protecting us from whatever lurked beyond.

"Nox, what do you do?" I smirked. "Besides rescuing women? Oh, and wearing a cape?"

"Like I said, you're my first rescue, and I reserve my cape for at least the third date."

So this is a date.

"I run businesses," he said between bites.

"Businesses?" Maybe the presidential suite wasn't indicative of *his* wealth. Maybe he was there on the company's money.

"Yes. It's really not that exciting. I travel a lot. That's how I knew that Max and his friend were up to no good. I've stayed in Del Mar on numerous occasions."

"I'd like to think that I would've seen through him, but I still appreciate your rescue."

"I'm sure you would have. Maybe I stepped in for selfish reasons?"

"Selfish?"

"Well, yes. I enjoy having you indebted to me."

I raised my eyebrows. "Indebted? Tell me, Nox, what else do you enjoy?"

The glint in his eyes spoke volumes, but instead of answering, he asked, "Was that your sister? The blonde who went off with Max's friend?"

"Yes, and believe it or not, he tried to get her to pay for his drink."

Nox's brow arched in triumph.

"Yes," I admitted. "You were obviously right. However, she did see through him."

"Then perhaps my intervention was unnecessary."

I shrugged. "If you hadn't rescued me, I wouldn't be here right now."

It was Nox's turn to shrug. "I assure you, that even before Max's clumsy attempt to play you, you had my attention this morning. That doesn't happen often. I also assure you, if I wanted you to be here, with or without my intervention, you would be."

"Only if you broke that rule about your cape," I said, trying for some levity.

"No," he answered, with all seriousness. "I don't break rules, and I don't appreciate it when others do either."

I was afraid to look down, fearful that my increased heart rate was made visible by the bouncing of the silver chain between my breasts. "Why, Nox, you seem rather confident of yourself."

"Yes, Charli, I am."

I reached for my wine and worked to steady my pulse. I shouldn't be here. Nox was the type of man I purposely avoided at Stanford. The campus was full of them: strong secure men, men who knew what they wanted and took it. There was something in their demeanor that frightened me. It wasn't their need for power or control. I had that too. In the right situation I was confident and driven. No. The reason I avoided them was because of what was happening to me on the patio of the presidential suite of the Del Mar. With each of Nox's words or phrases, my insides tightened to the point of pain.

Stupidly, the pain itself didn't frighten me. What scared me was that an undeniable part of me liked it. It was the part of me I'd suppressed as Alex. The energy Nox radiated electrified me, bringing to life a forbidden desire that I didn't want to acknowledge.

Successful women stood on courthouse steps and spoke with poise and determination. They studied hard, worked tirelessly, and made a name for themselves. Alex Collins didn't need a Mrs. in front of her name or a man standing beside her. She had a future built on her own blood, sweat, and tears.

She shouldn't be a woman who melted at the sound of a deep voice. A successful woman didn't go to dinner with a stranger just because he told her to. Nor did they dampen their panties at the mere suggestion of what else he may tell her to do.

Panic boiled deep inside of me, erasing Nox's words. For a moment I was a voyeur watching the scene as a silent movie. With the faint lighting highlighting the railing, the illumination of the pool, and the glow of the candle, I saw the movement of his lush full lips, but I couldn't hear the words. My attention was focused on the small shadows that chased across his high cheekbones and in the hollows of his eyes.

Nox reached across the table as my name echoed through the salty air.

"Charli? Charli?" The name was spoken each time louder than the one before. "Are you feeling ill?"

"What?" I shook my head. Perspiration dripped between my breasts as a chill settled over me. "I-I'm sorry. I don't know..." I didn't know how to finish the sentence. Four years in one of the most acclaimed colleges and suddenly I was inarticulate.

"Give me your hand."

Mindlessly, I obeyed.

"Let's go inside. Maybe it's the chill."

I stood, allowing Nox to guide me back into the suite. With only the slight pressure of his large hand in the small of my back I became his puppet.

"B-But our dinner?"

"Don't worry. Mrs. Witt will bring it inside. If you're feeling up to it, we can finish it in here."

Hugging my midsection and calming the thoughts in my head, I nodded.

Once we were inside, Nox removed his suit coat and placed it over my shoulders. The intoxicating scent of cologne filled my senses. I wondered how I hadn't noticed it outside. It must have been the breeze. With the soft satin covering my shoulders, I was enveloped in a woodsy scented cloud. Nox led me to a sofa near the windows while Mrs. Witt set our dinner on a dining room table.

His blue eyes swirled with gray and navy, like the clouds to his rumbling voice. "What happened?"

I lowered my chin, unable to answer, not because I couldn't speak, but because I didn't know.

His grin returned, if only tentatively. "Your coloring is better. How do you feel?"

I nodded. "Better. I really don't know what happened. I-I don't want to admit that I'm nervous."

Nox's confident tone was back. "Nervous? Surely, Charli, you're accustomed to the attentions of men."

I shrugged. "I-I'm not." I looked up at his scrutinizing stare. "I mean, it's not like this is my *first* either. It's that I've been busy with school and, well, I haven't dated in awhile."

"School?"

"Yes, I recently graduated."

"Tell me that you mean from *college*," he demanded.

I couldn't help the smile. Did I look that young? "Yes. I promise I'm of legal consent."

"I didn't doubt that." His tone rose and he squeezed my knee. "Now, what it is that you're willing to consent to… that's what has piqued my interest."

"Nox, this week is supposed to be my—well, our, my and Chelsea's—*discover life* week. Discover and enjoy but take no souvenirs. I have a lot happening in the future."

"Charli, I may have called you my wife at the pool, but rest assured, that's not what I'm looking for. Simply put, I find you attractive—striking really. You're well-spoken and witty. I like that. Believe me, when I decide a woman is mine, I hold on tight. But if we set the ground rules of going into this next week with no expectations for more, I can do that."

I thought about his proposal as we moved to the table. Though the seared shrimp smelled delicious, I moved it around my plate more than I ate.

"Again with the rules?"

His forehead wrinkled. "Do you have a problem with following rules?"

"As long as they're plainly stated, I suppose not." Truthfully, I was too good at it. That was one of the things Chelsea has tried over the years to rectify. Live, be spontaneous, she'd say. "Take college for example…" I tried to steer the conversation away from the obvious.

We talked about my major. At first I told him it was quantum physics. After all, he'd said I was well-spoken. However, it didn't take long before I admitted the truth. I'd majored in English with a dual minor in business and political science.

"Those future plans don't include law school, do they?"

"Nox, I-I…"

"Yes, Charli, seeing as I still don't know your last name, I'm going to assume that discovering life means some questions are off-limits. I can follow rules too, but I prefer to make them."

I smiled. "Do you have a last name?"

"Doesn't everyone?"

"Touché."

With our meals as done as they were to be, Nox lifted up a new bottle of wine. "Shall we toast to a week of first names?"

I offered my glass. "I'd like that."

His brow twitched. "I'll add to that, a week of finding out what else you like and the *boundaries to your limits*."

I almost choked on my wine as he added that final statement, but it was too late. As the crisp liquid flowed, I drank to his exploration of my limits.

"Are you up for going back outside? The view is why I stay here."

I shifted to stand. The lighting within the suite was much brighter than what we'd had on the patio. With his drink in his right hand, he offered me his left, and I saw it—my limit.

Suddenly the handsome, powerful man in front of me was no better than every other man, no better than Alton Fitzgerald and all of his business trips.

My neck straightened. "I've changed my mind."

"What?" Nox asked, visibly surprised.

I pulled my eyes from his left hand. "I forgot. I promised Chelsea that I'd be back to our room tonight. This week is about us. It really isn't fair of me to leave her alone."

"I saw your sister. I doubt she's alone."

Though Nox tried again for my hand, I pulled it away, busy with removing his jacket from my shoulders. Shoving what undoubtedly was a very expensive suit coat his direction, I reached for my handbag.

"Goodbye, Nox. It was nice to meet you. I'm sorry, but I do know my limits and I've already, albeit unknowingly, broken a hard one." I hurried toward the elevator. "Please don't attempt to contact me."

As the elevator doors opened, I turned to see not only Nox's puzzled expression but also Mrs. Witt's. With my lips pressed together in disgust, not only at them, but also at myself, I stepped into the elevator and waited for the door to shut. When it did, I exhaled and tried to comprehend how either of them would assume that I'd be comfortable with this circumstance.

I didn't care how good looking or charismatic Mr. Nox—no last name— was. I didn't see married men. The tan line on his fourth finger was too prominent to be anything but recent.

CHAPTER 6

Past

"MISS CHARLI?" FREDRICK asked with concern in his voice as I rushed from the private hallway. "Is everything all right?"

All right? No!

I took a deep breath. If I couldn't stop whatever game Nox was playing from getting to me, I sure as hell could stop from showing it to others. Pausing only briefly, I replied, "Thank you, Fredrick. I'm not feeling well."

"May I help you? Do you need assistance getting to your room?"

"No, I just need to lie down."

"Really, Miss Charli, I don't mind. I'm sure your host wouldn't want anything to happen to you."

My host. I wasn't born yesterday. Maybe I was being paranoid, but I believed as soon as Fredrick escorted me to my room, he'd report my room number directly to Nox.

"No, thank you." I began to walk away. "That won't be necessary. I'm sure your resort is safe enough for a woman to walk unescorted."

"Yes," he admitted coming out from behind his stand. "It is. However, if you need anything…" He handed me a card. "…you can call me direct."

I took his card and dropped it in my purse. "I'll be sure to do that. Good night, Fredrick."

I hurried away and toward the guest elevators. As I waited for the elevator, my chin dropped to my chest, and I tried to stop the memories of our evening from replaying in my head.

Anger, shame, disgust—all of it swirled like a cyclone.

I was not only furious with *him* but also disappointed in myself. Then again, I tried to reason, we hadn't done anything, not really. We'd talked and eaten dinner. Yes, I'd had some wine, but there was no touching. Well, he'd kissed my hand and helped me into the suite, but nothing overtly intimate.

It was still wrong.

I did my best to ignore the other resort guests passing by me. It didn't matter what I told myself, how I tried to justify it, I was appalled with Nox *and* with myself. I lifted my unseeing eyes and faced the truth; this was exactly what I deserved for going on a mystery date. I may never have made my prospective dates fill out a ten-page résumé, as Chelsea had joked, but at least I knew their names and marital status before I agreed to go out with them.

I could justify my situation as all Nox's fault, but if I did, it made me the victim. I wasn't a victim. I refused to be one. I'd been there and done that. Alex Collins was not a victim. I'd made the decision to meet Nox for dinner, me and no one else. He wasn't to blame for my decision.

When the doors of the elevator finally opened, a happy couple stepped from the elevator. If I hadn't noticed the way they looked at me, I wouldn't have even realized I wore a scowl.

Stupid, naïve people.

Happiness in another person wasn't real. All people did was betray one another: if not on the first date, then eventually. Look at Alton and Adelaide. They were supposed to be my example of love, of a healthy relationship. Hell no! They were dysfunctional on more levels than I cared to admit. Alex Collins was better off without someone. Just because continuing the Montague bloodline had been pounded into my being, since I was old enough to understand, didn't mean that I intended to do it. There was nothing Nox or any other man could do for me that I couldn't do for myself. This was the twenty-first century. I didn't even need a man, if and when I wanted to continue that bloodline. That's what sperm banks were for.

Riding up to our floor, my neck straightened with determination. *I'm Alex Collins and I have a future and plans.*

Shit!

I stepped from the elevator onto the multicolored carpet. Each slap of my shoes more determined than the last. The last thing a future hotshot attorney needed was an affair scandal in her closet of skeletons. How dare he lure me in? So what if he had a sexy voice and even sexier eyes. Who cared if he had a body like a Greek god? Not me. None of it mattered because that pale line on the fourth finger of his left hand told me all I needed to know.

Nox was a filthy cheater. Just like Alton and just like seventy percent of the married men out there. Well, I shrugged, as I dug in my handbag for the key to my suite, I actually made up that statistic. It was probably higher. Once I was out of this damn dress, I would Google that shit. Maybe civil law wouldn't be so boring. If there were that many cheating assholes out there, I could have a rosy future as a divorce attorney.

My lips snaked upward into a smile. This night had just been a learning experience, something to point me in the right direction. Tapping my keycard on the lock, I opened the door to our dark suite and stood silently for a moment, suddenly concerned I was walking in on something, or more precisely, Chelsea and someone. Instead, I was greeted by more silence.

The curtains were open. Without turning on the lights, I made my way to the balcony and opened the glass door. The mild air fluttered the hem of my dress, and I wrapped my arms around my waist remembering the softness of Nox's jacket as it blocked the chill. In the darkness the rush of the surf created a low rumble. Our view might not be as spectacular as the one from the presidential suite, but it was nice. As I kicked off Chelsea's high heels, I suppressed the emotions that threatened to bubble to the surface. Nox wasn't worth my anger or my tears. I wouldn't give him any more of either.

By the time room service finally answered my call, I had my silver necklace and earrings lying in a pile on the desk. "Hello, this is Al—this is Charli Moore. I'd like to order a glass—no a bottle—of your house red." I didn't wait for him to figure the total. "Charge it to my room and if you have it here in less than ten minutes, I'll double your tip."

Hanging up the phone, I pulled the blue dress over my head. I had wine coming and I planned to enjoy it. Some rotten cheater wasn't going to ruin my second night of vacation. No, I was going to make a night of it. Before sitting alone on the balcony and listening to the ocean, I would soak in a nice, warm bubble bath.

"I can do this," I said aloud to no one. "I don't need Nox." I worked to remove the bobby pins from my hair. "I don't even need Chelsea." I raked my fingers through the red-brown waves. "Pretty soon I'll be living alone in New York." I nodded to myself in the mirror. "And I'm nearly twenty-four years old. It's about time I get used to spending some time alone."

Realizing that I was carrying on an audible conversation with myself, I stepped from the bathroom and took another look around the suite. It was one thing to talk aloud to myself. It was another to have anyone hear me. Maybe I'd get a cat when I moved to New York. Then talking aloud wouldn't be considered crazy.

I read the different bottles of bubbles, oils, and salts while warm water filled the tub. As I tried to decide which one to use, which fragrance I'd choose to replace the lingering memory of Nox's cologne, I washed the makeup from my face. It was ridiculous that I was so nervous about our dinner. He didn't deserve the time I'd spent in his suite or the time I spent getting ready for it.

With each passing second my indignation grew.

I turned off the running water in the tub as a knock echoed throughout the suite. Wrapping the white satin Del Mar robe around my body, I walked barefoot toward the door. In a few minutes I'd have wine and a nice bath filled with bubbles. Who needed anything more?

Looking through the peephole, I saw the customary navy jacket on the young man through the lens. His face was slightly distorted with the dome of the glass, but I could see him plain enough. Had it been less than ten minutes? I wasn't sure. Hell, I'd go ahead and double his tip. He'd made it before my tub got cold. Besides the way this week was working out, I would probably become very acquainted with the room service staff. It was best to keep myself in their good graces.

I opened the door, but before the waiter could speak, my eyes went to the man standing off to the side, the one with the pale blue eyes I wanted to forget. Regret and sorrow morphed into hunger as Nox scanned my new attire. Although the robe was long, nearly to the floor, the rich satin did little to hide my body's reaction to his gaze.

I crossed my arms over my traitorous nipples. "What are you doing here? How did you find me?"

"May I come in?" The low thunder rumbled my insides.

"No," I answered too quickly, suddenly conscious of my lack of clothing beneath the robe. Even the loss of the high heels put me at a marked disadvantage. The man with the ravenous stare towered over me, taller than only an hour before.

"Miss Moore?" the young man in the navy jacket asked. "Would you like me to bring your wine into your suite?"

"I hope you don't mind," Nox said. "I may have changed your order—a little."

"Yes," I said louder than I intended. "I do mind." Turning toward the waiter I mellowed my tone. "Please go back to the kitchen. Bring me the house red and if you can manage to return alone, I'll triple your tip."

Still wearing the suit from our dinner, minus the jacket I'd thrown at him, Nox grinned as he pulled a money clip from the front pocket of his gray trousers. Without speaking, he peeled back a few bills. I tried not to look, but saw that each one was a hundred.

"Here you go," he said, offering the cash to the waiter. "The lady will be fine with the wine you currently have on your cart. Take it into her suite."

I pressed my lips together and moved aside to allow the waiter entrance.

As he moved the small linen-covered cart, he smiled bashfully. "Miss Moore, would you like me to open the bottle of Screaming Eagle Cabernet Sauvignon?" His smile grew as he proclaimed, "It's our finest wine."

"It's from Napa Valley," Nox whispered, leaning close to my ear, sending warm breaths over my neck.

"Yes, sir," the waiter replied. "We only serve California wines at Del Mar."

I shook my head. "No, thank you, just leave the opener and I can take care of it."

"Yes, miss. Thank you. If you need anything else…"

"That'll be all," Nox answered. "We'll call if we do."

The waiter nodded and disappeared down the hallway. Reaching for the door, I cocked my head to the side. "You're rather confident for a man who's still standing in the hallway."

"I am." His blue eyes shone with newfound determination. "However, you're right about my location, very astute of you. I'd much prefer to be in there." He nodded toward me.

Thankfully, there wasn't anyone else in the hall. "Nox, I don't see married men."

"Mrs. Witt was right. Would you allow me to explain, inside your room?"

I swallowed as he inched closer, his eyes never leaving mine as the intoxicating, woodsy scent filled my senses. I tried to stay focused. "No. That won't be necessary. It's very simple."

"Charli, it isn't as simple as you think. I don't usually ask the same question twice, but for you, I'll make an exception. May I come in and explain?"

He took another step my direction. If I remained still, we'd be close enough to touch. Unwilling to allow the contact, I took a step back. "Fine," I snapped, waving my arm in a grand gesture, "make it quick. Apparently I have some expensive wine to drink."

"The best California red Del Mar has to offer," he said with a smirk as he entered.

I didn't move farther into the suite or invite him to sit. Instead, I tugged on the lapels of my robe and said, "You have thirty seconds. Explain."

Nox's neck straightened as his shoulders broadened before me and the seams of his shirt pulled against the strain. His head moved slowly from side to side as he searched for the right words. "I also don't take orders well, but once again, I'll make an exception."

"Then you must be a great employee. I'm surprised your bosses allow you to stay in such expensive suites."

"My bosses?"

"You said you run businesses. They must belong to someone."

"Yes, you're right. They do."

I waved my hand in the air. "You know what? I don't care. I don't care if you take orders. I don't care if you repeat yourself, and I don't care whom you work for. Your time is almost up."

"I'm not married."

My jaw tightened. "I don't see married men *and* I detest liars."

He took another step towards me. "Charli Moore, I also don't explain myself... to anyone. I want you to listen and listen closely." He seized my shoulders. Before I could protest he continued, "I'm not married. I was. I won't elaborate any more than that. You're right that I took the ring off recently. I took it off for you—for our dinner. I didn't take it off because I'm cheating on someone. I took it off so that you wouldn't get the wrong impression."

With my face tilted toward his, I stared at his mouth and listened to his words. When he paused, I said, "I-I don't understand."

The lips I'd been watching forcibly captured mine, pulling me upward, closer to his mouth, his chest, and to him. Nox reached for the back of my neck, his fingers lacing through my long hair, holding me captive as his other arm wrapped around my waist. My hands flew to his chest as a moan escaped my lips and fire surged through me. The electricity of his earlier touch was but a spark to the wildfire that was growing inside of me. If I fought his actions, I couldn't remember.

Beneath the palms of my hands, I felt the erratic beat of his heart. He felt the same attraction that I did. The magnetic pull was too hard to resist. Finally, I pushed against his chest, needing air and space. "Nox..."

"I'm no longer married. I swear."

I stared up at his handsome face, and sucking my bruised lips between my teeth, I searched for any sign of deceit. I barely knew this man, yet, the way my body melted against his, I wanted to know him. I wanted to believe him.

When I didn't respond, he asked, "Do you believe me?"

"I want to," I answered honestly.

He caressed my cheek, the softness of his touch a stark contrast to the fervency of his kiss. "I had no idea what happened—why you left. You were there with me, and then you were gone."

I shook my head, trying to recall his words. "You said 'Mrs. Witt was right.' What did you mean by that?"

"She said that something upset you and asked me what I'd done."

"I thought you didn't answer to people?"

"Mrs. Witt isn't people. She's also not my boss."

I smiled. "I didn't think she was, but she is *someone*?"

"She is."

"But you won't tell me?" I asked. When he didn't answer, I tried another question. "How did you find me?"

He tugged my hand and pulled me toward the sofa. As we sat, he said, "You mentioned your sister's name was Chelsea and that your reservation was under her name."

His recollection of my dishonesty reminded me that I didn't deserve to know any more about him. "Nox, we said one week, with no commitment. If you swear that you're not married, if I can trust that, then I don't need to know any more."

I melted toward his lips as they again captured mine. With my chest against his, the soft fabric of the robe did little to hide my sensitive nipples.

His gaze dropped to where our bodies touched and his smile grew. "I swear." The thunder of his tone pulled me toward him as he teased the neckline of my robe. "Charli..." He lifted the end of my hair. "...you were stunning tonight at dinner. But now, here..." He caressed my cheek. "...is the beautiful woman I saw at the pool. I'd like to do all I can to learn more about you and those limits we discussed. If I only have a week, I don't want to waste any more time."

Mutely, I nodded.

"Besides not seeing married men, tell me your hard limits."

"I-I don't know," I answered truthfully.

CHAPTER 7

—•O•—

Present

"MRS. FITZGERALD, WOULD you like a glass of wine?"

"Mimosas, for me and my daughter."

"Right away, ma'am."

Mother and I settled into large comfortable chairs as we lowered our feet into the warm bubbling baths. From the reception we'd received, it was obvious that every employee of the private spa knew my mother, the great Adelaide Montague Fitzgerald.

"Darling," she said, with just the right amount of Southern twang, "please watch what you say, especially around Alton. Dear, you know how busy he is. He doesn't deal well with petty comments."

Copper filled my mouth as my teeth increased the pressure upon my tongue. I'd promised Jane that this visit would come and go without incident. I promised for her, not my mother and most definitely not Alton. I had missed Jane more than I'd realized. If I could manage to lower the tension level, perhaps I could arrange to visit more often, especially if I could schedule it when Alton was away on one of his trips.

The idea of having Jane and my mother to myself helped me ignore my mother's glowing endorsement of her husband. With a smile plastered on my lips, I replied, "I would like this to be a stress-free visit. I just wish you'd tell me why I'm here."

She patted my hand. "To see your family, dear."

I nodded at the young man who delivered our drinks. "I saw you in California, at my graduation."

"But that's not the same as being *home*." Her blue eyes turned toward me. For as long as I could remember, I knew my mother was the master of disguise, yet looking at her now, I saw a change. She was still attractive, but at one time, her eyes had danced with passion. I remembered a time when she was happy. She used to adore the arts and worked tirelessly with the Savannah Museum of Art. Her work was solely volunteer, because Montague women didn't need to work. Adelaide did it because she wanted to, because she enjoyed it. But then, as time passed, she had other duties, ones that were higher profile, ones that required more and more of her time. She said she wanted to do them—organize fundraisers and meet with Alton's clients and colleagues. It may not have been as noticeable when I saw her daily, but now after being away, I saw that the passion she'd once possessed was gone.

That wasn't to say that my mother wasn't still beautiful. She was, like a flawless caricature, from her slender figure to her unwrinkled face and brown hair. While I blamed Alton for her lifeless eyes, my mother was the one who allowed it to happen. She was the one who smiled on his arm while he introduced her to his mistresses. Not that he was ever bold enough to give them that title in Adelaide's presence. After all, she would always be his connection to the Montague name and fortune. No, he'd introduce them as his *assistant*, his *representative*, or maybe, as the *wife of his dear friend*.

While his exploits weren't limited to the women whom my mother knew, she never appeared unhappy. It went against her upbringing. A wife's duty was to support her husband, no matter his faults.

"Montague Manor is your home, and I think you should consider returning."

I bristled at the thought. "Momma, I have three years of law school ahead of me. I'll be in New York."

"I'm so proud of your accomplishments. You know that, I hope."

"Yes."

"Columbia is very prestigious. But you could change your mind and attend Savannah Law School or maybe Emory. That's only in Atlanta."

What? Savannah instead of Columbia? Does she think it's that simple, like changing a restaurant reservation?

I shook my head in disbelief. "Do you even hear yourself?" I kept my voice hushed. "Columbia will open doors."

She pressed her lips together and looked about. No one was near and if anyone was listening, they were polite enough not to be obvious. "Your name opens doors, Alexandria. This law dream is nice, but why? What's the point?"

My spine stiffened and jaw clenched. "Point? I don't know. Maybe the point is to be an attorney."

"You went off and had your fun in California. I wanted you to do that. I never had that chance. Now you're home. Savannah is where you belong. Continuing the Montague name is your destiny, not working in some dingy courtroom." She drained her glass of champagne with a touch of orange juice and motioned for another. "I see nothing wrong with you completing the degree, even the Georgia bar, if you want; however, it's really unnecessary. A Montague woman does not need to work.

"I'd hoped that while you were gone you'd meet someone. Then again," she added with a smile, "perhaps it's better that you didn't."

I couldn't keep up. First, my own mother thought my postgraduate work was frivolous and then she was talking about suitors. Momentarily, my thoughts went from Adelaide's preposterous dialogue to Nox. I hadn't spoken to him since Del Mar, even though he'd broken our rule and given me the means. Though I'd considered it, I hadn't broken the rule by doing it.

"Who said I didn't."

Mother motioned again for another mimosa. "What, dear?"

"Who said I didn't meet anyone?"

"Well, you never said you did." Her lifeless eyes opened wider. "Did you?"

"What does it matter? You seem to have my life planned."

"No, not planned. I just think it's time that you thought about your options. You know, the Spencers will be at our gathering tonight."

The heat of the footbath was lost as my internal temperature rose. Bryce Spencer—Edward was his actual first name, but many of us in the South had multiple names, and he'd always gone by his middle name, Bryce—was two years older than me and the son of my mother's closest friend, Suzanna Carmichael Spencer. They'd been friends since they were babies.

Another annoying trait of life in the circles of Savannah was that no one ever got out and rarely did anyone new get in. This place was like a spinning vortex sucking select people in and gluing them in the position where they were born. As I looked at my mother, I thought about how it also sucked the life right out of them.

I hadn't seen Edward Bryce Spencer since the day before I left for Stanford.

"Why, why would you invite them?" I asked.

"Well, Suzanna is still my closest friend. She's your godmother and she wants to see you."

I exhaled. "Suzanna was furious when I left for Stanford. Why would she want to see me?"

"Because you're back, dear. Did you know," she asked with more excitement than I'd heard in awhile, "that Bryce recently graduated from Booth? He has his MBA and has started working at Montague."

The mimosa churned in my stomach. Of course he was working at Montague. One of Bryce's many faults was that he worshipped the ground Alton walked upon. He always had, and strangely enough, Alton had always been attentive to him. I always assumed it was because my mom encouraged it. She was never able to give Alton a son, and Bryce didn't have a father.

Suzanna's husband left her when Bryce was young. No doubt, he couldn't take the pressure of marrying into the Carmichael name. It was never as prestigious as Montague, but at one time it was close. His departure was quite the scandal for our small-town aristocrats.

I didn't know any of that until I was older. I just knew that Miss Suzanna, Bryce's mother, and my mother were often together, which meant Bryce and I were together. We were friends, almost like siblings, until one day we weren't.

"I didn't know that," I answered honestly.

"I thought you two stayed in touch."

"No, we haven't. I stopped answering, and he stopped calling." I didn't know for sure if that were true. I stopped answering and I couldn't see if he called or not. Chelsea had encouraged me to block his calls and texts and change my privacy settings on Facebook. She helped me see that I couldn't reinvent myself into Alex with Alexandria's unofficial fiancé suffocating me.

"Hmm. That's funny," my mother murmured.

"Why? Why is it funny?"

Our stylists appeared and sat at stools near our feet. I knew protocol. I knew our conversation was essentially on hold. Nevertheless, I pushed one more time. "Why?"

"He knows all about you."

As our stylists began to work, my mind slipped back to when I was fourteen and Bryce was sixteen. We'd been close all our lives, and he told me he noticed a change in me. He was right. Carrying the Montague mask was wearing me down. He made a point of spending more time with me.

His advances started innocently enough, but each one made me more and more uncomfortable. Where once we'd held hands as friends, as his intentions became clearer, everything felt different. When I told my best friend, Millie Ashmore, that Bryce Spencer had tried to kiss me, instead of supporting me, she told me I was lucky, and she was jealous. It was then I realized how the other girls at the academy looked at him. The next time he tried, I let him. It was like kissing a brother I never had.

Bryce wasn't satisfied with a kiss. He wanted more. When I was fifteen, I purposely allowed my mother to see the two of us together. I'd managed to keep Bryce's attentions to kissing and light petting, but each day was a struggle. I figured if my mother saw us, she'd tell him to stop. She'd tell me to stop. I don't know what I thought, that maybe she'd be a mother.

She didn't do any of what I expected. Instead, she smiled and walked away. Later she came to me and told me how happy she and Miss Suzanna were. Even though Bryce was only a junior at the academy, I swear my mother and Miss Suzanna began making wedding plans. Not literally, but they'd make comments about a Montague and Carmichael heir.

When Bryce graduated from the academy he chose to go to Duke, even though he'd been accepted to Princeton. Duke was closer. For two years he drove back and forth to Savannah for every academy dance or family obligation. It wasn't that I asked him; he just did. I couldn't have dated anyone else even if I'd wanted to. Everyone in Savannah knew I was Bryce Spencer's girlfriend.

When it was my turn to apply for colleges, Bryce pressured me to apply to Duke. I did, and I was accepted. I'll never forget the day I told him I was moving to California. He lost it. I'd never seen him like that. It was a full-blown Alton rage, complete with red cheeks and screaming. According to him I'd ruined everything. He'd planned on proposing once we were together at Duke. He even had the ring.

For the first time, my childhood friend and first boyfriend scared me. I ran to my room and locked the door. The next day he arrived with flowers, to celebrate my acceptance to Stanford, he told my mother. Later he apologized and made me promise that we would stay in touch.

I promised, but we didn't.

How then does he know all about me?

WHILE WE RODE in the backseat and Brantley drove us toward lunch, my mother fingered one of my long auburn curls, making it spring against my shoulder. "Your hair looks lovely. This is so much more becoming than the dreadful way you pull it back. Look how it frames your face."

I refrained from shaking my head as I gave her a closed-lip smile. Sadly, I believed she thought she'd just complimented me. I'd agreed to the pedicure, manicure, and hairstyle. I drew the line at having my makeup done. It was only lunchtime. I didn't need to be painted to perfection for the tearoom.

"You'll look stunning tonight at your welcome-home party."

"Welcome home? I thought you said this was to celebrate my graduation?"

"It's one and the same, don't you agree?"

No. I don't agree.

"Who else have you invited to this celebration?"

"Oh," she said, dismissively waving her hand, "a few people. Of course I invited Millie Ashmore and her parents. She can't wait to see you. I'm sure you know she's engaged to that young man she met at Emory. His last name is Peterson. I really don't know much about his family. They're in the wine business. I believe that's what I've heard."

I clenched my teeth tighter. This was going to be hell.

"Your aunt and uncle will be there," she continued.

While Millie and I had at one time been best friends, our story didn't end as happily as momma and Miss Suzanna's. I had limits. *Hard limits.* The thought of my hard limits brought a much-needed smile to my face.

"I knew you'd be happy to see them," she said, misconstruing my expression. "They were disappointed that they couldn't attend your graduation."

I could argue that Gwendolyn and Preston Richardson weren't my aunt and uncle, that Gwendolyn was Alton's sister and therefore not related to me, but if I did, it would be a petty comment like my mother had asked me not to make. So instead, I just thought it.

"I'm sure they were. Will Patrick be there?" If Gwen and Preston were my aunt and uncle, then their son Patrick would be my cousin. He was the one Fitzgerald I actually liked. We'd spent many days and nights calling bullshit on our parents' messed-up code of social status.

"No. You know that he's living in New York now."

"I didn't," I said, genuinely interested. "Where? What's he doing? It'll be good to have him close."

"Close?"

"To me, Mother. Close to me. I have a small apartment on the Upper West Side, close to the university."

"You've already rented an apartment?"

Is she serious?

"Mother, classes start in a few weeks. Of course I have an apartment."

"But you still have an apartment in California and classes don't begin until September."

"Orientation begins in August and July is almost over. I know I still have an apartment in California. That's why I don't have time for this." I motioned around the backseat, my gaze catching Brantley's in the rearview mirror. His narrowed eyes reminded me to watch what I said around my mother. I could hear his unspoken warning: don't upset Mrs. Fitzgerald. I took a deep breath. "It is why I need to leave as soon as our meeting is done on Monday. I have a lot of packing and shipping to do."

Brantley pulled up to the front of the Gryphon Tearoom. As he got out to open Mother's door, she said, "Let's take this one day at a time, shall we? We need to discuss this with Alton."

I was living in a time warp. That was the only plausible explanation I could come up with. Nothing ever changed in Savannah or around Montague Manor. It never would.

Adelaide lowered her voice as we walked toward the entrance. "Of course, I would've much rather had high tea at the Ballastone, but as you know that isn't until four o'clock and with our guests arriving as early as six-thirty, we just couldn't." She reached for my hand. "But once you're home, we can do that. I remember how much you used to enjoy dressing up for high tea with your grandmother."

When I was four.

Monday could not come soon enough.

CHAPTER 8

---•O•---

Present

I HEARD THE voices from the grand hall as Jane entered my room. As soon as she closed the door they disappeared. If only she could make them really disappear. I exhaled and sat on the edge of my bed.

"What's the matter, child?" Her dark eyes sparkled. "I mean *madam counselor.*"

I squeezed Jane's hand as she sat beside me. "I'm sorry I didn't keep in touch with you. I think I wanted—"

"Don't you fret. I know what you wanted. You wanted to have a new life away from all of the Montague stuff. I'm part of that *stuff.*" She rolled her head around in a circle, gesturing with the last word.

"The best part of it."

"Your momma's down there telling everyone you'll be down in a minute. It's been more than a minute and you ain't there."

I scrunched my nose. "Do you think they'll notice if I don't show up?"

"And miss out on showing all them uptight stuffed shirts what a beautiful and successful woman Alex Collins has become? Oh no! You're going to walk down there with your head held high."

My cheeks blushed as I remembered someone else telling me the same thing. I hated how Nox kept finding his way into my thoughts. Chelsea had

65

said to have fun, not get close, and use him, like men used women all the time. I tried, and I did. But I didn't. Even though I'd left him in Del Mar, he was constantly on my mind.

How is he? Who is he really, his real name? Who does he work for? Where does he live?

"...done invited half of Georgia!"

My attention went back to Jane's words. "What? Momma said a few people."

"Well, chi—Alex, if thirty-six, no, thirty-seven people is *a few*, then that's what she did."

I exhaled and lay back on the bed. "Why?"

Jane pulled my hand to make me sit up. "Don't you go messing that beautiful hair. It's so pretty and long and look at these curls."

Pride at her encouragement was momentarily overshadowed by the memory of when my hair wasn't long and pretty.

Jane pulled me close and wrapped her arms around me. "Don't," she said. "Don't you let those shadows back in your eyes. You keep them out where they belong. You stand proud and show all of them what a Montague woman can be."

"Collins," I corrected.

She released me, and her grin was back. "That's my girl, Miss Alex Collins, and look at this dress. You'll be the center of attention down there."

I let out a long breath. "I guess it's time."

"It sure is. Let's get this dog and—"

"Pony show underway," I said, finishing her sentence. I went to the full-length mirror and did one last appraisal, pressing down the taffeta of my light blue dress.

Light blue... like eyes.

"You know," I commented, "if I really were Alex and not Alexandria, I wouldn't look like I just stepped out of *Steel Magnolias*."

"You ain't wearing no hat or white gloves. You look like a formal Alex."

"Then why do I feel like Alexandria?"

"Because Alexandria's a fine woman, too. It don't matter what you call yourself. It matters what's inside. You have a heart in there, one that knows what's right and what's wrong. That's why one day you're gonna make a great, powerful lawyer… maybe even a judge! Justice Collins."

My smile faded. "Momma doesn't want me to practice law."

Confusion clouded Jane's expression. "What? Not Mrs. Fitzgerald. No, you misunderstood her. She's been telling everyone who'll listen about you and what you doing."

"I don't think I misunderstood her, but that's nice to hear."

"Now git! Or that pony show will start without you."

I nodded. *Let the show begin.*

Heads turned as I made my way down the winding staircase. There had to be at least ten people in the grand hall not including staff. With each step down, I saw more people in the front sitting room and more in the parlor. Keeping my smile plastered on my lips, I nodded and responded appropriately as each person welcomed me. "Alexandria, look how you've grown." "Alexandria, it's so nice to have you home." "Congratulations, dear, on doing so well in college." The front door continued to open allowing gusts of humid Georgia air to permeate the entrance as more and more people arrived.

The entire time, I searched the crowd for my mother. *Where is she? She's the reason I'm here.*

"Alexandria!"

The muscles in my neck tightened as I turned toward my one-time best friend. She bobbed with excitement as her blonde hair, piled in some kind of curly bun, bounced and more curls fluttered around her perfect porcelain face. This was a world of smoke and mirrors. Everyone appeared ideal on the outside, but it was only an illusion.

"Millie."

My neck stiffened and eyes rolled as she hugged me. With the eye roll, I caught the smirk of the tall, lanky man beside her. As soon as she released me, I offered my hand his way. "Hello, I'm Alex," I said, fighting the urge to add *andria*. "You must be Millie's fiancé?"

He shook my hand. "Yes, Ian. Ian Peterson."

Millie thrust her left hand into my line of sight. The diamond was, well, a diamond on prongs. "Isn't it wonderful?" she asked. "We're so happy!"

"Yes, wonderful. Congratulations."

"Ian has one more year of graduate school at Emory. So we set the date for next June, right after his graduation."

"What about you, Millie?" I asked. "Are you going on to graduate school?"

She suddenly looked as if she'd eaten something sour. "Of course not. I have a wedding to plan."

My plastered smile became increasingly thin. "I can see where that would take all your time."

"Oh, you have no idea." She leaned closer. "You don't, do you? Last I heard you weren't dating anyone."

"I'm so glad my dating status is a matter of conversation."

"Well, it wasn't—really. It just came up when I was having lunch with Leslie and Jess. Jess said you never change your status on Facebook."

Leslie and Jess were girls we'd gone to school with. At one time we were all part of the same crowd.

I shrugged. "Some of us are too busy dating to update our status."

"Oh! Does that mean you *are* in a relationship?" The idea of having fresh gossip had her practically foaming at the mouth.

"It means it's no one's business but my own. I know from experience what can happen when others get involved." I nodded toward Ian. "It was nice to meet you. Welcome to Savannah." And I turned to walk away.

"Alexandria," Millie called.

I exhaled as I spun back around. "Yes?"

"Since you're home, you should have lunch with Jess, Leslie, and me. I know they're coming tonight, but we need some girl time. You all have a shower to plan."

There were more incorrect statements in her two sentences than I cared to clarify. "That sounds amazing." This time I successfully walked away.

I finally found my mother in the parlor, a glass of white wine in her hand. I had to check my watch. Surely it was time for red. Hell, I was considering some of Alton's Cognac. It was then I noticed Alton and the man he was talking to. They were laughing and patting one another on the shoulder—a refined pissing contest. Whichever man's hand was higher was the alpha. I almost giggled as each pat moved increasingly higher. Pretty soon they'd be bopping each other on the back of the head.

"Mother," I whispered in her ear. "Is that Senator Higgins?"

"Yes, dear."

"Why is Senator Higgins at my party?" Remembering not to upset Adelaide, I refrained from labeling it graduation or welcome home.

"Well, you see, he's working with Alton on a few things, things that will help Montague."

The Montagues originally made their fortune in tobacco. Investments had diversified; however, tobacco was still a big piece of the pie. Taxes and other legal restraints on the cancer-inducing crop were always a battle.

I shook my head. "Well, it's nice that we can get some bonus points with the senator at *my* party."

"It's quite an honor." She stood taller. "How many of your friends have a senator at their party?"

"Gosh, Mom, I'm not sure. I'll look into that." I turned to walk away and murmured, "Right after I update my Facebook status."

As I entered the sitting room, I caught a glimpse of Bryce at the far end of the room. Since he seemed occupied, talking with a man I didn't know, I took a glass of wine from one of the caterers and turned. Being the guest of honor, I'd undoubtedly need to talk to him eventually, but I could delay that reunion as long as possible.

"Welcome home."

Shit! I should have gone toward Bryce.

"Suzanna," I tried for my most confident tone. "It's nice to see you."

"And you."

"How are you these days?"

"Disappointed."

My attempt at friendly small talk was shot to hell. *Do I bite, or do I smile and walk away?* I tilted my head and gave her my most sympathetic sigh. "I'm sorry to hear that. I hope things get better."

"I have every reason to believe they will."

"That's great." —

Her tone lowered. "Don't do it again."

I straightened my neck. "Excuse me, don't do what?"

"You know very well what I'm talking about. Don't break his heart."

"Suzanna, I haven't seen or spoken to your—"

"I'm well aware of your lack of communication. But now that you're home and he's working for Montague—"

Interrupting her, I spoke in a hushed whisper. "I'm not home. I'm here for a visit. I will be leaving for law school in a matter of—"

A large hand landed on my shoulder as his voice whispered menacingly between Suzanna and me. "I hope *we're* having a nice time at your party, Alexandria."

My skin crawled at his touch. Stepping forward I turned toward my stepfather. "*We're* just having a private discussion."

Suzanna stood mute as I faced Alton.

"Don't embarrass me or your mother. Perhaps private discussions would be better held in private."

I returned my smile to my lips. To an outsider, I was having a nice conversation with Alton. "Perhaps if you were concerned about my embarrassing you, you should have thrown *my* party without me."

"Alexandria, there are plans in the works. You don't want to be the catalyst that changes them."

"Someone needs to tell me what's going on. I can't support or change plans that I know nothing about."

Alton reached for my arm, his grip tighter than it appeared. "Come with me."

I planted my feet into the lush carpet, willing my heels to grow roots. "Unhand me this instant," I said through gritted teeth, "or I promise you the biggest scene you've ever witnessed." Red seeped from the collar of his shirt turning his neck crimson. Before it reached his face I added, "I'm sure the senator and some of your other cohorts would love to see *your daughter* lose her shit."

He released my arm and leaned closer. "In my office in five minutes." With that he turned and walked toward Bryce and the other man.

Suzanna's eyes were wide as she stared at me. Instead of responding, I shook my head. The waiter was back with the tray of goblets of wine and I reached out and stopped him. Tipping my glass back, I emptied it, placed it on the tray, and took another. With a boost of liquid confidence, I turned back to Bryce's mother. "It was a pleasure." I allowed my usually-suppressed accent to grow thicker. "Let's do lunch, shall we?"

I turned before she could reply.

As I resumed my duties as guest of honor, I fell into a nice conversation with one of my mother's friends about Stanford. I hadn't realized that she too was an alumna. It was so nice talking about the campus and hearing her memories that I lost track of time. Maybe it wasn't that I lost track. Maybe it was my coping mechanism, the way I survived. I blocked out my confrontations with Alton like others blocked out a bad day at work. Once it was over, I put it aside. It didn't do any good to dwell or recount it. Years of medicine for anxiety taught me that. I had forgotten all about my summons to his office until my mother appeared at my side.

"Excuse us, Betty." My mother turned toward me. "Dear, we need you for a few minutes." Speaking to both of us, she added, "It won't take long."

"What is this about?"

"I should have told you this afternoon. It was just that we were having such a lovely time. I—" She stopped talking as we came to the closed door. Then, before opening it, she said, "Please, Alexandria, don't say anything rash."

My step stuttered as she opened the door and three sets of eyes turned our direction.

CHAPTER 9

Six weeks earlier

DARKNESS DANCED IN the paleness of Nox's gaze. "You don't know your hard limits?"

I shook my head. "I-I've been very focused on school. I told you I just graduated. I really haven't..." I lowered my chin. It wasn't that I was a virgin. I wasn't. But everything in my life as Alex had been sweet and overtly planned. Limits weren't an issue. If I were to be completely honest, everything in Alex's sex life had been boring. That was probably why I rarely dated. On the few occasions when I did become intimate, it was usually anticlimactic, in all meanings of the word. My vibrator and I had a better time than I did with the few men I'd known in college.

Chelsea said I overthought it and needed to put myself out more. I worried about the long-term consequences of following her advice. I suspected that many of my classmates would go on to impressive careers. The idea of running into one of them—a one-night stand—in a courtroom one day didn't sit well with my long-term career goals. I was safer with my vibrator. It had no aspirations for the judicial system.

"You've had sex, haven't you?" Nox asked.

"Yes," I replied indignantly.

"So you know what you like? Right?" He was still looking at me

72

with wide eyes.

I stood and wrapped my arms around my midsection. "Nox, I don't think I know you well enough to have this conversation."

Immediately, he was off the sofa and pulling me close. "You will."

A shiver shuddered through me as his words rumbled from his chest to mine. His response was not only a promise, but also a threat. By the way my pulse skyrocketed, I was certain that the threat part intrigued me more than the promise.

"B-But we said one week. That's it. That means no delving into one another's lives."

He lifted my chin. "Charli, it's not your *life* I want to delve into."

Oh shit!

My cheeks filled with heat. I wanted that too, but not yet. I was still trying to come to grips with the pendulum of emotions that Nox evoked within me. The way his voice ricocheted through my body, the way his touch surged with electricity, and the realization that even when I'd been upset, I still wanted him.

Then again, I reminded myself that I had been upset only an hour ago. I didn't want *make up sex* to be what we did for our first time—first times were supposed to be special. "Can we take it a day at a time?"

He sighed. "We can. I want to reestablish the ground rules."

Unknowingly, I rolled my eyes. "Again with the rules."

"Yes," he replied, undaunted by my reaction. "We touched on them in my suite, before you so rudely walked away."

I pulled back from his embrace and crossed my arms over my chest. "I wasn't rude. I thought—"

"You thought I was married."

"I thought you were a cheater," I clarified.

"Married men and cheaters… we're establishing your list of hard limits. That's good," he added. "Charli, you don't have to tell me any more about yourself than you want to. But I have a hard limit too—a rule: honesty. You need to be honest with me and I'll do the same. You don't need to tell me everything, but what you do tell me, I must be able to believe without question. I'm straightforward to a fault. I'm used to saying my mind, and I want others to do the same. I'm not a cheater or a liar nor do I get my feelings hurt. Don't run away like you did tonight ever again. Tell me when something is bothering you—I can handle the truth."

The guilt rushed over me. I lowered my arms and chin, no longer feeling as defiant as I had. My dishonesty about who I was had already broken his *hard limit*—his rule.

He reached for my chin and pulled my eyes back to his. "I mean it. Some of my tastes are *unique*—they aren't for everyone. I understand that." His thumb caressed my cheek. "And I'm willing to adapt if…" He paused. "…I like someone." He leaned down and brushed his lips over mine. "Charli Moore, I like you. I have since the first time I saw you." He shifted. "When Max was trying…"

I smiled at the change in his tone as he recalled this morning's escapades. *Jealous much?* When he finished his account, I said, "I think I should go find Max."

"Why?"

"Because I owe him a thank-you." Fingering the small buttons of Nox's shirt I added, "Because he brought you to my chaise."

"I believe I mentioned that I would've gotten there one way or the other."

"Well, I should thank Max anyway, because he provided you a way. And…" I leaned closer. "…I'm glad you got there."

He held my hand, the one on his shirt. "If I only get one week with you…" His voice came breathier than before. "…I want it to count. Charli Moore, I want you to remember your stay at Del Mar."

The guilt I'd felt earlier came rushing back, compressing my chest, and making breathing increasingly difficult. I hated cheaters and liars and wasn't willing to be one of them. If this week was going to work, it was now or never. "Before that…" I lowered my chin and looked up at him through my lashes. "…I think I should confess."

"Confess?"

"Though I only *thought* you broke my limit, I've broken *yours*, your *hard limit*—not intentionally," I added. "More by omission."

He stood taller, the ridges of his torso more defined under my touch. "How? What have you done?"

I exhaled. "I let you assume that Chelsea and I share a last name. We don't. We have different fathers." That wasn't being dishonest. We also had different mothers, but I wasn't sure I was ready to go that far.

"Is your name Charli?"

"It's a nickname," I answered honestly. Meeting his stare I asked, "Is your name Nox?"

The corner of his mouth twitched toward a grin. "It's a nickname, too. So if Moore isn't your last name, what is it?"

I tilted my head to the side. "Let's spend the next week as Charli and Nox—no last names, no commitments. Can we do that?"

"You didn't research who was staying in the presidential suite? You really don't know my last name?"

I shook my head. "I didn't. Not because I wasn't curious—I am. But, I'm ashamed to admit that I didn't think of it until you mentioned it."

His large hands traveled to my waist as his side grin turned into a full-blown sexy smile. As he tugged at the sash of my robe, his tone found the timbre that resurrected the butterflies deep inside of me. "Just know, Miss Charli no-last-name, the next time you break one of my rules, I won't respond as lightly."

"You won't?" I asked, more aroused than curious. "What exactly does that mean?"

He moved closer, seductively teasing my breasts with the presence of his wide chest. "I guess we'll need to find that out together."

I had to lift my chin to see his eyes. The light blue sparkled with suggestions. The longer I stared, the more a part of me wanted to find out exactly what he had in mind. There was also a part of me that knew that wasn't a good idea. I shrugged nonchalantly. "Then I guess I better not break any of your rules."

"Where's the fun in that?" he asked.

"Oh, I believe I can be all kinds of fun." I gasped as he pulled me nearer.

My nipples—the ones that had softened during our conversation—were now hard nubs burning with desire as they were pressed against his broad chest. That wasn't our only connection that made my insides tighten. Lower, his hardening erection pushed against my stomach.

"Perhaps we could begin that *fun* tonight?" Nox asked.

No doubt he could feel the rapid beat of my heart reverberating from my chest to his. I wanted everything about this man, and if I let my body have its way, we'd be horizontal in fifty-one seconds flat. But I couldn't. If we were to explore my limits, I needed to know that they would be honored. Gathering my strength, I stepped back. The bit of space gave me purpose. "Nox, I'd rather spend the *entire* week getting to know you." My lashes fluttered. "You, me, and all the fun that may entail. Let's not do it all in one night."

Straightening his back and nodding, Nox reached for the bottle of cabernet. "Let me open this and we'll toast to Charli and Nox and…" He cocked his head. "…to *fun* and *getting to know one another.*"

The pop of the cork echoed through the suite, momentarily overriding the rushing sound of blood coursing through my veins, as Nox poured two glasses. Musk and desire filled the room as we both worked to ignore the peaked points of my nipples through my satin robe and the obvious tenting of his gray slacks. With a knowing glint in his light blue eyes, he handed me my glass. "Charli, another thing I rarely do is suffer from sexual frustration. The only reason that I'm able to tolerate it tonight…" His gaze pointedly went to my chest. "…is that I know you're suffering the same."

Before I could cover my chest, he lifted his glass and went on. "Let's toast to us—to a week of discovering not only one another but the people we can be when we're together. Because in the last two hours, the most beautiful and intriguing redhead that I've ever had the pleasure of meeting, has had me saying and doing things that I, L… Nox, don't, as a rule, do." He lifted his glass. "To an unforgettable week."

Our glasses met with a clink and we took a sip. The rich, thick liquid warmed my tongue and throat. The aroma reminded me that we weren't drinking the house red.

"This is very good."

Nox shrugged. "For a California wine. I told you: I have very particular tastes."

The way he looked at me, the way his pale stare zeroed in and took my breath, told me that Nox wasn't talking about wine, not anymore. My insides twisted, and I knew that I wanted to learn more about Nox: his tastes, both for wine and for everything else.

Chelsea said to stay uncommitted and to learn very little. Nevertheless, as I watched him swallow and his Adam's apple bob, I wanted more. Unfortunately, anything more than a vacation hookup wouldn't work with Alex's future.

I sighed.

I had a week as Charli, and I planned to take it.

Nox reached for my hand. The warmth of his touch was a contrast to the cool air conditioning of the suite. When I looked up, he said, "Just because I've made exceptions to my usual behavior doesn't mean I'm willing to give up on my quest."

"Your quest?"

"At the end of the week, I may not know your last name, but trust me, Charli: I will know every inch of that beautiful body and we will both know your limits."

He'd asked me earlier if I believed him. I'd wanted to then. Now I had no doubt. Nox would take me to those limits, but the fact that he wasn't pushing now made me comfortable enough to simply say, "I believe you." I tugged his hand. "Let's go out to my balcony. It's not as grand as yours and there's no private pool, but we can hear the ocean."

He picked up the bottle and followed me outside.

"YOU DRANK WINE? That's it?" Chelsea asked for the fifteenth time.

"It doesn't matter how many times you ask, the answer is still the same."

Chelsea eyed me over the rim of her orange juice glass as we ate breakfast.

"Besides," I said with an air of superiority. "Where were you until, like, three this morning?"

She reached for her temples and pushed from both sides. "Do you have to accuse so loudly?"

I leaned forward. "Babe, I'm whispering."

Her head moved from side to side. "No way. You're yelling. You're going to get us kicked out of here."

I laughed a full-belly laugh. "I hardly think that will be me."

"Well," she said, her hazel eyes darting from side to side. "I may have ordered a few drinks and charged them to our room."

"I'm shocked!" I said mockingly.

"Well, after Mr. Fancy Pants tracked me down, I knew I couldn't come back to our room."

"Nothing happened in our room! And you didn't tell me that Nox found you."

"Found is such an odd word. I was talking to a few new friends and Mr." She paused. "Nox—is that what you called him?"

I'd said the name ten times. Obviously, she was still inebriated from the night before. "Yes, it's a nickname."

Her bloodshot eyes widened for a second. "Like Charli? That's a nickname."

"Yes," I confirmed. "Now tell me more."

"Well, it's kind of fuzzy, but I was in the bar. He came up and asked me a question about my sister. I kind of stuttered." She leaned forward. "Well, because my sister is still in California." Her giggle disappeared as she took another drink of orange juice. "This is the worse mimosa I've ever had."

"It's because I told them, no champagne."

"What the hell? That means it's just orange juice."

I nodded. "Yes. Now, Nox asked you about your sister?"

"I remember. I told him my last name and our room number."

"Why? What if he were some ax murderer?"

Chelsea pursed her lips. "Apparently, I made the right choice."

"Yes," I whispered. "Thank you."

"So will you see him again?"

"I want to," I confessed. "I'm more attracted to him than I've been to anyone…" I hesitated. "…ever."

"Haven't you noticed that this place is crawling with good-looking, rich men? I met this guy last night. Dan. Don. Ron." She closed her eyes. Just before I thought she'd fallen asleep, her eyes popped open. "Jon. That was his name. Don't worry about me. I think we'll both be fine."

"Jon? Jon who?" I asked, concerned.

"Nox who?" she replied.

"Touché."

Yes. Who the hell was I to judge her and Jon, Ron, or Don? I wasn't any better.

CHAPTER 10

——•○•——

Past

THE SUN CONTINUED to rise in the east and set each night beautifully in the west. With each passing day, Alex's career goals and Alexandria's ghosts slipped further and further away, evaporating into Charli. Between days with Chelsea and days and nights with Nox, there was nothing I'd ever enjoyed more.

While Chelsea and I spent time together at the pool or in our suite, I admitted my growing feelings for Nox, the ones I didn't want to face. I didn't want to admit the way my heart beat faster when I was around him or the way things that he did or said made me feel special, because with each tick of the clock, our time together waned. If our vacation were an hourglass, the bottom had more sand than the top, and I knew I couldn't turn it over.

"Girl," Chelsea said one morning as we were putting on our normal breakfast-by-the-pool attire—bathing suits, cover-ups, and flip-flops. "Don't overthink it. That's the beauty of it. No commitment. Besides…" She wiggled her eyebrows. "…don't you think the non-committed sex is steamier?"

I shrugged as I threw the sunscreen in my beach bag and looked for my Kindle.

She reached for my shoulder and spun me toward her. "What?! You haven't done the dirty deed with Mr. Tall-Dark-and-Handsome?"

"It's only been three days."

"Which means there are only two more nights left. Jeez, I've seen the way he looks at you. That poor man must be suffering a serious case of blue balls." Her voice lowered. "Are they blue?"

I hadn't seen them, so I couldn't answer indisputably, but I'd been close to them and their impressive third wheel, with only the material of his slacks, jeans, or bathing trunks in between. I'd even rubbed my hand over him and felt his size and power trapped behind the clothes. I'd also had that same restrained power against my body, pushing against the small of my back, my tummy, and thigh. I'd been with him in the private pool on the balcony of the presidential suite with warm, glowing water surrounding us as my legs wrapped around his torso and arms around his neck. It wasn't that I was being a tease. We'd been *almost* there.

He'd caressed my breasts and even sucked my nipples. The mere thought of his lips against my skin caused them to harden. I'd unashamedly arched my back and allowed him access. More than that, I'd wanted more.

I wasn't sure how to explain it, to Chelsea or to me. I was different here in Del Mar than I'd ever been. The way Nox's body reacted to mine didn't scare me. For the first time I could remember, despite our obvious difference in size and strength, his hunger empowered me. He made me see that it was me who affected him. I had the ability to arouse this powerful man with the deep velvet voice. When my small hand rubbed against him, I was the cause of the guttural growl. The way it rumbled from the back of his throat sent shivers down my spine. With his chin in the nape of my neck, it sounded like a predatory lion.

When I wasn't with him, I wondered what it would be like to have someone like Nox in my life—my real life.

Could Alex do it? I didn't know the answer.

Nox and I had both made a conscious effort to limit the information we shared. We worked to stay away from our backstories and agreed to live in the here and now. I'm not sure which one of us laid down that rule, but we were both following it.

That didn't mean I hadn't gleaned a little personal information here and there. From what I'd picked up, Nox hadn't been with one singular person for a while. He'd dated. He had beautiful women who adorned his elbow to functions for both pleasure and work. But that was all they'd been— accessories. He didn't mention his no longer wife, and I didn't ask. Were they divorced or had she passed? I didn't know.

It would break our rule.

I also didn't know what he did, other than ran businesses.

Often he'd spend the morning in his suite working long distance. Noon in California was already three in the afternoon in New York and the close of the day in London. He could have almost a full day's worth of phone calls and web conferences complete before I was ready for lunch. A few times he'd left the resort, but never for long.

"His balls aren't blue," I responded matter-of-factly.

"And you know this because..." She paused, but when I only looked at her with wide eyes, she continued, "...you've seen them and you... Oh! I know. You've at least given him a—"

"Chelsea, stop! I'm not giving you the gory details."

She wrinkled her nose. "Gory? So he's a looker but doesn't have the equipment?"

"Stop. He has the equipment. I believe. I mean from what I've observed."

She shook her head. "If you leave Del Mar without getting laid it's totally your fault. And if you ask me, that man will be the best you've ever had. Stop letting Alex get into your head. You have three more days and two nights as Charli." She straightened her shoulders and looked at me over the rim of her sunglasses. "Don't come home tonight."

"Hey, it's my suite. I can come home," I responded playfully.

"It's in my name."

She had me there. "Even if we, you know..."

"Have wild-ape-crazed sex?" Chelsea offered.

"Do it," I corrected. "I'm not spending the night. He gets up at some ungodly hour to do whatever it is he does. Besides, I'm not taking the walk of shame down that private hallway." I visibly shivered. "The doormen who work that desk and private elevator already know my name."

"No, they know *Charli's* name. And I bet they already think you've had crazy-gorilla sex every time you leave the suite."

"Gorilla? I thought it was ape?"

She laughed. "Well, they both can do it hanging upside down." She kissed my cheek as we stepped into the hallway. "Give that some thought and I bet you don't come home tonight."

EARLY THAT EVENING, I winked at Chelsea as I smoothed the black silk material of my dress. "I can't believe I'm really doing this."

"Who are you doing it for?"

I turned toward her and gained strength from the sparkle in her hazel eyes. "Me."

Her smile broadened. "Right answer!"

"I'm not sure I'll even tell him."

"Where did you say he's taking you? I mean he took you to that rooftop place last night, Pacifica?"

I nodded like a giddy teenager. "The resort had a driver for us and oh... the place was gorgeous. The view was amazing. Tonight he said he has a car and we're going up Highway 101 to Oceanside."

Her eyes were wide. "Charli may not be getting laid, but she's doing some fine eating."

"Tonight's 333 Pacific." I lowered my voice. "I Googled it. That's why I bought this new dress."

Chelsea crossed her arms and inspected me from head to toe. "And you're rocking it, too. You look beautiful. Remember what I said. Charli has come a long way, but you're still not Chelsea. Wasn't that the plan?"

I inhaled deeply and the tightly fitted bodice of my dress pulled against my breasts. With only thin spaghetti straps, the way the dress accentuated my curves and held tight to my breasts was what kept it from falling. The lightweight material flowed to just above my knees.

The week of relaxing by the pool had left my normally pale complexion a nice golden brown. Even though my hair had red, the deep brown from my mother's side prevailed, giving me the bonus of vibrant hair without the disposition to freckles and sunburns. As long as I was faithful with my hat and sunscreen, the sun and I played nicely together.

"I'd say there's more Chelsea in Charli than Alex, but it's not that easy..."

She hugged me. "Do what you want. This is your vacation. I'm just happy seeing that perpetual smile on your face. Go... don't be late for Mr. Handsome."

"We know his name—it's Nox."

"Yes, but not his last name. I've dubbed him Nox Tall-Dark-and-Handsome, Mr. Handsome for short."

I laughed. That was a lot of names, but for someone who had four names herself, six if I included Alex and Charli, *Nox Tall-Dark-and-Handsome* wasn't outside the realm of possibility.

A few minutes later I stepped into the front lobby of the resort and walked toward the large glass entrance. My breathing hitched when Mr. Handsome came into view. Without thinking, I scanned him up and down. Each time I looked at Nox from afar, I wondered what it was that he'd seen in me and why he hadn't been dating anyone. The man was sex on a stick, and for a few more days he was all mine. The way his gray suit fit perfectly in all the right places tightened parts of my insides while melting others. He was talking to one of the hotel employees. As I approached, I concentrated on my steps across the shiny floor, but from the corner of my eye, I saw the employee nod my direction and Nox turn.

Any semblance of composure I'd been holding floated away with the breaking of the proverbial thread. From nearly fifty feet away, his blue gaze drank me in and devoured me whole. I was the prey to the lion I envisioned when he growled. Instantaneously, one of his cheeks rose, pulling his lips into a lopsided grin. His approving expression filled me with the confidence I needed to move forward.

The Del Mar employee disappeared into a haze, as did everyone else.

Nox and I were the only two people on earth. I'd seen this happen in special effects during a film. Everyone except the main characters was out of focus. As I came to a stop in front of the only person in the lobby, I begged my heart to slow its stampede.

Lifting my hand, Nox brushed his full lips over my knuckles. "You are stunning."

Before I could respond, he turned toward the employee who had reappeared.

"Don't you agree, Ferguson? My date is the most beautiful woman you've ever seen."

"Sir, you're a lucky man."

Taking my hand into the crook of his elbow, Nox turned us toward the doors. "Luck," he responded to Ferguson, just before we walked away, "has nothing to do with it. It's all about knowing what you want."

"Yes, sir. Have a good evening and you too, Miss Moore."

"Thank you," I managed to say.

Nox's closed-lip grin widened, revealing his white teeth and a bright smile. Though he was still talking to Ferguson, his eyes were only on me. "Oh, we shall. We shall."

I was about to ask about our plans, if we were going to do more than the restaurant in Oceanside when Nox stopped in front of a black Porsche Boxster convertible.

"Your carriage for the evening, m'lady."

"Really? You're going to drive? I guess I thought when you said a car—"

"Are you disappointed?"

"No," I answered honestly. "Not at all. This is a great car."

Opening the passenger door and helping me in, he replied, "It's a rental, but I like to drive." Once he was in the driver's seat, he said, "I could arrange to have a driver tomorrow night, if you'd prefer."

"I like this better."

"Good." He put his hand on my knee. "I want you all to myself."

I couldn't hold back my smile as I fastened my seatbelt. As he pulled out from under the awning, the evening sun washed over us. We made our way down the winding road off the resort. Since I'd decided to leave my hair down for the night, I searched through my handbag and found a hair tie and fastened the auburn waves into a low ponytail.

I wasn't making Nox feel better when I'd said I preferred his driving. I detested limousines. They reminded me of Alton. Savannah wasn't that large. There was no reason for Alton Fitzgerald to be driven to his job each day or for he and my mother to be driven to dinner. It was simply him being ostentatious.

As we headed north, I scoured the breathtaking scenery along Highway 101. With the roof open, I could scan every direction. Out Nox's side of the car, the Pacific Ocean glistened with prisms of light as the sun sunk lower in the sky. Throughout the entire trip, whether we were talking about the ocean or the sky or just enjoying the *whoosh* of the wind around the Boxster, Nox held my hand or my knee.

The touch of his skin to mine no longer shocked me. That didn't mean the connection was gone. It was different. Instead of the electricity I'd felt the first time we touched, now our link was more like a familiar blanket. Even though he might only be holding my hand, my entire body warmed with his presence. Still driving along the coastal highway, with the city growing larger in the distance, Nox turned toward me, and I immediately noticed something different in his expression.

"Charli?"

"Yes?"

"Our time is…" He inhaled. Squeezing my hand, he narrowed his light blue gaze. "Damn, I don't know what to do with you."

"Excuse me?"

Shaking his head, he slowed the Boxster and pulled off the road onto a scenic vista. Though sunset was still over an hour away, the sky before us was filled with colors. Purples and pinks dominated the horizon as the orange globe of the sun cast yellows and reds in all directions. The blue water shimmered. "I know you don't really know anything about me, but I can tell you, I am rarely—no never—" he corrected, "hesitant about my demands."

"Your demands?" My voice came out an octave higher than I planned.

"Do you remember my telling you that my tastes are unique?"

"Yes. No California wine."

His smile returned. "Well, there is that. I wasn't speaking of wine."

I nodded. "Yes, Nox, I remember."

"Have you had a nice week, so far?"

"I would say *nice* is an understatement."

He moved his hand higher on my thigh. "I don't usually ask for what I want."

My eyes widened. "You don't. Does that mean you take it?"

He shrugged. "Yes, but when it comes to sex, I'm not saying it's ever been against anyone's will. I can't remember a time it wasn't plainly offered or at least assumed."

"Are you asking if I'm offering?"

"I'm glad you've enjoyed yourself this week. I'm ready, more than ready, for you to enjoy yourself more. I've tried to go slow on pushing those limits. But damn, time isn't on our side."

I tried to swallow, but my mouth seemed suddenly dry. Chelsea's words came back to me, telling me to have fun and also to think about *me*. "I promise to let you know if I'm not comfortable."

Nox nodded. "I've been giving this a lot of thought."

I held my breath.

"And I want to explore those limits tonight. I want you to do something for me. Will you?"

I looked from side to side. There were other cars parked along the highway. In front of us there was a railing and steps. The people in those other cars had probably parked and gone beyond the railing, down the hill, to watch the sunset. That didn't mean we were alone. There were cars passing by at a regular rate.

He squeezed my thigh, bringing me mentally back to him. "Charli?"

I let out the breath. *Does he seriously want a blow job right here, before our dinner?*

"What do you want me to do?"

"No, it doesn't work that way. I want you to trust me. I want you to trust me with this one night. I want to spend tonight showing you a small sliver of my unique taste. Then, tomorrow night, our last night together, you can decide if we go back to nice or we explore more limits. Do you trust me?"

I nodded. His offer excited me in a way I'd never imagined. "Yes, I do."

"And?"

"And..." I gathered my courage. "...I'll do whatever you want."

The relief in his expression at my answer took away any doubt. Yes, if for only two more days, I would trust him. "I'm not sure exactly what this means," I admitted honestly.

"It means tonight you do exactly as I say. Don't question or overthink it. If you can do that, I promise you more than nice. I promise you a night you'll never forget."

Though I felt as though I, Charli, was betraying Alex, the woman I'd worked so hard to be, I agreed.

Nox leaned forward and opened the glove compartment. "First, I want you to slip off your panties and put them in here."

My eyes must have given me away, because that wasn't the first demand I'd expected him to make.

He splayed his large fingers under the hem of my dress. "The point of this is that I shouldn't have to explain. However..." He grinned. "...I seem to make exceptions for you and I'll do it again, just this once. Take off your panties, as I said, so that I can think about you—imagine you—exposed under this lovely dress. I want to know that as we dine, with you seated in the chair next to me, if I move my hand..." His hand inched higher. "...I have access to you. I want to touch you in plain sight while no one but us knows what's happening. After we eat, I want to take you by the hand and lead you down the long wooden pier, knowing that you're aroused. I want to watch your beautiful face as the sea breeze touches what I did. Charli, I've taken this as slow as I can..." He reached for my hand and pushed it against his erection. "...I've imagined your pussy. Tonight, I want it and since you've agreed, I'm going to take it."

If he'd moved his hand any higher, he'd have found exactly what he wanted. With only his words, I was painfully aroused. That didn't mean that I could do as he said. "Nox, I'm sorry."

The sparkle that had been in his eyes only seconds earlier disappeared as his neck stiffened. "I see."

"No." I grabbed his hand before he could pull it away. "No, you don't."

"What?"

"Nox," I explained, "I can't remove something I'm not wearing."

The look of complete shock quickly morphed to amusement. "Can you repeat that?"

I unbuckled the seatbelt and leaned closer to his ear. With purposely breathy words, I repeated, "I can't remove something I'm not wearing. You can do everything you said. I'm not wearing anything to stop it, and," after a kiss to his cheek, I added, "I don't want to stop you."

With his large hands framing my face, he stared into my eyes, and I nodded, trying to tell him with my eyes that I trusted him and was being truthful. Somehow our fantasies had become one. A moan filled the evening air as he forcefully pulled me toward him. Our lips united as his tongue probed, willing mine to part. His kiss was mint and whiskey, invigorating and calm. Nox was a walking contrast, a dichotomy of everything I'd known and everything I thought I'd wanted. His unique combination of force and tenderness should be illegal, because with just one taste I was instantly addicted. I scooted closer like the addict I was.

"Damn," he said when our lips parted. "I'm thinking about forgetting those reservations for table 101,"

I read about table 101 when I'd Googled 333 Pacific. The website said that it was famous for its view and needed to be booked far in advance. How did Nox get that table? Who did he work for?

I wanted the reservation, but I also wanted other things. Tonight was up to him—I'd already agreed to that. Nevertheless, I did my best to sound bold. "If you do that," I said seductively, licking my bruised lips. "Then I won't be able to do all the things you mentioned: the table, the seat beside you, the sea breeze." Saying them made my insides tingle with anticipation.

"No, but I know of other things I want too."

Rearranging my dress, I sat back into the deep bucket seat. And with a sideways glance, simply stated, "Me too."

"Oh fuck!" Gravel flew as he threw the car into reverse and spun us toward Oceanside. "To the fastest dinner in history."

My laugh resonated from deep inside as the sky's golden hues combined with the purple. I wasn't sitting in a fancy car. I was floating in the colors, overwhelmed with the euphoria of Nox. I wished I could bottle the sensation and save it for the future. In that moment, I doubted I'd ever feel this empowered and desired again.

CHAPTER 11

———•○•———

Present

THE CONVERSATION BETWEEN Alton, Suzanna, and Bryce stilled when we entered. I held my breath as my mother closed the door.

"Apparently you forgot to check your watch," Alton said. "Or is it an issue with telling time?"

"What is this—?"

"Five minutes, Alexandria. Five minutes. It seems a college degree has done little for your ability to follow simple instructions."

"I was told to play nice and be polite to the guests. That's what I was doing. You're not a guest and playing nice isn't in your repertoire."

My mother stepped forward. "Alton, we're here now. I realize this is my fault."

I narrowed my eyes trying to comprehend the conversation. *Her fault?*

"Yes, Laide, it is, and we'll discuss that later."

My mother shifted as she looked from person to person. Both Suzanna and Bryce met her gaze, but in true Savannah style their expressions revealed nothing.

"Would someone tell me what's going on?"

Mother led me toward the conference table. It wasn't as large as a corporate conference table, but it was dark, glossy, and ostentatiously regal. It fit in Alton's office perfectly. There were four leather chairs on each side and one at each end. The ones at the end had arms and resembled small thrones. When I was little it helped to perpetuate my princess theory. It was probably the table my grandfather had and his father before that. Despite the heritage, I hated that table almost as much as I loathed my bedroom. Each time throughout my childhood when I was caught or accused of wrongdoing, my correction began with a family conference at this table. There were three of us—three. Sitting at this giant-ass table was ridiculous. It was part of Alton's power play, his demonstration of strength. When I was five, it probably worked. By the time I was old enough to understand overcompensation, I found it humorous.

I stopped walking and laughed. I wasn't five nor was I seventeen. The Spencers weren't family, and we weren't discussing my correction. This was pure bullshit.

My forced laughter filled the room. "Are you all out of your minds?" I moved my outstretched hand toward each person. "What is this? I'm not sitting. I'm not doing anything. And if you want me to go back out to those guests—my guests, ha!… If you want me to go back out there and play the dutiful daughter then someone better answer some damn questions."

"Alexandria—"

"Alex," I corrected my mother.

"Alex," Bryce offered. The years of our friendship rippled through the sound of his voice as he said my name. But that quickly disappeared when I looked at him and remembered the rest of our story, after our friendship.

Bryce had grown up well in the past four years. His shoulders were broader, his chin was defined, and his light blonde hair longer than I remembered. It wasn't too long, but had a slight wave I'd never noticed when we were younger. He was a swimmer at the academy and had always kept it short. Over the past few years, his lean swimmer's body had broadened. That wasn't to say he was heavy. The weight looked good on him, or maybe it was the suit. He definitely looked the part of a Montague minion, all the way to his Italian loafers.

"Hi, Bryce."

He took a step toward me. "I wish we had more time to explain."

I shook my head. "Explain what?"

"We have a situation, something that you can help with. Something I'd—we'd—like you to do."

My mother nodded while Suzanna and Alton shared an expression somewhere between pain and disgust.

I forced another laugh. "A situation? Does this have anything to do with the senator or perhaps the man you were speaking to?"

"No, not really," Alton offered. "It has more to do with Bryce."

"I don't understand. How can I help? We haven't spoken in four years."

"No one needs to know that," Bryce said.

The entire scenario didn't make sense.

"Alexandria," Mother began. "Do you follow the news?"

"The news?" I repeated incredulously.

Suzanna exhaled and leaned back against the edge of Alton's desk, her arms crossed over her chest.

Finally, Alton sat at the table and began to fill in the blanks. As he spoke, I stared at Bryce and tried to judge if any of what Alton was saying were true. By both Mother's and Suzanna's expressions, I believed every word. With each sentence, my desire to stand diminished, and my legs grew weaker. Eventually, I collapsed into a chair at the table I despised. By the time Alton was done, all five of us were seated: Alton, Mother, and I in our assigned spots with Suzanna next to Mother and Bryce at the other end.

No matter the severity of the shitstorm blowing around us, Montague Manor had its hierarchy and it didn't matter that Adelaide and I were the only true Montagues, males still perched like proud peacocks at the top. This place was a prison—an eighteenth-century torture chamber.

I needed to call Chelsea as soon as I could. If anyone could break me out, it was she.

Alton explained that an undergraduate student, a woman, who attended Northwestern, claimed that she and Bryce had been in a relationship last semester. Booth was in Chicago, near Northwestern.

She claimed that Bryce assaulted her, physically and sexually. She went to the police, and they took pictures of her bruises. The rape kit showed sexual activity, but the only DNA was a hair, and Bryce didn't deny consensual sex. He did deny harming her. Montague attorneys have gotten the unfounded and unsubstantiated charges dropped, and a gag order in place. Unfortunately, about a week ago, someone leaked the story in an on-campus publication at Northwestern, during an early freshman orientation. The author of the article cited the incident as an example of a continued cover-up by university officials regarding sexual abuse of female students. No names were listed in the article. Alton believes that the author was aware of the gag order and didn't want to pay the excessive fine. However, that didn't stop other outlets from picking up the story. It was immediately run by a Chicago network and within hours was plastered all over social and news media.

The description of the perpetrator was vague, but there have been reporters sniffing around. The human resources and publicists for Montague suggested withdrawing the offer to employ Bryce, but Alton wouldn't hear of that. Bryce continued to claim his innocence and Alton believed him. As CEO of Montague Corporation, Alton insisted that they find another way to lessen any possible negative impact to Montague Corporation if the full story were to be released.

The temperature of the room rose as everyone turned toward me.

"Darling," Mother began. "This is your name, your company. You've had your time to see the world."

I could scarcely believe my ears. "California is hardly the world."

"You know what I mean."

"No, I don't know what you mean." I looked around the table. "I don't know what any of you want from me."

Bryce cleared his throat. "Alex-x," he stuttered, not completing my whole name. "I didn't do it. You know me. You know who I am. No one knows that we haven't been in contact."

I did know him, and that didn't reassure me.

When I didn't answer, he went on, "Sure, I took that girl out on a few dates, and yes, we had sex, but look at me. Look at my family and the job I had waiting. I'm not only a Spencer but also a Carmichael. I don't need to force anyone for sex. Why would I risk everything over some piece-of-trash college freshman?"

My stomach turned. "Freshman? Like eighteen?"

"Yes, she was legal."

Oh God. That wasn't where I was going with that. I may only be twenty-three, but Bryce was twenty-five, almost twenty-six. That was an eight-year difference. I pressed my lips into a straight line, reviving my Montague mask, the one that revealed nothing.

"Alexandria, dear," Suzanna's angry tone from the parlor had been replaced with saccharine sweetness—as artificial as ever. She wanted something from me and suddenly, we were friends again. "I've been upset with you, as you know, because your choice to move to the other side of the country upset my son. Once you have children, you'll understand how we mothers feel everything our children do, but even more intensely."

"How did it feel to rape a girl?" I asked.

Suzanna and Mother gasped, both sitting straight as if my words had the power to physically harm them. Simultaneously, the room echoed with the slap of Alton's hand against the shiny wood. "Alexandria!"

Bryce's brief look of anger magically morphed to hurt. I remembered seeing that transformation once before—no, more than once actually. It was that time I told him about Stanford that the anger lasted longer than a short moment, but there were other times I'd seen him upset, when we were young and then as teenagers. Did I think Bryce Spencer was capable of physical assault? Yes. An incident at the academy came to mind when he'd used a younger student as a punching bag simply because he'd made some comment about swimmers. If I recalled correctly, that incident was quickly brushed under the proverbial rug as well. After all, universities like Princeton and Duke didn't look kindly at applications from students with records.

Did I think Bryce would hit a woman—a girl? I didn't know.

With large gray puppy-dog eyes, Bryce asked, "Alex, how long did we date?"

Date? Was it still dating when he was at Duke and I was forbidden from seeing anyone else? Forbidden, or exiled?

"From the time I was fourteen until I graduated: four years," I answered.

"How long were we friends before that?"

"Our whole lives."

"How many times did we have sex?"

Are you kidding me?

I felt my cheeks redden, but not from embarrassment—from anger. "What the hell? You want to have this conversation in front of our parents?" I was too upset to separate Alton from that generalization.

"Yes," Bryce replied. "I do. If I remember, we had the same conversation many times, alone."

It was my turn to slap the table. "I'm not having this discussion with you again, alone or in front of an audience. It doesn't matter."

"It does, Alexandria. It does. I dated you for four years. You were my best friend. I miss you. Mom was right. I was devastated when you left for Stanford. I just prayed that you'd realize where you belong—back here with me. I didn't follow you out to California because I knew you needed to make that choice yourself. It's like that poem you always liked. Remember the one about loving something and setting it free?

"You were free," he went on. "Now you're back, and I want to resume where we left off. Why would I risk losing that by raping some gold-digging tramp?"

Disgust emanated from my eyes. I felt it. For not the first time in my life, I wished looks *could* kill. Bryce wanted us back together but more than that, he wanted me to help with his cover. That was why he'd said that no one knew we weren't in contact.

"Never. Never. Never!" I said each word louder than the one before. "We *never* had sex, and we never will. So if you're waiting for me, you should go ahead and screw every young thing out there. However," I added, lowering my voice a decibel, "you might want to get their consent first. It'll cut down on the legal fees. And I don't plan on being your alibi."

"Dear, lower your voice. You don't want our guests to hear you."

"Our guests, the people who we're rudely ignoring. Are those the *guests* you're referring to?"

"She's right, Laide," Alton said. "You and Suzanna go back out to the guests. Let them know that Alexandria will be out shortly, and we have an announcement."

Like dutiful Southern women, they both stood.

"Alton," Suzanna said, "I think it would be better for Laide and I to talk to *Alex*." She smiled my direction, as if using my preferred name won her points. "Woman to woman."

This is absolutely unbelievable.

I stood. "I tell you what. I'll go out to the guests. I only know about two-thirds of them," I said, shrugging. "But that's all right. Supposedly, they're here to wish me well. The only announcement we'll be making is that I'll be leaving Savannah on Monday and currently have no plans to return."

I turned toward the door and was halfway there when Alton's command reverberated through the paneled room.

"Stop."

Though my feet obeyed, I kept my eyes fixed on the door, refusing to turn back around.

"Bryce," Alton said. "Your mother is probably right. Let's give the ladies a few minutes. I'm sure Alexandria will make the best decision for her family, for Montague."

I spun toward them all. "What in the hell decision do you think I'll make? What exactly are you asking?"

"I told you that I had a ring—"

"No!" I cut Bryce off. "Hell no."

"We can start slowly. We'll just mention how we never really lost contact. We agreed to an open relationship, one where we could both mature."

Open relationship. Nox's confident demeanor as he offered to tell Max we had an open marriage came to mind. My attention went back to Bryce and I raised my eyebrows. "So we could *mature*? Is that code for something, because as I recall as soon as I was out of the picture—no, before I was out of the picture—you were *maturing* with Millie."

"Those were only rumors, ones that she started because she was jealous."

We were all now standing, and Suzanna reached for Bryce's arm. "Dear, go with Alton. You two have clients out there. Let Laide and I have a moment with Alex. It seems like it wouldn't hurt."

When she looked back at me, I shrugged. What the hell? This whole messed-up family wanted to gang up on me; they wanted to betray me.

Let them give it their best shot.

CHAPTER 12

———●O●———

Present

ONCE THE MEN were gone, I gave my mother and godmother my best *have-at-it* look.

Suzanna began on the offensive. "Dear, men have needs. Did you really expect my son to remain celibate if you weren't willing to help him out?"

"Help him out?" I asked incredulously. "Are you saying that if I wanted to keep your son, which I didn't nor do I now, I should've *helped out* or *put out* at fourteen? Or maybe I should have waited until I was fifteen?"

"No," Mother replied, her hand fluttering near her neck like it did when she was upset and it was missing its customary glass. "There are two sides to this. On the first side, the most important side," she emphasized, "is that you are a woman of breeding. You did the right thing by abstaining. It's just another reason I'm proud of you. But dear, one day you'll need to help a man out, as Suzy said."

I sat back down and crossed my arms over my chest. This was priceless. My mother decided to have the *sex talk* with me when I was twenty-three, in front of her best friend. After my high-school boyfriend forced the issue in front of all of our parents. Oh how rich. Adelaide always did have impeccable timing.

"Yes," Suzanna agreed. "How do you think grandchildren are made?"

I shook my head. "You two are unbelievable. I'm not a virgin. I know how babies are made, and I know how to help a man out. What I don't know is why you think I want that with Bryce."

"You two were close."

Were.

"And," Suzanna went on, "this will benefit everyone. Once the press learns that Bryce has been in a long-term relationship, they'll be less likely to assume he's the man in that article."

"But he *is* the man in the article," I pointed out the obvious. "And we haven't been in contact. If anyone digs, we'll both look like we cheated on one another. And that doesn't even scratch the surface of the absurdity of this whole thing. Whether he raped her or not, he had sex with a child."

"She was of legal age," Suzanna defended.

"He also screwed around on me with my best friend. It's great you two have this lifelong friendship, but I have limits. My best friend screwing my boyfriend is one of them. Cheating is another. As far as I'm concerned Bryce and Millie can spend the rest of their lives sneaking quickies on the side. I don't care. They just need to do it without me in the equation."

My mother took my hand. "You're not a virgin, but that doesn't mean you understand the things that some men... need. They aren't all proper."

"Momma, don't." I was certain I'd vomit what little bit of food I'd eaten if she started to give me examples.

She shook her head. "It's true. Isn't it, Suzy?"

Suzanna nodded.

"Dear, if Bryce can get what he needs with Millie Ashmore or any other willing whore on the side, it will make your life better."

I threw my hands in the air. "I just can't."

"Yes, you can. I'm not saying you need to marry him... yet. We'll work our way up to that. For right now, the two of you can just be... what is it?... going steady?"

"You're certifiable, both of you. I'm leaving in two days."

"And you'll be concentrating on your studies," Suzanna said. "What harm is there in pretending?"

"Don't you see," Mother asked, "why attending Savannah Law would be better?"

No. I didn't see that.

LEAVING ALTON'S OFFICE a few minutes later, flanked on either side by the women who were supposed to be my biggest advocates, felt more like being led to a firing squad. I hadn't agreed to do anything except to decline to dispute the assertion that Bryce and I had been in contact over the last four years. Essentially what I agreed to was letting others make assumptions, not to perpetuating them myself. A cold chill ran through me as we entered the grand hall. This really was a dog and pony show and I was the one being led around by a lead.

As we mingled and passed the groupings of people, it was clear that the party had progressed without us. I ventured that most of the guests never realized we were missing. They probably assumed we were in one room or the other. Since night had fallen and Georgia's summer heat had lost the glare of sun, guests socialized both inside and outside on the rear stone terraces.

Keeping my Montague mask in check, I moved from room to room until I spied him near the bar in the den. Each room had its own bartender and selection of food. From the strong aroma of Cajun spices, the den seemed to have a New Orleans theme. Earlier I'd eaten a little of the hors d'oeuvres in the parlor. Unfortunately, the tempura-battered oysters and blue crab beignets were probably all I'd be able to stomach tonight. My appetite was gone.

It wasn't Bryce I had looked for; it was Alton. He was conversing with the same man Bryce had been speaking with earlier. Instead of interrupting, I stood behind the man, and with my lips pressed into a straight line made eye contact with my stepfather.

"Excuse me, Severus. My daughter needs me."

I grimaced at both the label and sweaty grasp as he took my elbow and led me away. It took all of my self-control to remain composed until we reached a secluded corner of the room. Once we were there, the first thing I did was free my arm.

Before he could speak, I began, "I'm talking to you directly for one reason: I want you to understand that I'm not bluffing. If you go further than I want on this agreement, I will talk and I'll talk loudly."

His lip twitched before he asked, "What did you agree to do?"

"Bryce and I have stayed in touch. Now that I've returned to the East Coast, we have agreed to talk and see more of one another. That's it," I qualified. "Nothing more. No big announcement. No secretive, passionate love. Take it or leave it."

Alton nodded at another guest I didn't know and lowered his voice. Leaning closer he whispered, "Alexandria, I will not be threatened. I'll take your offer—for now. This isn't done, and when it all plays out, remember you have only yourself to blame."

The fruity stench of his breath churned the seafood in my stomach, making the earlier acrobatics it had been doing a pleasant memory. "When what plays out?" I asked. "What do you mean, and why?"

People continued to move nearby. Alton's liquor-stained teeth peered between his thin lips as he forced a smile. "Why what, dear?"

"Why go to all this trouble for Bryce?"

"We can discuss this at another more appropriate time. This isn't the place."

I kept my voice low and raised my brows. "I'm playing nice. Give me something. I want to know *why*."

The hairs on the back of my neck came to attention as his large hand splayed across my shoulder. To the outside world—to people two feet away—we were a happy family, father and daughter, having a pleasant conversation. "Your mother," he said. "She cares about Suzanna. It affects Montague Corporation."

"Alton, I don't mean to interrupt." Senator Higgins' booming voice rippled over my shoulder.

"Not at all, Grant. Alexandria and I can continue our talk another time. Isn't that right, dear?"

Instead of responding, I turned toward the politician. "Senator, thank you for attending my party. It's an honor to have you here."

He shook my hand. As I was about to retrieve it, he held tight and said, "I'm always happy to meet with your dad and lovely mother, but tonight I'm pleased to meet one of the future litigators of our fine state." He looked past me to Alton and back. "And such a pretty little one, too."

Chauvinist!

I forced the tips of my pressed lips to rise. "Thank you. If you'll excuse me?"

He released my hand after a condescending pat. "Certainly, young lady. It was nice to meet you."

My skin crawled as I walked away.

Alton never did tell me what would play out, and I sure as hell didn't buy his answer about why he was helping Bryce. I didn't. It didn't make sense. This entire scenario didn't need to negatively affect Montague Corporation. That was Alton's call, at least from the story he'd told me. He could have agreed to withdraw Montague's offer to employ Bryce. Most large companies had ethics clauses. Montague Corporation could have easily cited that as a reason to withdraw their earlier offer.

"Alexandria."

I turned toward the kind voice.

"I have to warn you, you're going to miss it."

My Montague mask morphed into a real smile as I looked at Miss Betty. "Stanford, you mean?"

"Yes," she replied wistfully, "and the freedom."

"Freedom?"

She took another drink from her glass. Small bubbles moved upward in her sparkling wine. From her tone and the way she swayed slightly side to side, I presumed it wasn't her first glass. Not everyone could hold their liquor like my mother. It also seemed that my alma mater had brought back memories that she'd tucked away.

She squeezed my hand. "You still have three more years. Take it from me, life happens too fast. Marriage, children, shit." Her eyes popped open, and she playfully covered her mouth. "I didn't say that aloud, did I?"

I giggled and shook my head. "Say what, Miss Betty? I didn't hear a thing."

"You, young lady, will go far. And I'm not just saying that because of Stanford." She held onto my arm and scanned the grand hall. "This is such a lovely home. I've had a wonderful time, but I think it's time I get my driver, and we head home."

"Thank you for coming."

I helped her to the door and made sure that one of the staff alerted her driver. I'd known Miss Betty most of my life, yet for the first time, it was as if I'd seen the real woman behind the mask.

Smoke and mirrors.

Dog and pony shows.

Why would anyone choose to live in this world of delusion?

Hearing my name, I turned toward a group of people. *Shit!* It was Millie, Ian, Jess, Leslie, two men I didn't recognize, and Bryce. I'd been wrong earlier. *Now*, the show was about to start. Why the hell did it need to be with Bryce and Millie?

"ALEX, CAN WE talk?" Bryce asked with a grin. The small dimple on his chin revealed a glimpse of the boy who'd been my friend.

Most of the guests had left, Mother had retired to her suite, and Alton was in the den with some men whose names I couldn't remember. The household staff as well as the caterers, were working tirelessly to clean away any evidence of the celebration. Soon Montague Manor would be exactly as it had been earlier today, last year, a hundred years ago.

I'd been ignoring Bryce for most of the party. Our story was that we'd spoken, not that we were close. Besides, standing by his side and talking with old academy friends was almost as appealing as a Brazilian wax. It only took me a single time to decide that wasn't for me. I knew before I walked over to the group of vultures that I didn't want to be among them.

He reached for my hand.

"We can talk," I confirmed as I retrieved my hand. "Touching is prohibited."

He nodded. "Some things never change."

"Around here nothing changes."

Warm air surrounded us as we walked out onto the back terrace. Stars dotted the night sky while the incessant hum of crickets replaced the clatter of dishes inside the house. Although I detested everything about Savannah and my childhood home, there was something peaceful about the leaden humidity and silence that came with the estate.

"Do you really plan on never returning?" Bryce asked. "I mean, I know you have memories. You never said exactly, but this is your home." He spun around and looked up at the massive structure. "How could you not want to live here?"

I shrugged and brushed my hand along the rough stone banister. The large limestone steps descended to the lower lawns. Fireflies twinkled in the distance. When I was little I thought they were fairies, like Tinkerbell. I was convinced if I caught one, it would change into a fairy and grant me my wish. It was another childhood fantasy that didn't come true.

The house was constructed on a hill, allowing it to oversee the vast land behind. Hundreds of years ago that land was filled with one-room houses, tobacco fields, stables, and barns. The old structures were gone, as if erasing that time in our family's history was that easy. Now it was covered with the best that money could buy: a large pool, flower gardens, and better-constructed buildings. The biggest addition to the property was a lake.

Who can decide they want a lake and get a lake? A Montague can.

This time of year, the manmade creation would be nothing but a puddle in the Georgia clay if it weren't for the pump that pulled water from the depths of the earth, filtering it through sand to keep the lake not only full, but fresh. It was still astonishing how well it worked, but near the turn of the twentieth century, when my great-great grandfather had it installed, it had been an amazing feat of engineering.

Nothing but the best at Montague Manor—on the surface at least.

I slipped off my shoes and stepped onto the perfectly manicured lawn.

Even under the cover of night, Montague Manor was a beautiful prison. Trying to keep the shadows at bay, as Jane had said, I concentrated on fond memories. They were there. And as much as I hated to admit it, many of those from my childhood included Bryce.

"Do you remember swimming in the lake?" he asked.

I grinned. "Yes. Our mothers would get so mad. They were sure it wasn't safe and wanted us in the pool instead."

"Nessie," we both said with a laugh.

"I think they were the ones who told us about her. You were never afraid of Nessie. I was," Bryce admitted.

"You were? You never acted like it."

"Because I'm a guy. Guys can't show fear, and you were younger than me. I couldn't let a little girl be braver than me."

"I don't know if it was so much being brave as it was defiant. And unbeknownst to my mother, Jane had explained the pump to me. So I knew the hum wasn't really a monster."

"Why didn't you tell me? That would've saved me a lot of sleepless nights."

I softly laughed. "Because you never told me you were afraid."

Bryce stopped walking a few feet from the shoreline. "I can still hear it. Can you?"

Camouflaged behind the crickets and occasional croaks of a toad, was a faint hum vibrating through the ground more than the air. "I can."

Bryce reached for my hands and as I tried to pull them away, he said, "Alex, give me a second, please."

Swallowing, I nodded.

"Thank you for helping me."

"I-I'm not..."

"You are. More than you know. It was bad—the police, the station, the holding cell. I can't go back. I can't. I'm telling you what I've never told anyone. I was scared, more scared than I was of Nessie."

I clenched my teeth. "I'm sorry, but I'm not helping you or anyone else cover up a crime."

"Then you're going to make a lousy lawyer."

I knew he was kidding, but I was tired of people telling me what to do with my future, what to become, and how well I'd do. I pulled my hands away. "I will make a great attorney, because I'll stand up for what's right."

"There are two sides to every argument."

"Why did you do it?"

"I didn't." He ran his hand through his blond waves. "We had sex. She wanted more than a few dates and sex. I didn't. She had some grand illusion about marriage. When I told her we were done, she promised she would get back at me. She said I'd led her on."

"Bryce, Alton said there were bruises."

He shook his head. "She didn't have bruises the last time I saw her. I swear."

I paced a few steps and turned back toward him. "I don't know."

"Yes you do. You know me. I'm the guy who was afraid of Nessie. Please consider transferring to Savannah Law."

"What?"

"New York is far away. Not as far as California, but still far. If you'd transfer to Savannah Law, we could..." His voice trailed away.

"We could what?" I asked, with more attitude than I intended.

"Just see where the future leads."

The caterers were gone by the time we made our way back up to the manor and lights were off in many of the rooms. It wasn't until after Bryce was gone and I headed up to my room that I heard the voices—his voice. The tenuous calm that had settled over me at the lake's edge disappeared. I wrapped my arms around my midsection and tried to drown out his shouting and her tears.

As I quietly shut and locked my bedroom door I realized that I was a child again, and at Montague Manor that's what we do, we pretend not to hear and not to see. We live in the illusion hidden within the smoke and mirrors.

CHAPTER 13

———●○●———

Six weeks earlier

OUR DATE AT 333 Pacific was everything Nox promised and more… down to the sea breeze. Our covert scandalous behaviors had me twisted tighter than I'd ever been. Everything was erotic: the scent of his cologne, the thundering rumble of his voice, and the confident, assured touch of his skin against mine. Though part of me knew what we were doing—what I was allowing Nox to do to me—went against everything Alex stood for, I was virtually on the edge of explosion. Sometime during the evening, the tightening inside of me moved from pleasure to pain. I needed release and knew my only source was the man beside me. However, instead of offering relief for the smoldering fire, Nox simply continued to fan the flames.

The menacing gleam in his eyes was the spark. The way the navy swirled in the paleness as he leaned close and whispered in my ear turned butterflies into bats. At first his directives were simple, almost mundane: take a sip of your drink, tilt your head to your right, spread your legs, wider. Then I realized his plan. He was testing me step by step, to see if I would play his game.

I did.

I wanted to.

By the time our main course arrived my thighs were slick with my dedication to Nox's entertainment, yet he'd barely touched me. My stuttered breathing and noticeable arousal was mostly accomplished with merely his words and velvety tone. On the few occasions he'd ventured to ease his skilled fingers higher and lightly brushed my folds, I squirmed involuntarily toward his touch. Instead of rewarding my effort, he'd calmly rebuke me, reminding me that *he* was the one testing *my* limits. This was his night. My part was to follow his rules. Though I did everything but verbally beg for more, his teasing continued, never delving deeper or satisfying the part of me that longed for his attention.

After dinner he took my hand and led me out past the palm trees to the long Oceanside pier. Despite the beautiful atmosphere, my frustration had grown beyond want to need. I silently cursed myself for the last few wasted nights. I cursed him for what he was doing and what he could do. My urgency was palpable. I wanted—no needed—to hurry back to the resort so that he could explore my limits in private.

"Patience," he murmured close to my ear, his warm breath sending shivers down my spine. As if he could read my thoughts, he added, "We'll both get what we want. But before we do, I need to be sure you're ready."

Ready?

"I'm ready. I promise."

His deep chuckle was quickly lost to the roar of the surf.

The water and sky were no longer blue and sparkling. Old-fashioned street lamps, every fifty or so feet, cast circles of light upon our path. The soft illumination gave the illusion that the boardwalk was suspended in space. With the cover of night, the sea had become a black tide, invisible but for the whitecaps and the gentle rocking of the pier. The sky shimmered with stars. We paused at a simple wooden bench just outside a circle of light, and Nox gestured for me to sit. My pulse quickened and mind spun when instead of sitting beside me, he knelt before me. Electricity ricocheted through me as he leaned down and kissed the inside of my knee.

"Nox?" I asked. Drawing out his name, the one-word question revealed a hint of my hidden Southern drawl. With his warm breath skirting my thighs, I nervously looked from side to side, wishing we were alone.

Ignoring my silent plea, the menacing grin I'd grown to adore made

ALEATHA ROMIG

Nox's eyes sparkle as he gently pushed my knee to the side. I sucked my lip
between my teeth, stifling a moan. The cool sea breeze was a stark contrast to
his warm breath against my drenched sensitive skin. Slowly, he brushed his
large hand over my leg, moving it down, and capturing my ankle. Just as I was
about to speak, though I wasn't sure what I would have said, he lifted my foot
and removed my shoe. Then he did the same with the other one.

"Damn," Nox said, standing and offering me his hand. "Even in the
dark, that was a fucking fantastic view."

A rush of blood filled my cheeks as I stood, barefoot, short, and
confused. "Why did you...?"

He touched my lips. "Remember, tonight is about no questions, just
trust."

I nodded against his finger. He took my hand in his and began walking
toward the end of the pier, while my shoes dangled from the long fingers of
his other hand, the hand that I wanted somewhere else. After a few steps I
understood what he'd done and why. It was the wooden slats of the pier. In
the dark it would have been difficult, if not impossible, for me to walk without
getting my high heels caught. I leaned closer to his arm as the strong wind
blew inland, pushing the skirt of my dress against me. It wasn't just my skirt.
The cool air made the evidence of my arousal tingle, reminding me how close
Nox had been, yet still so far.

As we walked, we talked casually about the ocean and our shared love of
water. Our fingers intertwined as we discussed dinner. It was as if I wasn't
nude beneath my skirt and our lives wouldn't diverge in only two more days.
We laughed about the people around us and made up stories about their lives.
Nox was certain that I wasn't the only woman in my predicament, confident
that each one who passed in a dress was enjoying the sea breeze as much as I.
Though my vulnerability was potentially public, with him I felt safe and
private.

By the time we made it back to the car, my tension had mellowed, but I
was still ready to return to Del Mar. The man who'd placed my shoes back
upon my feet was indeed my prince charming; however, my best friend was
wrong: the clock would strike midnight.

110

Not wanting to think about the end to this fairytale, I concentrated on the here and now, on us, in a bubble, traveling back south on Highway 101. Only the headlights and the illumination of the dashboard dared to lessen the dark security that surrounded us.

"Charli?"

I turned my mindless gaze from the star-blanketed ocean toward Nox. "What? I'm sorry, I wasn't listening."

He reached for my thigh, skillfully moving the hem of my dress upward. "I asked if you enjoyed the restaurant."

Enjoyed?

"Dinner was delicious."

"The atmosphere?"

I bit my lip. "It was beautiful and so was the pier."

"Then why do you seem…" He hesitated. "…unfulfilled?"

Because I'm freak'n aroused and you've done nothing but tease me.

"I'm not."

A small gasp escaped my lips and my body twitched as Nox's hand moved higher, nearing my core. "You're not?" He quickly turned my direction and back to the road. By the glow of the dashboard and oncoming headlights I saw the accusing stare as his lids narrowed. "Do you know what happens when you break my rules?"

I'm not sure I could think about that. Would the answer push my limit?

My pulse quickened. "I'm not breaking your rules. I've done everything you said."

"So you were just truthful? You're not horny? You don't want relief?"

My eyes widened. *Shit!* "I didn't say that. I do."

He flipped my skirt higher. "Then do it."

I shifted in the seat, my untethered hair blowing around my face. "I-I don't know what you mean."

"You've never pleasured yourself?"

"I have. But…"

"But what?" he asked.

I sat straighter. "Isn't that *your* job, to pleasure me?"

"It is. And I will. Like I said, I want to be sure you're ready."

"Shit, Nox," I practically spit the words out before I gave them any thought. "I'm ready. I am."

"Put those fancy shoes I carried up and down the pier on the dash."

I contemplated his demand. *On the dash? Does he mean while I'm still wearing them?*

"Don't make me keep repeating myself. I don't like to repeat myself. Put your shoes on the dash and lay your seat back. Not all the way."

Shit! He does mean while I'm still wearing them.

"Nox?"

"My night. Have I surpassed your limit?"

I didn't answer, not verbally. My tummy fluttered as I found the button and reclined the seat.

"That's enough. I want to be able to see *everything*, including your beautiful face."

I released the button and one by one put my feet on the dashboard. The position gave me the sensation of a gynecological appointment. That was, until the velvet voice began.

While expertly steering us toward Del Mar, Nox's commands choreographed my every move. Step by step, he verbally moved me, to his optimum viewing pleasure, and to the promise of my relief. By the time he was satisfied with my positioning, my dress was bunched around my waist, my knees were awkwardly spread to the side, and my fingers were working feverishly. It wasn't like I'd never done this; however, I'd never done it with an audience.

"Don't think about it."

My fingers stilled.

"Charli, don't stop and don't think—feel and listen. Listen to me."

I closed my eyes and concentrated on the rush of wind around the car, the rumbling timbre of Nox's tone, and the tension building inside of me. "Listen to me." His voice dominated my thoughts. "Don't stop. Think about the sound of my voice and the touch of my hand. Imagine it's me working that beautiful pussy. Pretend it's me: my fingers, tongue, and cock."

My fingers moved in circles, small and slow, sliding my essence across my core. Faster and faster they worked, concentrating on my sensitive nub. A moan echoed through the night as the passing cars and trucks disappeared and my back arched.

"That's it. I'm going to be the one doing what you're doing. But first, beautiful, you need some relief."

I plunged in one finger, then two, as I shifted my weight to my shoulders and sucked my lip.

"Oh that's it. You're close, aren't you?"

I am. I'm so freak'n close.

I tried to respond, but when my answer emerged more as sounds than words, I merely nodded.

"Stop."

What the hell?

I heard his command, but my orgasm was too close. My fingers had a mind of their own.

"Stop." He seized my hand and pulling it toward him, sucked the evidence of my pleasure from my fingers. "Put your seat up. We have a stop."

Stop? I couldn't comprehend.

"Put your feet down and adjust your skirt."

The dark, isolated world inside the Boxster turned bright as the tires bounced, and Nox turned the car off the main highway. We were at a gas station. The car needed gas? You had to be kidding me.

I was wrong. This man wasn't my prince charming. He was a sadist.

Before I could do much more than right the seat and myself, we were parked but not at a pump. I gasped as my door was opened and Nox pulled me from the car, my feet doing their best to maintain his gait. The fluorescent lights assaulted my eyes as we passed the counter filled with lottery tickets, and watched over by an attendant. There may have been other people. Were there cars? I couldn't think or remember as he tugged me forward.

He threw open a door and pulled me inside. Disinfectant assaulted my nose as the lock's tumblers reverberated through the small bathroom. I stared up at Nox, confused as hell.

"Wha—"

Gleam and want shone from his pale blue eyes, making the world beyond us disappear. Our breaths, shallow and fast, filled the silence. I didn't have a chance to finish my word, much less my question, before my back collided with the cold tile wall, and Nox pulled my tangled hair, tilting my head.

A gasp escaped my lips only a moment before his mouth captured mine, swallowing the sound of my protest.

Protest?

I couldn't fight him off if I wanted to. But as my body melded to his, I knew it was all right. I didn't want to fight.

The scent of disinfectant was soon lost to the musk and desire that filled the air. His movements were no longer refined as his hunger overtook him. Nox wasn't hungry—he was ravenous, a man on the brink of starvation and I was his meal. Tugging at the zipper of my dress, he released the fitted material and freed my breasts. They were his first course as he kissed, sucked, and abraded my sensitive skin with abandoned disregard for the coarseness of his cheeks.

"You are a magnificent woman," he praised, "a princess in another life." His words came between kisses—no, nips and bites behind my earlobe, collarbone, and breasts. "You *deserve* a man who worships and makes tender love to you."

My entire body trembled with need.

His gallant words were in severe disparity with the roughness of his actions. He spun me around to face the sink and his voice lowered. "And I think you've had that. You've had chivalry. Charli, tonight I'm going to give you the opposite. You deserve candlelight and walks on the beach."

Nox forcefully placed my hands on the edge of the sink and yanked my ass backward. Looking up to the mirror, I watched the erotic scene unfold. With my breasts exposed and auburn hair mussed, I looked into my own eyes and saw the golden color clouded with desire. Spreading my legs with his knee, he pushed my feet apart.

I closed my eyes and willingly surrendered, knowing that what he was doing was wrong and went against everything Alex had worked to become.

That didn't change the reality: I wanted this. Nox was right. I'd had sweet, and just like the woman in the mirror, I was his for the taking.

He bunched the skirt of my dress around my waist. "Our first time," he said, "because there will be more than one time, won't be what you *deserve*." His words skirted in hot breaths against my ear, making my knees tremble and skin pepper with goose bumps. He lowered his lips to my collarbone. "Our first time will be what you *want*, what you fantasize about. I'm going to take you, right here, right now." He tugged my hair, bringing my eyes back to the mirror to make our gazes meet. His blue swirled with dark navy as he stared into me, into my soul. His tone demanded honesty. "Limits, Charli. I'm going to fuck you like you've never been fucked. Tell me now if I've crossed that limit. Tell me now if you don't want this."

Words didn't form; instead, I pushed my ass backwards until it brushed against his erection. Sometime during his speech he'd freed it from the confines of his slacks.

"Last chance, Charli."

"Please." My word was barely audible.

He tugged my hair again. "What did you say?"

"Please, Nox. I want you. Take me."

He didn't need to be sure I was ready. The evidence glistened under the awful fluorescent lights. The sound of the condom package tearing was soon replaced by my whimper as he plunged deep.

I tried to brace myself against the sink, but his unrestrained passion was more than I could handle, and my grip began to slip. Just then, his strong arm wrapped around my waist and held me steady as he fulfilled every desire. In two, three, no, four thrusts, my back arched and he buried himself inside of me.

"I want to hear you." The command came out as a growl against my neck as he moved slowly in and out.

The tension, building since our drive to Oceanside, intensified. Those flames that earlier he'd only fanned began to rage. The friction inside of me was the fuel feeding the growing blaze. I bit my lower lip to stop my screams. I was almost certain there were people out there.

Nox thrust over and over. Reaching forward, his fingers on my clit masterfully added to the growing wildfire.

"Oh!"

"That's it. I want everyone out there to hear us." He continued to move in and out. "When we walk out of here, everyone's going to know exactly what we did." His fingers mimicked the movements I'd done in the car. The waves building within me blocked out the cramped bathroom, the terrible lights, and even the world. It was only us and what he was doing and saying. "They're going to know that I fucked you, not like a princess..." He continued to move in and out. "...but like a slut in a public bathroom. And every one of them will know you wanted it." He slapped my ass, the sting kindling to the ever-growing inferno. "Now, Charli, say it. Tell me you want this."

"Yes."

"Louder."

"Yes! I want this."

"What? What do you want?"

Oh God. I'm about there.

"You," I said breathily.

He pulled out, leaving my insides clenching at nothingness. "Tell me *exactly* what you want."

I thrust my body backward. "You, please. Inside of me." My inhibitions evaporated. "Damn it! Asshole, I need your cock inside of me! Now!"

My words were rewarded with a deep laugh as he went deeper, stretching me, filling me, moving faster and faster, finding my breasts, and tweaking my hard nipples.

"Oh yes!" I cried out as we fell deeper into the fog of musk.

"I-I..." My fingers gripped the sink as my legs stiffened.

Nox pulled out, turned me around and lifted my body to his. Pressing my back against the cold tile, I hugged his neck and wrapped my legs around his waist. We were like two locking pieces of a puzzle. Once I'd accommodated him completely, I screamed and surrendered to the most earth-quaking fall I'd ever experienced. With my face buried in the nape of his neck, I gasped for breath. The woodsy cologne filled my senses as the stars exploded like fireworks, the sparks lingering until the world around me came back into focus. With one final thrust, Nox's growl rumbled against my bare chest and bounced off the bathroom walls. His massive shoulders fell against me and pinned me to the wall.

Shit! They'd probably heard us all the way to the gas pumps.

Tenderly, Nox kissed my lips and lowered my feet to the floor. I stood on wobbly knees as he lifted the front of my dress over my breasts and pulled the zipper up.

"Adjust your dress," he said with a smirk.

He discarded the condom in the toilet and turned back to me. Lifting my chin, he said, "Walk out of here with your head held high, princess. When we get back to Del Mar, you're getting what you *deserve*."

CHAPTER 14

───●○●───

Past

WHAT I DESERVE... the words rang through my consciousness as Nox parked the Boxster under the large awning and gave the keys to Ferguson.

"Welcome back, sir and miss." *Did I imagine his grin?*

As we walked toward the private elevator, Nox leaned down and whispered, "You're a princess, and I'm going to show you how a princess should be treated."

I hadn't thought about it earlier, but no one since my real father had called me princess, not in a positive way. While my body ached from his last demonstration, the name made my heart soar. Curiosity about his plans pulsated through me, tightening my insides, erasing the soreness.

We both smiled and politely conversed with Fredrick as we waited for the elevator. It appeared so natural, no one would know that I was still without panties and we'd just had sex in a filthy public bathroom. All right, it wasn't filthy, but it wasn't a five-star hotel either. It was a roadside gas station.

"Thank you, Fredrick," I said as we stepped into the elevator.

"Good night," Nox said, handing Fredrick a bill from his money clip and pushing the close button for the door.

I smirked at Nox's polite and not-so-subtle way of letting Fredrick know that we didn't need his assistance to push the one button.

"Good night, sir, miss."

We both giggled as the doors closed.

"I have plans for you."

His deep tone sent chills across my skin. "Plans?" I asked with my most innocent tone and expression.

The corner of Nox's lips moved upward. "Oh princess, you do that doe-in-the-headlights look very well." The elevator began to move. "But I just fucked you in the bathroom of a gas station." He pushed me against the dark paneling as his lips covered mine and his tongue took my breath. "That fuck'n innocent act... that ship has sailed."

I swallowed, unsure what to say. Nox did that to me, took away my breath, words, and maybe my heart. When the doors opened and we stepped from the elevator hand in hand, I peered around, looking for Mrs. Witt. I'd never been to the suite when she wasn't there.

"Are you looking for Mrs. Witt?"

I swear the man could read my damn mind.

"Yes, is she here?"

He tugged my hand, pulling me toward the ostentatious floral arrangement. The sweet aroma of orchids eclipsed his woodsy cologne. Flinging his jacket onto a bench, Nox's smirk returned as he effortlessly lifted me onto the edge of the marble table. Spreading my knees he leaned between my legs. "Would it matter to you if she were?" His arm surrounded my waist and pulled me closer as his other hand moved higher on my leg. "You told a whole gas station full of people you wanted my cock inside of you. My *cock*," he repeated with the lifting of his brow. "That was the word you used. It doesn't seem like someone who would do that would be concerned about the presence of *one* woman."

I lowered my forehead to Nox's shoulder. A rush of blood colored my cheeks as I murmured against his jacket, "I know Mrs. Witt. I didn't know—"

"Matt and Sally...?" He lifted my eyes to his. "They were the only two wearing name tags."

I shook my head. "I used the wrong word."

"You did?"

"Yes, I should have said *dick*, as in you're being one right now."

Nox laughed as his pale eyes sparkled. "Am I now?"

"Yes," I said defiantly; however, with my chin still held captive and a grin on my face, I didn't think he believed me.

His thumb caressed my cheek. "I don't think so. You see, princess, I doubt that crowd gives many standing ovations, and we were fortunate enough to get one."

Oh! I was so embarrassed.

I met his wicked eyes, and asked, "Mrs. Witt?"

"She has her own suite. For the rest of the night..." He spread my legs wider. Brushing his lips to mine, his fingers found my folds. "...you're mine. All mine."

Tilting my head back, Nox nuzzled my neck. His stubble abraded my sensitive flesh like the prickling sensation of a thousand needles sending sparks from my neck to my core. When my breathing increased, Nox lifted me from the table and cradled me against his chest.

"This is where I get to decide," he smirked.

"Decide?"

"Should I be the *dick* you mentioned?"

I reached up and kissed his cheek. "Do I have any other options?"

He carried me toward his bedroom. "I promised you what you *deserved*. I don't break promises."

My eyes opened wide in astonishment as he opened the door to a sea of flickering candles—hundreds of candles everywhere—on the armoire, windowsills, and tables.

"How?"

He set me on the floor and pulled me toward the bathroom, also illuminated by candlelight. I turned a full circle in awe. The large tub was filled with bubbles and the scent of lavender hung heavily in the air.

"The other night," he explained, "my visit to your suite interrupted your bubble bath, and I told you earlier that you deserved walks on the beach and candlelight." He gently spun me around and lowered the zipper of my dress, all the way down. "We've walked," he murmured against my skin. "Now it's time for candlelight." Slipping the straps from my shoulders, he allowed my dress to flutter to the ground, creating a puddle of black silk around my feet. Nox gently pulled the tie from my low ponytail as I stood with my back still toward him, wearing only my heels. "You have the most beautiful hair." He spoke as he gathered it higher and wound the tie around it. "In here," he went on, "with the candlelight, it's the color of mahogany, rich and distinguished, but in the sun, I see red and yellow." He twisted the length and tucked it under the tie, creating a bun. "It's just like you: beautiful, layered, and unpredictable."

I stood statuesque as the puddle near my feet grew with the inclusion of Nox's shoes, shirt, tie, and slacks. He turned me toward him. "You deserve to be treated like the princess you are, like a queen."

I couldn't stop the grin when I realized that he had dressed similarly to me, also commando, standing before me in his purest and sexiest form. I reached for him, seeing clearly, for the first time what I'd only felt. The tendons in Nox's neck strained as I ran my hand over his length. Grinning at the pile of clothing that didn't include his boxers or underwear, I asked, "Did the sea breeze thrill you as much as it did me?"

"No." Velvety smoothness cut through the fog of the warm bath water and steam on the mirrors. "I believe your dress gave you a distinct advantage over my slacks."

I lifted myself to my tiptoes and kissed his cheek. "Pity. You don't know what you were missing."

After slipping out of my heels, Nox helped me into the tub of warm water. Bubbles covered my breasts as the water rose and he slid in behind me. I settled between his legs, my back against his chest and erection.

Cupping the water, Nox showered my breasts and collarbone, caressing and fondling as he worked. Tilting my head back, I closed my eyes while the flicker of candlelight danced behind my lids.

"How did you do this?" I asked.

His words skirted over my neck. "I may have sent a text, and Mrs. Witt may have left just as we entered the elevator."

"I never saw you do that. I didn't even notice your phone."

Nox laughed his chest vibrating behind me. "That means I was doing a good job of keeping you preoccupied. Now I plan on doing more than distracting you."

Oh God.

With the twitch of his erection against my back, my once satiated core clenched with wanton lust.

"I believe it was you," he cooed, "who mentioned that *pleasing* you was *my* job."

I nodded as I closed my eyes again and yielded to his ministrations. His fingers found my core, rubbing, stroking, and caressing. I craned my neck toward him offering my lips as our tongues moved together. He continued to stroke the fire inside of me, building the pressure until I was afraid I'd explode too early. My nails dug into his thighs as my back arched and legs stiffened.

"Not yet," Nox said, lifting and guiding me. I sucked in a deep breath as he moved me until we were face to face. After he made sure we were protected, he aligned himself with my core and pulled my hips down, sheathing his cock with my already tender body.

"Oh! God!" My whimper echoed off the tile as he stretched me in one painful yet pleasurable plunge. I bit my lip and lowered my forehead to his shoulder as he moved my hips up and down.

Nox coaxed my lips to his. "There's no one else around to hear." Nox kissed and teased my lower lip free with his teeth. "But don't let that stop you. Hearing you turns me on." He sucked my taut nipple. "It makes me harder."

I wasn't sure how he could possibly be *harder*, but if letting a few sounds come out was all it took, I was ready.

Up and down I moved, my knees against the side of the tub, the water sloshing about. I wasn't sure what sent me over the edge, the marvelous friction building inside of me or the sated expression as his blue eyes clouded with pleasure, but either way, I couldn't muffle my cries as my body detonated around his.

By the time we made it back to the bedroom and he laid me on the bed, some of the candles had burnt themselves out, making the room darker than it had been. With my head on the pillow, Nox fanned my hair around my face and lifted a votive. Swirling the warm melted wax, Nox asked, "It's still my night, princess. Have I reached your limit?"

"No. But I don't—"

His finger touched my lips. The flickers of flames danced as reflections in his eyes. "Just tell me if I do. I'll listen."

Oh God. What is he going to do? Do I trust him?

I nodded.

Never taking his eyes from mine, Nox tenderly wrapped a long piece of satin from the bedside stand drawer around my wrists. Each twist made my heart soar faster and faster. Questions came in rapid succession as he secured my arms above my head, but each time I opened my mouth to ask, his gentle kiss took away my words.

I'd never allowed anyone to bind me—Alex hadn't—and I shouldn't. I pushed Alex away. This was Charli's night with Nox, not hers.

My body was on high alert. Everything was magnified. The aroma of musk with a hint of the lavender filled my senses, while his breaths filled my ears.

"Do you want me to stop?"

My hips swayed with need. "No."

His smile melted what was still whole inside of me, as his fingers moved to be sure I was ready. I was. I wanted him and was ready to let him do anything, until... he turned his attention from me to a flickering candle. I suddenly remembered the way he'd swirled the wax. My heart raced as I debated my hard limit.

"Nox?" I'd never experienced hot wax on my skin. I didn't know if I was ready.

"Do you trust me?" Nox asked, as he lifted the candle from the table, pursed his lips, and blew out the flame.

I did. I wanted to.

"Princess?" I asked, reminding him of what he said I deserved.

"Fire doesn't burn the dragon."

Oh shit! Sexy and a Game of Thrones *quote.*

I stifled a scream and pulled violently against the satin as the first dollop landed on my breast. The hot wax hurt like hell.

"Limit?" Nox asked with that menacing gleam to his eye.

It was that shimmer that kept me mute, that shimmer that stopped me from yelling *yes* at the top of my lungs. It was that glint that twisted my insides to a painful pitch. I inhaled and shook my head.

"I trust you."

I don't know what happened during the next few minutes, or was it days? I couldn't recall any of it, even if I were under oath. I hated the hot wax upon my tender skin, and at the same time, it was the most erotic experience of my entire life. Each time the molten liquid landed on me, Nox found another way to make it pleasurable: a suck and nip of my hard nipple, his fingers angled perfectly inside my core, or the saltiness of him deep in my throat. By the time he'd peeled the cold wax from my skin and released my wrists, I was lost to a high only he could provide.

Gently he eased his covered rod into me. "You *deserve* a man who will make tender love to you."

Though my energy was spent, my core clenched around him, hugging him with a ferocity I couldn't muster and milking him for everything he could give.

There was at least one more detonation before I conceded to my limit. It wasn't my hard limit, but the amount of energy I could possibly expend. The last thing I remembered was Nox's embrace as I floated away, lost in the aroma of woodsy cologne and musk.

WAKEFULNESS CAME SLOWLY as I stretched over the soft sheets and cuddled under the fluffy comforter. It wasn't until my body protested with the ache from last night's exploration, that I remembered I was in Nox's suite. I hadn't planned on staying. With my eyes still closed, I listened for anything, but only the hum of the air conditioner could be heard. Slowly, I opened my eyes. I was alone in the large bedroom. Pulling the sheet around my breasts, memories of the night before came rushing back.

I checked my wrists for bruising and found none. On the end of the bed was a robe, like the one I had in my suite, complete with the Del Mar emblem on the breast. As I reached for the robe, I saw the note beside the bed.

Good morning, princess,
I trust you slept well—since you did it through most of the night and most of the day.

I looked at the clock and smiled. It was after ten-thirty. I had slept well, but there was still a lot of day left.

Mrs. Witt has coffee for you and can get you anything you'd like to eat. I'm in the office—of the suite. Come find me. We have more exploration to do.
~Nox

I eased out of the big bed and wrapped myself in the robe. Though my body wasn't sure it could take any more exploration, the goofy smile on my face told me that I wanted to try.

In front of the bathroom mirror, I apprehensively opened the robe. I wasn't sure what I expected from the wax, but whatever it was, there was very little evidence. A few light pink circles on my breasts, but that was it. I checked my wrists again. They were a little tender to the touch, but no discoloration.

The large tub returned the smile to my face.

Debating between a shower and finding Nox, I cleaned myself as best as I could. The washcloth and sink sufficed as I secured the robe and set off to find Nox.

"Good morning, Miss Charli," Mrs. Witt said as I rounded the corner to the kitchen.

My cheeks blushed knowing the thoughts she'd probably had. If I hadn't tamed my hair before coming out of the bedroom, no doubt, she'd have thought crazy-ape sex.

Oh shit! I needed to call Chelsea.

I did my best to act nonchalantly; after all, she worked for Nox. The man

125

was gorgeous. She was probably used to having women in robes wandering about.

"Good morning, Mrs. Witt. I'm sorry to bother you…"

"No bother," she said with a smile as she reached for a coffee pot. "How do you like your coffee?"

"Cream, no sugar."

Handing me the mug, she asked, "Can I get you anything to eat? Fruit? Muffin? Mr.… umm… Mr. Nox said you might be hungry."

Damn! The blood rushed back to my cheeks. "I think maybe I should go to my suite."

"No. I know he's waiting for you in the office. I believe he'd be very disappointed if you left."

I knew I didn't have any claims on Nox. That was our agreement: one week—that's it, but I couldn't help but ask the question that popped into my head. "Mrs. Witt?"

"Yes, dear."

"I suppose this isn't unusual…"

Her smile widened. "That's not for me to say."

I nodded.

"But," she went on, "Mr. Nox has spent the entire morning ensuring that his afternoon and evening are free. *That*," she emphasized, "is highly unusual. Don't you see why you shouldn't run off? Besides, he wasn't very happy when that happened before."

I grinned. "That was a misunderstanding, as I'm sure you're aware."

"And it was understandable. His removing that ring… let's just say, between us, that this past week has seen a string of *unusual* occurrences."

"Are you sure I won't be bothering him if I go in the office?" I still didn't know what Nox did for a profession. What if he were talking to one of his bosses? I thought about Alton and how he didn't like people coming uninvited into his office.

"No, dear. He asked for you to go to him, right?"

I nodded. "Well, in a note."

"Then there's your answer. Mr. Nox doesn't say what he doesn't mean."

"Thank you, Mrs. Witt."

She nodded. "You let me know if I can get you anything to eat."

"I will."

Carrying my coffee, I padded barefoot toward Nox's office. I knew the layout of the suite from my other visits. Thankfully, the door was slightly ajar.

"I don't care." His gruff tone came through the crack. "The debate has been going on too long. I want this resolved—yesterday."

I pushed the door wider, afraid there was someone with him, or he was on webcam. Instead, I found him standing at the window, wearing gym shorts and a worn Boston t-shirt, with a phone to his ear. The stern tone I'd heard in his voice showed in his face as he turned toward the creak of the opening door. And then his expression morphed: his blue eyes shimmered as his scowl curved into a smile.

I probably looked like an ogling schoolgirl, but the sight of Nox with sex-mussed hair, a day's beard growth, and casual clothes had me smiling from ear to ear. I hadn't thought it was possible for him to look sexier than he did in a silk suit or swim trunks, but it was. The familiar tightening inside me returned. It seemed to be a constant ailment in his presence.

"Good morning," he mouthed, still listening to the person on the other end of the phone. "Edward, I'm going to need to continue this discussion another time. Something just came up."

My gaze lowered to his shorts.

When I looked back up, he winked. "Resolve it. Goodbye."

I took a step toward him as Nox did the same.

"Not one of your bosses?"

Nox's eyes widened. "That call? No. Nobody really. I could tell you all about it, but that would break our no-information rule, and then I'd have to..." He pursed his lips.

"You'd have to *what?*"

"I was thinking about that." He reached for my waist and pulled me close. "I'm sure I can think of something." After a quick kiss he asked, "How are you this morning?"

I tilted my head against his chest. "Good."

Lifting my chin, he asked, "Good? Is that all?"

"No, I'm better than good."

CHAPTER 15

—•O•—

Present

WHEN THE LIGHT of day finally leaked around the edge of the heavy draperies and the sound of staff passed my locked door, I let myself drift off to sleep. I couldn't do it while the darkness gave cover. I couldn't do it as I stared at the glass doorknob and willed it not to turn. I wouldn't do it knowing that the old silver key that was supposed to keep my door closed could be pushed out with the right tool.

It was almost noon by the time I woke to the knock.

"Who is it?" I asked through the wood after I groggily made my way across the room.

"Me, child. Are you going to sleep the day away?"

I opened the door to Jane's smiling face. "Maybe," I replied with as much cockiness as I could muster.

She walked past me and looked around my room. Shaking her head, she opened my drapes.

The bed was disheveled from my sleepless night, but other than that, everything seemed ordinary. "Why are you shaking your head?"

"I was just wondering if you was alone."

I forced my squinted eyes to open in the now too-bright room. "What? Of course, I'm alone."

"Well," Jane said, in a tone that meant she was letting me in on some big secret. "Word around the kitchen is that Mr. Spencer be here until late. Nobody sure when he left."

My hands went to my hips. "Mr. Spencer and I walked to the lake after the party. Then he left. End of story."

"Uh-huh."

"No, uh-huh, Jane. Last night was the first time I've spoken to him in four years."

She tilted her head. "Then why I hear you two stayed close."

"Where? Who told you that?"

"You know how it is? Bethany, in the kitchen, she's friends with one of the Ashmores' girls. She said she heard Miss Millie talking to Mr. Peterson 'bout you. Said she wasn't surprised. She knew you two were just keeping it on the down low."

Oh my God!

"Down low? Are you serious?"

It made sense. That was how stories and rumors got going in Savannah. It was the system long before Facebook or Twitter and now with the help of cell phones, it was probably faster. The house staff didn't repeat what they didn't see or hear, but give them a rumor and it not only made its way around Montague Manor, but to every other house in town with help.

I reached for my phone on the nightstand. I needed to talk to Bryce again. If this weren't corralled, the people of Savannah would have us engaged before I left town tomorrow. The icons flashed. I'd missed two calls from Chelsea. We'd been texting halfway through the night. It wasn't so bad for her—she was three hours behind. For me it was after three when we stopped chatting. I'd played a few mean games of whatever the latest game app was for a little while before I'd gotten lost in the book I'd recently downloaded.

Once law school started I anticipated my time for fun reading would be severely diminished.

I scrolled down my contacts, and while I let the screen linger on one name, I forced myself to scroll back up to the B's. "I don't even have his number." Exasperated, I looked at Jane. "You can see how close we are."

Her face scrunched together. "So you two's not…"

"No. We're not."

"That's my girl. Don't let no man stop you from your dreams. You're going to be a famous judge!"

I love her so much.

"I don't know about judge or famous," I responded, "but lawyer is the plan."

"You get cleaned up and dressed, and I'll bring your lunch." She shook her head with attitude. "You done missed breakfast."

"Thanks, Jane. You don't need to do that. What time is lunch? I can eat with Mother."

A shadow passed over Jane's gaze, the same one that spent the night lurking the hallways and doorways, and then just as quickly it was gone. "Your momma's not feeling well today. She's resting. You know how those headaches of hers can be. And I don't mind bringing you some food. I'm so happy you're here."

My appetite disappeared again. If I stayed here too long, I'd waste away. "All right. But after I eat, I'll go see her."

"Let me see if she's awake."

Awake? That wasn't what Jane needed to check and we both knew it. We just didn't say it.

Smoke and mirrors.

I started to walk to the bathroom and remembered my door. "Jane, when you go get that food…"

She nodded and patted the pocket of her slacks. "Of course."

Jane had said Mother was sleeping, and since I had nothing else to do while I waited for the mystery meeting tomorrow, after my shower and lunch, I spent some time on my laptop scheduling the movers. They were supposed to pick things up on Thursday. That didn't give me much time. Chelsea and I had already started packing a few things, but the big stuff needed to get across the country, and fast. I wasn't sure where the summer had gone, but it had. It was crunch time. Even though the company promised coast-to-coast service in under two weeks, I figured I'd be sleeping on a sofa in New York for awhile, waiting for my bedroom suite to arrive.

I wasn't taking all the furniture. First, I doubted it would fit. My new apartment was nice looking from the pictures, but I knew New York well enough to know nothing was large. The other reason I wouldn't take it all was my best friend. We still had two months left on the lease in Palo Alto, and I promised her I'd pay my part while she figured out exactly what she was going to do.

I also looked at flights to get me back to California. I wished I could take one of the early ones, but I didn't know for sure what time our meeting was. As I let the cursor float over the different flights, I decided to wait until I had more information.

Living in a huge house was like going to the local supermarket. The analogy had nothing to do with food, but made sense anyway. When you went to the supermarket in sweatpants, ponytail, and barefaced, not wanting to see anyone, you ran into everyone you knew. It was the way it worked. If you're freshly showered or had just come from work or class, and you had time to run into people, you wouldn't. Living in Montague Manor was like that. The corridors could be quiet and empty, or I could run into people at every turn.

I'd made an effort with my hair, but as much as my mother complained about the ponytail, the humidity in Savannah wasn't my friend. I settled for a messy bun, but went to the trouble of putting on another of the casual sundresses she'd bought. It was the one Jane had pulled from the closet the first night. I couldn't believe after all this time, Adelaide still thought I liked pink. Red heads don't wear pink. Yes, usually the brown dominated the auburn, but my stay in Del Mar had brought out the reds and a few streaks of blonde.

My stay in Del Mar had done more than that, but I wouldn't let myself think about it—about him. We'd said one week. It may have been the best week of my entire life, but that was all we had. Besides, if we ever did find each other again, it wouldn't be the same. Del Mar was special because it was fantasy, not real life. I didn't think my heart could take Nox in my real life. He was too... too... Nox. That didn't mean I couldn't daydream about him. Real life can't ruin daydreams.

Each room I passed on my way to the rear terrace was pristine and empty. If I'd have walked around in the shorts and t-shirt that I slept in, I would have surely met Mother and Alton along the way.

I walked around the grounds. Perhaps it was because it was Sunday, but everywhere I went, there was no one but me. I wasn't looking for anyone, but it seemed strange that no one was about.

Even with the heat of the summer, the gardens were beautiful. Path after path wove through flowers, some as tall as me. Iron benches dotted the path. As a little girl I'd pretended it was a maze and only I knew the way in and out.

When I passed by the pool, the crystal clear water beckoned and I thought about swimming, but decided it wasn't worth redoing my hair. Instead, I sat on the edge, pulled my dress higher on my thighs, and let my feet dangle in the tepid water. My mind slipped back to the last morning in Del Mar.

It was the sunrise I'd been dreading—we'd been dreading. If I didn't wake up, if I lay perfectly still with my body pressed against Nox, maybe I wouldn't need to get on the plane, maybe I could stay in Del Mar forever. The warmth radiating from his skin covered and shielded me from the cool air-conditioned chill of the suite.

Skin to skin, nothing separated us.

"Are you awake," he asked, his deep voice gravelly with sleep.

"No." I buried my head against his chest.

"Isn't this early for you? Yesterday you didn't wake until, what... ten?"

My cheeks filled with crimson. "I think you wore me out the other night."

"Oh?"

Nox rolled me onto my back, his hands upon my shoulders and chest against mine. "Does that mean I didn't do a good job wearing you out last night?"

I looked into the pale blueness of his eyes. It was barely light outside, but his gaze held that hint of menace that twisted my insides. He'd done a fine job of testing my limits. I still didn't know where they were—not with him. It wasn't that I'd ever imagined some of the suggestions Nox made. It was that when he proposed the limit, no matter what it was, I wanted to test it, for him and for me. I saw the happiness he derived, and I knew the happiness he could provide. Nox made each and every prospect sexy and pleasurable. Even if, like the wax, it didn't start that way, Nox made sure it ended that way.

I shook my head. "No, you did a fine job. It was just…"

The pad of his thumb tenderly caressed my cheek as his prominent brow furrowed. "Charli, why are you crying? Did I..?"

I swallowed and shook my head. I didn't want Nox to think he'd done anything wrong. I also didn't want to admit how strongly I felt for him, or how I didn't want our time together to end. "I don't want to wake up. If I stay asleep then today will never come."

His lips gently brushed mine. It was meant as an affectionate kiss, but I didn't want that. I wanted more, needed more. I wove my fingers through Nox's dark hair and pulled him closer. The taste of his lips and his tongue as it wrestled with mine was the catalyst to my desire. Breathing no longer mattered as my back arched and I pushed my pebbled nipples against the hardness of his chest.

We didn't rush. For what seemed like an eternity, we lost ourselves in one another. It was much different than our first time, and different from every time after that. Nox had said he'd made love to me the night he brought me back to Del Mar after 101, but this was more. Every movement of his hands, tongue, and body was deliberate. He played me like an expert musician plays a prized instrument.

My body ached with need and desire as he took me to amazing highs with catastrophic earth-shaking conclusions. I gripped the sheets and called out his name, afraid I'd fall, and yet each time he was there to catch me. When we both descended from the final high, I collapsed against his shoulder and slipped off to sleep.

He'd granted my wish. The day wasn't ready to begin.

A warm breeze brought me back to reality, and I shifted against the edge of the pool. I had no idea where Nox was, but even from far away he could do things to my body. Looking down at my breasts, I thanked God that I was alone. My thin strapless bra and pink dress did little to conceal the thoughts my nipples broadcasted.

I leaned back on my arms, lifted my face to the sun, and twisted my head from side to side. The slow movement allowed the warm wind access to my perspiration-moistened skin and freed the few stuck renegade strands of hair that had escaped from my messy bun.

Is it the Georgia heat that turned up my internal thermostat or my thoughts?

I wasn't sure how long I'd been outside when I made my way back toward the house and up the stone staircase, but when I entered the house,

Mother and Alton were in the sitting room. They didn't hear me enter and for a few minutes I stood and watched them. Last night I'd heard their exchange, but today, from their expensive casual clothes to the way Alton waited upon my mother, filling her wine glass, they appeared the perfect couple.

It wasn't until my shoes clicked upon the hardwood floor and Adelaide's red-rimmed eyes met mine that I knew there was more to their current charade. She didn't speak, but sighed, bit her lip, and turned toward the window.

"Alexandria," Alton said, "have a seat. We need to speak to you about our meeting tomorrow morning."

I sat, but spoke to Adelaide. "Momma, what's the matter?"

"I just can't... I can't..."

Alton stood taller by her side. "Your mother has been upset since our office discussion yesterday."

I moved to the edge of the chair. "It's fine," I placated, like the good daughter I'd been taught to be.

Tears coated my mother's cheeks as she reached for Alton's hand.

"Momma, are you sick?"

"No." She shook her head. "Alexandria, if only you would have tried."

"Tried? What are you talking about?"

Her chin dropped to her chest. "The meeting tomorrow is to update you on your trust fund."

"I thought it might be, but why are you so upset. If I get it early, I won't do—"

"You're not getting it *early*," Alton said. "You no longer have access to it. It's gone."

CHAPTER 16

———◦○◦———

Present

"GONE? I DON'T understand. How is a million dollars gone?" I stood, unable to contain my fury.

"You've lived on it for four years," Alton said. "Stanford isn't inexpensive. I guarantee it wasn't a million any longer."

"I review the online statements every month. It was *not* gone the last time I looked."

"It's been re-appropriated." His tone slowed. "Before you decide to make any more threats, I assure you, it's completely legal and within the guidelines of the clauses set forth by your grandparents."

"Darling," Mother interjected. "I didn't want you to be blindsided at the attorney's office like you were yesterday with Bryce. That was my fault. I should've talked to you about Bryce earlier in the day, but we were having such a nice time." She dabbed her eyes with a handkerchief.

I didn't give a rat's ass about Bryce. I did about my trust fund.

"Columbia?" I asked collapsing on one of the many sofas.

"That's what we were saying yesterday. You don't have the funds to attend Columbia."

"Your first semester is paid," Alton interjected. "You'll need to transfer, or you could withdraw and receive a refund. It's time you stop wasting money and concentrate on the future."

I palmed my temples and pushed. This wasn't happening. It couldn't be happening. The future? Law school was my future.

"Dear, are you all right?"

"No, Mother, I'm not. I'm not all right. I was accepted into *Columbia Law*. Do you have any idea how difficult that is? No, you don't. You don't because as soon as you finished your degree—in art appreciation—at Emory—you married my father. You didn't apply to graduate school. And you…" I stared at Alton. "…your master's is from Georgia State!"

"I don't need to defend my degree to you or to anyone else," Alton said, the crimson creeping up his neck. "The difference is that I use my degree. You need to face the fact. It's time to move home, stop playing student, and get married."

"This isn't 1920, 1950, or even 1980! I don't need to marry."

"Dear, calm down."

I blinked my eyes hoping that if I did it enough times the scene in front of me would change. "I'm not saying I'll never marry. I'm saying I'm only twenty-three years old."

"You'll be twenty-four soon enough, and weddings take time. To really do it right, we'll need at least a year to plan." Mother lowered her voice. "We don't want people thinking you had to get married."

My head began to twitch. The world was jumpy, like an old television that had difficulty keeping a signal. "You *are* saying I have to get married. It may not be because of pregnancy, but what you're discussing is a shotgun wedding nevertheless."

"No one is putting a gun to your head. Stop being so dramatic," Alton said dismissively as he stood and refilled his tumbler of Cognac.

I stood with a huff and paced back and forth in front of the large windows, my palms clenching and unclenching. Finally, I turned. "You said clauses. What *clauses*?"

"We can discuss that tomorrow."

"No, we can discuss it *today*."

Raising his chin, Alton's eyes closed. "Hmm. I don't have the wording memorized exactly, but there's a clause about education. Undergraduate is specifically mentioned. Thankfully, Ralph was reviewing the document and found it."

Thankfully?

"So you're saying that it was intended to pay for my undergraduate degree, but not postgraduate? And you're telling me after my first semester has been paid?"

"It was an oversight, dear." She looked to Alton and back to me. "We discussed it at some length. It all became more pressing when Bryce's incident became public."

"You want me to marry Bryce. I don't even have a say in who I marry?"

"It's a matter of name. The Carmichael name and Montague, it's a match made in blue-blood heaven. Your grandfather would approve."

"Re-appropriated?" I asked Alton. "My money has been re-appropriated to where?"

"Again, the wording escapes me. However, the intended reasoning was for your focus, following college, to be on Montague. If you refuse to honor your obligation, in your absence the funds remaining in the trust revert back to the estate."

I stared in disbelief. "To you. To both of you. You have my money available to you and you're not giving it to me? Mother, you're holding my education hostage so I'll become you? Is that what you really want? You want to see me in an unhappy arranged marriage and not fulfill my dream?"

"Dear, we all have dreams. That's what sleep is for. Life has responsibilities. Your responsibility is to Montague." She reached for Alton's hand and squeezed. They'd put on the performance for so long, they probably believed it themselves—when they weren't arguing. "My marriage isn't unhappy. Marriage takes work and compromise..."

I stopped listening to her before she began. Instead, I was preoccupied doing mental math. I had a few accounts and credit cards. I didn't want to be in debt, but maybe if I could start class, and find a job, I could look into student loans. I'd never had a job or needed credit, but surely, a law student at Columbia was a good credit risk.

"…coming for dinner tonight. He wanted to see you."

I turned my attention back to my mother. "Repeat that."

"He wants to see you."

"He, as in Bryce?"

"Well, yes. Whom else would I be talking about?"

"No."

"Excuse me?" she asked.

I walked toward the archway. "No. I have one semester. I'm taking it."

"Alexandria," Alton said, "technically, we could withdraw the payment for this semester. It was made in error."

I swallowed my pride and concentrated on my mother. Moving to her, I knelt beside her knees and reached for her hand. "Momma, give me the one semester. Let me try to do this. I'm not saying I'll never marry. Let me do what you never could."

When she started to look at Alton, I squeezed her hand. "*I* am a Montague. *You* are a Montague. If you support me, no one can stop it."

Her chin dropped as she exhaled. "No more money."

"I have some cash. I'll get a job."

Tears moistened her blue eyes. "You're so strong."

I wasn't. I was scared to death. I also wasn't going to be railroaded into a lifetime sentence.

"This is a waste of your time and money," Alton repeated his case. "If you do the sensible thing and withdraw from classes, we'll let you keep the tuition."

I straightened myself, stood tall, and pulled my shoulders back. "Say that again."

"If you do the sensible thing, we'll let you keep the tuition."

I smirked and looked at Adelaide. "Did you hear that?" Before she could answer, I continued, "That tuition money is mine. I want to use it for Columbia."

"What about your rent? What about other expenses?"

"I'll find a job."

Alton scoffed while my mother shook her head. Finally, she said,

"Montague women aren't meant for jobs. We're meant for carrying on the name."

"What name? My grandfather put this archaic clause in my trust fund and he was the one who let the name end. There are no more Montagues. Forever, it's destined to be a middle name."

"Alexandria Charles Montague Collins, whether it's a middle name or not, Montague blood runs through your veins as strongly as Collins blood. It doesn't matter if it's passed on by a female or male, you are heir to one of the most prominent families this state or nation has ever known."

I shook my head. "Bravo, Mother. If you're right that it doesn't matter, then make the decision. Give me one semester, because the way I feel right now, I'm not discussing this calmly over dinner with Bryce. I'm not marrying Bryce, and I'm not moving home. I'm leaving Montague Manor today with or without your blessing. If you ever want me to return, my leaving and one semester will be with your blessing." I crossed my arms over my chest. "The choice is yours."

"Laide, we discussed our daughter's ploys."

"I am *not* your daughter!" I snapped.

Faster than I knew he could move, Alton stood and his open palm slapped my cheek.

Stunned, I took a step back. Turning to my mother I asked, "What do you say?"

MY HANDS SHOOK as I got into the backseat of the taxi outside of Montague Manor. "To the airport."

I didn't say another word to the driver as he drove the long oak-lined drive. I couldn't form words, not in coherent sentences. I'd done well, in my opinion, during the confrontation. It was afterward, in my room with Jane, that I lost it.

Jane told me that Brantley would drive me wherever I wanted to go, but I didn't trust him. She was the only one I trusted at Montague Manor. I sucked in my breath and clenched my teeth together when the taxi reached the gate. I wouldn't have put it past Alton to have the watchman stop the taxi. It wasn't until we were free of the grounds of the estate that I remembered to breathe. Sitting silently, with my Montague head held high, I watched the passing landscape as we drove into Savannah. This driver wasn't on Alton's payroll, but that didn't mean he couldn't be bought. I didn't want him to know where I was truly going.

I'd left the manor in too much of a hurry to book a flight. Besides it was Sunday, and the Savannah airport wasn't that big. Sunday evening departures were few and far between. My plan was to be dropped at the airport and then take another taxi to a nearby hotel. I would find an early morning flight or I'd rent a car and drive to Atlanta. I didn't care, as long as it was away from Montague Manor.

My mind slid to Jane. I loved her as I should love my mother. She was the one who was always there for me. She was the one who rocked me when I was little and put the bandages on my scraped knees. She was the one who worked to protect me from the monsters that lurked in the shadows. My mother hadn't been there then. Why did I think she'd be there now?

Tears threatened as I considered the possibility that this could be the last time I was ever home, ever in Savannah, maybe even in Georgia.

I'd walked calmly out of the sitting room when silence followed my question to Adelaide. I didn't want to hear any more of Alton's reasoning or Adelaide's excuses. I made it all the way to my bedroom before I let the pain register.

Everything I'd worked for, everything I'd accomplished while away at Stanford was for naught. According to them, it was a four-year reprieve, my chance to see the world. It wasn't about education or bettering myself. They didn't know how hard I'd worked to bury Alexandria and create Alex. None of it mattered.

Alexandria Charles Montague Collins had her time away, now she had a duty. They didn't care about my dream of law school, because the only dream I should have had was to marry, continue the bloodline, and live the genteel life of illusion.

As I threw my possessions into my suitcase, I left the dresses my mother bought for me wadded up at the bottom of the closet, along with all the other gifts she'd left around the room. They weren't for me. They were for Alexandria.

For maybe the last time, my comfort came from Jane. She wrapped me in her arms as the hurt and rage came out of me in deep hiccupping sobs. I hadn't cried like that since... since him. Though she rubbed my back and told me it would be all right, I knew, just like last time, it wouldn't.

The blessing I'd requested from my mother in the sitting room came via Jane. It was my mother who gave it, just not in person. I had one semester and some money in my checking and savings accounts in California. It wasn't much, but it would get me to New York. Even if I survived until the holidays, even with my mother's blessing, Jane and I both knew the beginning of the year would signal my death.

If I didn't return to Montague Manor, I never could. I'd be dead to my family.

If I did return, I'd be dead to me.

Either way, my diagnosis was terminal.

My phone vibrated with a text message:

Chelsea: "CALL ME!"

I'd turned off my ringer. I wasn't ready to talk to anyone.

Me: "I WILL. GIVE ME A FEW."

Chelsea: "WHAT THE HELL HAPPENED? ARE YOU COMING HOME?"

Me: "LATERS."

In all the madness, my best friend still made me smile. This time she'd done it without even knowing. She did it by calling our apartment *home*. As usual, Chelsea was right. The two-bedroom flat we shared had been more of a home to me than Montague Manor had ever been. My shoulders straightened and I sucked in a breath as we pulled under the *Departures* sign.

I had a home in Palo Alto and I would find one in New York.

The Montague name didn't own me—no one did.

CHAPTER 17

--●o●--

Six weeks earlier

NOX REACHED FOR the lapels of the robe and teased them apart.

"Hey, Mrs. Witt," I reminded.

"Do you know how badly…" His husky tone was thick, sending tingles through me. "…I wanted to look under your robe the other night?"

I rested my hands on his arms, making no effort to stop him from doing exactly what he wanted. "No, how badly?"

He loosened the sash from around my waist. As the tie fell dangling in its loops, the robe gaped open, revealing just the sides of my breasts. The warm pad of his finger skirted across my skin, moving the satin aside. With my breasts fully exposed I looked up and quickly away. His pale gaze swirled with an intensity that reverberated to my bones. With nothing more than his eyes, my breathing hitched and nipples hardened.

I had absolutely no control or willpower when it came to this man.

Nox lifted my chin, bringing our eyes back to one another. His lips gently touched mine. I moaned as his fingers captured my pebbled nipples.

"Very, very badly." His velvet words were a blowtorch, melting my insides. "I imagined what I'd find."

I leaned into him. My head, suddenly heavy, fell backward as he continued to caress my breasts.

ALEATHA ROMIG

"I already knew you were stunning, ravishing even. I knew you had a smile that beckoned, holding me captive. In the short time before you left me alone in my suite, I saw a glimpse of the depth of your intelligence and humor. Your quick wit still keeps me on my toes." He released my breasts and pulled me tight to his t-shirt-covered chest. "But I still didn't know what was under that robe."

I was lost in his words.

"Do you know what I found?" he asked.

I shook my head.

"I found an alluring body. Enticing breasts that I could caress for hours because I love how you respond. Your nipples fascinate me. I love how they not only harden but how the color darkens when you're aroused." His lips twitched as he stole a glance at my aroused nipples. "And your pussy... I found heaven inside of you. The way your body hugs me, the way it shudders as you come apart." He kissed me again. "My imagination wasn't even close to what I found."

The world no longer registered. Nox and I were lost in the fog of him.

"Excuse me, Mr. Nox," Mrs. Witt called from the hallway. I turned away and quickly fastened my robe.

Nox laughed. "Mrs. Witt, your timing is impeccable."

"I'm sorry, sir. I thought you should know that you have an email. I believe you'll want to see it before your... your plans for today."

"Thank you, I'll take a look."

Her footsteps disappeared.

"Your housekeeper reads your emails?"

Nox walked to the other side of his desk and looked at his computer screen, but his head quickly snapped upward at my question. "Housekeeper? Mrs. Witt isn't my housekeeper." A smile snaked over his lips. "I can't tell you any more. No information. I believe that was *your* rule, Miss *Moore*."

I knew what he meant. I knew he was referring to our lack of last names. He was right. Who Mrs. Witt was, what her job entailed, or even its description, were none of my business. I reached for the cup of coffee that I'd set on the edge of his desk.

"Because of you, my coffee is cold."

He was deep in thought with whatever he was reading. My words hung unanswered in the air, until he looked up. "I'm surprised. I thought it was getting rather warm in here."

I blew him a kiss, purposely avoiding the other side of his desk. I didn't want him to think I was looking at his email. Although, the fact that it more than likely contained his last name did run though my consciousness. "Nox, I should go back to my suite."

"No, stay."

His command wasn't said with any urgency, but the lack of request didn't go unnoticed.

"I'm interrupting you."

"No," his tone was brisker. "This asshole is interrupting me—us. This won't take long. I'm going to call him and put this to rest, at least for now. His sense of urgency and mine are different." Nox walked to where I was standing, and the menacing gleam that was heroin to my system flashed in his pale eyes. "Today my only urgency involves you. What would you like to do today?"

"I don't want to be the cause of any problems. I'd hate to have you lose your job or account or whatever that is, over me."

He caressed my cheek. "None of that is your concern. Don't give it a second thought. Now about today: I know what I wanted about a minute ago, but we have all day. Would you like to stay here, go to the pool..." He added with a smirk, "Maybe we can see Max?" When I only pursed my lips, he went on, "Or the beach. We could rent a yacht. Have you eaten?"

I shook my head. "I still need to go to my suite and get some clothes. I don't think this robe or my black dress make very appropriate beachwear."

"Then the beach it is." He tilted his head. "You know, if we stayed here and swam in the private pool, what's under that robe would be perfectly acceptable."

"Mrs. Witt?"

"May take the rest of the day off. She has family nearby. I think I can tell you that without breaking our rule or having to kill you. That's part of why she traveled here with me."

"Oh, but then who will read your emails?"

He pulled me close, our bodies molding together. "If you take a shower here, I'll have the shop downstairs send up a swimsuit in your size."

My head continued to move back and forth though I now had to look up. The result was my hair swaying over the satin on my back. "That's not necessary. I have plenty of—"

His finger touched my lips. "Size..." He eyed me up and down. "...4?"

"Yes, well before all the meals we've been eating. I'd go with a 6 now or maybe an 8."

Nox smiled. "We had a good amount of exercise last night, but... if the 4 doesn't fit, we'll need to add more cardio to our schedule."

I didn't know if I could take more cardio. "Fine," I said as I pulled away, but before I turned to leave, I asked, "Where's my phone?"

"In the bedroom. It's plugged in. I turned off the sound."

Nodding, I went in search of my phone and a shower while Nox went back to his email.

"WHERE ARE YOU?"

"ARE YOU SPENDING THE NIGHT WITH MR. HANDSOME?"

"OMG YOU AREN'T ANSWERING. YOU ALWAYS ANSWER."

"ARE YOU DEAD? TELL ME YOU'RE NOT DEAD."

"IT'S AFTER TWO. YOU ARE SPENDING THE NIGHT!!!!"

"YOU DID IT! GO GIRL! OMG, ARE HIS BALLS BLUE?"

"HIS EQUIPMENT????"

"HE'S A LOOKER NOT A PRODUCER... AM I RIGHT?"

"IT'S OK IF IT WASN'T GOOD."

"OR WAS IT SO GOOD YOU CAN'T RESPOND?"

"SEX COMA???"

"NO MATTER WHAT, I WANT DETAILS."

"OK, NOW I'M WORRIED. IT'S MORNING."

"SHOULD I CALL HOTEL SECURITY?"

"CALL ME! SEND A TEXT. YOU GET MAD WHEN I DON'T KEEP IN TOUCH."

"I'M GIVING YOU ONE MORE HOUR... THAT'S IT."

Tears blurred her texts as I scrolled down them and laughed at my best friend.

Well, that was until I got to the last message. I didn't think Nox would appreciate hotel security busting into his suite. I was beginning to think that maybe he didn't work for anyone, but no matter what, I didn't want anyone thinking he'd done something wrong.

He's done nothing wrong.

Even the thought of things he'd done right twisted my insides.

I checked the time Chelsea sent her last text message against the clock. *Shit!* I only had ten minutes to spare.

I touched the *CALL* icon.

She answered on the first ring. "Where the hell are you? Are you still with Mr. Handsome? I was just about to—"

"Stop. I'm fine, well..." Blood filled my cheeks. "...better than fine, really."

"Better than fine," Chelsea repeated. "I'm listening."

I turned away from the bedroom door and covered my phone with my hand. "Chels, I'm standing in his bedroom wearing a robe. I'm not giving you any details—yet."

"Just one, I need to know..."

"I thought you'd be..." Nox said, as he entered the room.

I spun toward him and pointed at the phone.

"So?" Chelsea asked.

"Not blue," I answered with a grin.

"Oh girl. I need more."

"Chels, I need to go. I'll be by our room..." Nox shook his head *no* as the menacing gleam I adored grew. "...or not. I'm spending most of the day with Nox."

Though I was talking to Chelsea, Nox had my full attention. He twisted the button inside the doorknob and stalked toward me. When he was mere inches away, he mouthed *locked*. Shook his head and quietly whispered, "No Mrs. Witt."

"Chelsea, I need to…"

Nox's gaze held me captive as he removed the phone from my hand and hit the red disconnect button. When he placed it back on the bedside stand, I considered protesting, but didn't. Movement and speech were beyond my ability. Simple life processes were now my concern. Filling my lungs with shallow breaths was difficult. My heart had a new rhythm. Rushing blood filled my ears and prickled my skin. My body was hypersensitive to everything—the satin of the robe and the scent of desire.

Nox's movements were deliberate and predatory as he tugged the sash of my robe. I arched my back and gasped for air as his lips seized one of my nipples and he pulled with his teeth. Musk and need filled the room as he lifted me to the bed and slowly removed the robe from my shoulders.

He led me back to the bed. The searing stare he'd given me at the pool the day we'd met was but a tepid glance compared to the way he looked at me now. In this moment, our roles were clear. I was his for the taking, vulnerable to his whims and malleable to his touch. He had complete control.

I'd never been as exposed or felt as worshipped.

That was what Nox did: he worshipped, adoring my body—every inch. Beginning at my ankles, he kissed the insides of my legs. Slowly, his attentions moved upward until I nearly pierced the soft sheets with my fingernails as his tongue and lips devoured my tender core. With my essence on his lips, his assault continued until our tongues danced. By the time we made it to the shower, my body ached from satiation as well as wanton need. Though he'd brought me to soaring heights, he'd yet to fill me.

Chelsea was wrong—Nox had the equipment. Running my grasp up and down his stretched skin, I wordlessly told him what I'd screamed in the gas station. I wanted him. I needed him inside of me.

I couldn't contain my smile as he produced the small silver packet from the shower shelf. Using my teeth to open the condom, I wantonly sheathed his rock-solid erection.

With the warm water washing over us, Nox lifted me against the tile and granted my desire. Clinging to his shoulders, I buried my face in the crook of his neck. Each thrust moved him deeper, pushing and stretching. My moans echoed within the glass stall as I sucked the saltiness from his skin.

Though my mind questioned my ability to find the high he'd already provided, my body knew better. The more he fanned the flames of my desire, the more my muscles tightened and toes curled. Higher and higher we flew until our blaze of passion exploded, leaving us both victim to the spectacular detonation. With a guttural growl, he collapsed against the wall, pinning me in place. With the water still falling, waves of pleasure washed through me.

When our eyes met, his lips curled into his sexy smile. "I don't have the words," he said. "Amazing seems woefully insufficient."

A GENTLE BREEZE blew the sheer curtains of our cabana bed. The covering did little to shield us from the sun or from the other patrons as we rested upon the soft mattress.

"I don't remember the last time I spent an entire day like this."

I rolled to my side, planted my elbow and popped my head on my hand. Staring into his pale eyes, I asked, "So you work a lot, even when you travel?"

He pulled me closer, flattening my breasts against his bare chest. "I do. I've had a few meetings since I arrived. That's what brought me here this week."

My cheeks rose. "I'm glad you had those meetings."

He tucked a rogue strand of hair behind my ear and caressed my cheek. "Me too." His menacing grin returned. "Have you spoken to your sister?"

My ongoing deception tugged at my conscience. "You mean since you so rudely disconnected my call."

"Yes, but I didn't hear you complain. Oh, I heard you," he smirked. "But it didn't sound like complaints."

"Back to your question." I couldn't think about what we'd done. If I did, I'd want more. "I did talk to her, why?"

"I hope she doesn't mind my stealing you for the rest of your vacation."

I shrugged. "We live together for now. So I think we'll be fine."

"I'm glad I heard your answer to her question."

I leaned back and narrowed my eyes. "What question?"

Nox rolled me over until my head was upon the pillow and he was over my chest. Raising his brows, he said, "I may have seen a few texts when I plugged in your phone."

"You looked at my texts?"

"No, I plugged in your phone and they were there. And…"

My irritation floated away with the sound of the surf and the kiss of his lips. "And," I replied, "I told her your balls aren't blue."

Nox laughed, his chest vibrating against mine. "Not anymore."

CHAPTER 18

━━━●○●━━━

Past

DREAMS, LIKE FAIRYTALES, all come to an end. We wake or turn that final page. There's no escaping it. It may take days, years, or an entire lifetime, but forever doesn't truly exist. No matter how hard we wish or try, the end always comes.

Nox's and my final day, the last day of my vacation, arrived. Though we'd both awakened early, we'd been granted a short reprieve when Nox successfully lulled me back to sleep. With the sun barely up, I'd drifted away in a sweet cloud of musk, wrapped in the arms of the man I barely knew.

I didn't know his last name, where he lived, or what he did, but I knew that in the six days and five nights we'd been together, I'd lost my heart to him. I didn't know if he'd stolen it or if I'd given it. I even tried to convince myself that it wasn't the entire thing... that it was only a piece of my heart that he now possessed. If that were true, it meant that I would survive. If it were only a piece and even if what I still had within me was broken, I stood a chance of repair. One day I might find the magic we shared. Someday when Alex was ready, when she wasn't about to concentrate on law school, she could discover what I would soon be leaving.

It was a good tale, a story of fabrication, and one I knew was a lie. The pain within me from the moment we woke was too intense. The evidence pointed to one conclusion: Nox hadn't taken a *piece* of my heart. He had the entire thing. Repair would never come. It wasn't possible to repair what no longer existed.

With each breath, the void of my missing heart ached in my chest.

Though I needed to pack my things and Chelsea and I needed to get to the airport, I wasn't rushing. Instead, I was sitting across the small table on the balcony of the presidential suite, sipping coffee and moving eggs and fruit around my plate. Our time together was ticking away. The figurative clock would soon strike midnight. If this were Cinderella, I'd be running down the steps and leaving my glass slipper.

For the first time since we'd met, our sentences felt forced—polite and proper. There were so many things we hadn't said, so many things we wanted to say, but now it was too late. When we were showering, Nox joked about my missing my flight, but other than that, we'd avoided the subject.

"Nox," I said, debating with myself if I could be at least partially honest. "I know our agreement, and I still believe we should honor it. But there's something I want you to know."

His pale eyes looked up from his barely-eaten breakfast. Apparently neither of us had an appetite. "What?"

"I guess I want you to know that this week wasn't me."

Putting his fork down, he asked, "What do you mean? You're not Charli?"

I didn't want to go there. "I mean that I've never before done what we've done. I want you to know that I don't go around meeting men and doing what we did."

His grin quirked. "You want me to know you don't sleep around."

I nodded. Why would he believe me? I let him fuck me in a public bathroom. I asked for it—for his cock. That didn't sound like someone with standards. "It's just that… well, I'm sure you have met… other women… had more opportunity…"

"Charli," he reached across the table and laid his hand down, palm up.

A tear escaped my eye as I placed my hand in his.

His surrounded mine with a squeeze. "I believe you."

I forced a smile.

"No matter how experienced you think I am or how many women there have been, I'm not what you think. I don't do *this* either. I've told you—I have unique tastes, and honestly, they don't bode well for most relationships. I have sources that keep me satisfied, but that's not the same thing. I haven't even tried to be in a relationship for quite awhile."

I looked at him through my lashes. On his face I saw the sincerity mirrored in his words.

"There was something about you," he went on, "about *us*, that was different—different than anything I've *ever* experienced. I was drawn to you that morning at the pool. There was—no, *is*—electricity that surrounds us like I've never known."

The void in my chest gaped open. It was so painful I feared looking down. If I did, I was sure I'd see bloody shreds of vessels and flesh where my heart had been. Nox felt what I felt. It wasn't just me. We had a connection and soon it would be over.

"I-I wish," I said through ragged breaths, "I wish this were another time and place. I wish this were longer than a week. I wish I could, but I can't."

He squeezed my hand again. "I'm not asking—not because I don't want that. I do. I'm not asking because we both went into this with the same expectations. Believe me, I've been racking my brain for ways to make you stay, for me to stay." He looked around, taking in the balcony and the ocean beyond. His cheeks rose as he said, "I don't really live here. I also have a life to return to."

My eyes darted to his when he said *life*.

"*Life*, Charli, not *wife*. I didn't lie. Both of us have lives. Maybe one day, if it's meant to be, they'll intersect. In the meantime, we'll always have Del Mar *and 101*." He added the last part with the menacing grin that made my tummy do somersaults.

Nox stood and lifted my hand. When I rose, he pulled me into his arms and our lips met. I wanted to stay in his embrace forever. His kiss was tender and giving. The urgency we'd had over the past week had been replaced by a need to share what little of ourselves we could. His lips and tongue tasted like coffee. I knew that every time I drank a cup, I'd remember Nox. I'd also remember the way we fit together. Whenever I was chilled, I'd recall the warmth of his solid body against mine. That memory would become my blanket as I resumed my life, my real one.

I longed to give him something, too. As his fingers raked the waves of my long hair, I wanted him to remember me, to remember us. I would have gladly given him anything he desired, but the pain in my chest meant I had nothing left to give. Nox already owned me—heart, body, and soul.

I was no longer my own to bestow.

"I'll take you and Chelsea to the airport."

I shook my head. "No, I can't. I can't do this again. This has to be our goodbye." The word was a knife gutting the void.

The vein and tendons in his neck told me that he wanted to argue, perhaps demand. After all, he hadn't asked. The navy swirling in his light blue eyes also let me know that his emotions were on overload. He was debating his next words.

"Please, Nox, please don't make this more difficult than it already is."

His lips captured mine. One last kiss—no longer gentle. This was rough and devouring.

I moaned as our bodies melted together.

When Nox released me, he brushed my bruised lips with his. It was as if he needed one more connection. "Charli, I'll never forget you." Taking my chin in his grasp, he said, "I'm not going to tell you which one or that I'm sorry for doing it, but when you discover the rule I broke, I hope you know that it was because of you."

I shook my head. "I don't understand. What rule?"

He kissed my nose. "I said I wasn't going to tell you."

"Will you tell me why it was because of me?"

"Because since the first moment I saw you, I've made exceptions. I've done and said things that I do not, as a rule, do. You do that to me. You make me rebel even against myself."

I nodded, understanding exactly what he was saying. Nox had done the same thing to me. He'd made Charli into someone Alex or Alexandria would never be. Because of him I'd cheated on myself. And I loved him for it.

My eyes closed as another tear cascaded down my cheek. I'd said the word, if only in my head. I *loved* Nox, a man with no last name.

"Goodbye," I choked as I turned and walked away. I couldn't turn back. I couldn't see him in his jeans and white button-down shirt with the rolled-up sleeves. I couldn't stare one more second into the stunning pale blue of his eyes or run my fingers over the scruffiness of his jaw. When the doors to the elevator closed, I collapsed against the paneling and the control panel's buttons blurred as I continued to blink away the tears.

Though my head ached from the pent-up pressure, it wasn't until I was safely inside Chelsea's and my suite that I let the sobs rain free. With my face buried in my best friend's shoulder, I cried as my body convulsed with each tattered breath.

CHELSEA AND I settled into our airplane seats as other passengers walked by. People thought first-class was something special, but as person after person passed, first-class felt like a display case. I wished for a seat at the very back, a place where I could hide and no one would see.

"Before we take off, can I get you anything to drink?" the way-too-perky flight attendant asked, placing napkins on the armrest between us. With a wink, she tapped my knee. "You know, honey, it's not that bright in here. You can take off your sunglasses."

"My friend has sensitive eyes," Chelsea said. "We'll both have champagne."

After she walked away, I whispered, "I don't feel like celebrating."

Chelsea removed my sunglasses, shook her head and returned them to my face. "You need to celebrate. You need to look at this the way it was—something amazing and unique."

The attendant handed us each our plastic glass with bubbling liquid.

"I thought they used glass glasses in first-class," Chelsea said, examining her cup.

"After we take off."

"Because it's safer to have real glass at 42,000 feet than sitting still on the ground?"

I shook my head. I'd never given it that much thought.

"Come on," she encouraged. "Let's toast."

"Chels…"

She tipped her cup toward mine. "To Charli with an *i*."

"To Charli with…" *Nox*. I said the last part only to myself. Then I added, "Welcome back, Alex."

Chelsea smiled. "You know, Alex isn't so bad." She shrugged. "I like her."

"Thanks. I'm glad. She's *not* bad, but she doesn't have an *i*." Sighing, I reached under the seat in front of us and pulled out my purse. It didn't matter that my eyes were red and puffy, I brought more attention to myself with the sunglasses than I did without them. I put them in their case.

"You know," Chelsea said, "I had a great time, even if you didn't."

My face snapped toward her. "I did!"

"There," she declared triumphantly. "I wanted you to hear yourself admit that. You *did* have a great time."

"I did." I turned on my phone. "Have you put your phone in airplane mode?" I asked.

"Hey, let me see that," Chelsea said, grabbing my phone from my hand.

Why are people constantly taking my phone? "What are you doing?"

"I've been thinking about what you said, remember?"

I shook my aching head. "No, I don't remember. Do you think they could get me something for this headache?"

"More champagne," she murmured before she repeated the story I'd told her. "You said that *he* told you he broke a rule."

My void grew. It was too early to remember *his* words. They weren't only words in my memory. They were deep, velvety tones that tightened my insides while covering my skin in goose bumps.

Involuntarily, I shuddered.

If anyone notices, they'll probably think I have the flu or some disease. If I don't get my shit together, the FAA will put us all in quarantine.

"Chelsea, give me my phone. They're closing the door."

"Look!" She pointed at the screen.

"Shit," I whispered. My pulse was suddenly racing as my puffy eyes filled with tears. "Why? Why would he do that?"

"I think if I remember what you told me, he said it was *because of you.* You make him break his own rules."

NOX- PRIVATE NUMBER was displayed on the screen of my phone with a telephone number below.

"When?"

Chelsea shrugged. "Probably when he had you in a sex-induced coma."

"Those don't exist."

"They do…" She wiggled her eyebrows. "…if you have too much sex."

"Is that even possible?"

"Comatose? Hell yes."

"No," I corrected, "too much sex?"

"Not if it's done right."

Oh, Nox did it right.

"I should delete it."

She pulled the phone away and spoke in a stage whisper. "Like hell you should. You're not thinking straight right now. Don't you dare delete that number."

"But we agreed to one week, no future, no past. This opens a door for a future."

Chelsea pursed her lips. "No, it doesn't. It's simply *the door. Opening it* would require hitting that little green icon."

"We said…"

"*He* broke the rule." She shrugged. "Maybe you should call him to yell at him."

"I can't call him. I can't."

"Fine, that doesn't mean that you have to barricade the door. It's not hurting anything sitting there."

Hesitantly, I put my phone in airplane mode, leaving Nox's number where he'd left it. With a sigh, I laid my head back against the leather seat, closed my eyes, and remembered. I wasn't sure my eyes would ever close that I didn't see the sexy pale blue stare, the menacing one that left me breathless.

CHAPTER 19

———— ●○● ————

Present

"FORGET THEM, ALL of them," Chelsea said, her voice coming through my phone loud and clear.

Sitting cross-legged on the bed of my Savannah hotel room, I shook my head. I knew I was in Georgia, and she was in California so I knew she couldn't see me, but I needed to move. I needed to explain. "I-I will. God! I can't believe they did this. I really thought this was about my getting it early. How? How could they do this? I guess Alton doesn't surprise me, but my mother?"

"I mean what the hell? Did they really think you'd say, 'Sure, let me just throw my dreams away' and fall in with their plan?"

I took another drink of wine. It was a cheap bottle from a drug store. On the way from the airport, I asked the taxi driver to stop. Sure, they had room service at the Hilton, but suddenly money was an object. It wasn't like I was ever a compulsive shopper. I wasn't my mother. My wardrobe was limited, but quality. That wasn't for any reason other than habit. It was all I'd ever known.

The wine I found at the store had two pluses: it was inexpensive and the bottle was big. I'd drunk this brand before with Chelsea, and while it didn't exactly taste like the Montague private reserve, now that half the bottle was gone, I hardly noticed. One of the facts I needed to face: my days of spending

159

more on wine were gone.

Not gone. Postponed.

If I could somehow stay in school, one day I'd buy the best that money had to offer. One day, I'd make Jane proud. I'd make me proud. Bryce said I'd be a lousy lawyer because I had standards. I disagreed.

"Chels?"

"Yeah?"

"Do you think I can do it? Can I be a good attorney?"

"Hell yes!"

I pulled the phone away from my ear as a smile curved my now-stained lips. "Bryce said I'd be a bad one. My mother doesn't want me to ever practice. And then there was the senator." My whole body shivered. "I don't know if I can do the good-ole-boy thing."

"Honey," she said, her tone mellowed, "they screwed you. Your family royally screwed you, and not the oh-that-was-fun kind of way."

"I do like that way better."

Chelsea laughed.

The label of the large bottle of wine caught my eye. Under the large drawing of a foot, I read the words *California Wine*. Despite my emotional breakdown, my thoughts went to Nox and my smile grew.

"I know you do," she said. "You could always give Mr. Handsome a call. Maybe he knows someone. We never figured out whom he worked for. Maybe he has some New York connections?"

I shook my head. "Let me get right on that. Hi, remember me? Charli? Well, first, that's not my name, and, oh yes, my whole life was just flushed down the toilet. I didn't call you when I was financially solvent, but now that I'm penniless, can you help me out?"

"You're making it sound like it's a bad idea."

"It's a very bad idea. If, and I mean *if*, I ever see him again, the last thing I want him to think is that I'm needy." I lay back against the headboard. "I hate being needy. Alexandria was needy…"

"Babe, you're going to do this. I know you are. First, you're not penniless. You have a full jar of those in your room. Second, you created Alex and Charli. You will…"

I closed my eyes and listened as Chelsea gave me the pep talk I needed. However, the person I was seeing behind my closed lids wasn't my best friend. The person who I saw had the palest blue eyes and chiseled jaw. He had hands that were strong but gentle. He wore the sexiest cologne, yet filled a room with the sweet aroma of musk and desire.

I didn't want to think about Nox, remember him, or dream of him. It just happened. Seeing *California wines* or the course number *101* made my insides tighten. Hell, just touching the high heels that had adorned the dashboard of the Boxster brought me to near orgasm. My vibrator had burned through more batteries than I cared to admit since we left Del Mar.

Nox was a piece of my history, my past, and I had come to terms with that. In a way, that made him better. We'd never have a first real fight. We'd never betray one another or end up in a sad relationship like my mother and Alton. Nox would always and forever be my prince.

Thinking about him was better than thinking about my family.

"What are you going to do?"

Chelsea's question snapped me back to reality. "I don't know. I was wondering if I could ask you a big favor."

"Whatever you want, you've got it. Do you want me to sell blood? I'm there for you. Eggs? I heard you can make a lot doing that."

"Stop," I said with a giggle. "It's not quite that dramatic. No *selling*. I draw the line at prostitution. No, it's just that I don't have my ticket for Palo Alto. The movers are scheduled to get my stuff on Thursday. I've already paid them so I know they're coming. It might be better financially for me to go straight to New York. My mother mentioned that my cousin Patrick lives in Manhattan. I'm not sure where, but I've been thinking I could call him. If he'll let me bunk with him until my apartment is ready… then maybe…"

"I was listening. I really was. What was your question?"

"Will you pack the rest of my stuff?"

"Hmm, I'm not sure I can be trusted with your shoes."

I took a deep breath. "I love you, I really do. But if you touch the black Louboutins, I will have to kill you."

"No way. After what happened in those babies, I think you should consider putting them in some kind of glass case—you know, like the museums have?"

"So?"

"Yes, I'll pack. First, call Patrick and be sure the plan's a go. If it is, I'm going to miss your face. And I'm not leaving you alone in New York. We're going to see each other again."

"I love you, sister." She was the sister I never had.

"Back atcha. Text me. Tell me what's happening."

"I will."

Just saying my plan out loud gave it strength. Alton and Adelaide expected me to submit to their plan. They thought I'd fold. I'm not folding, not without a fight.

I'd already paid the deposit and first month's rent on my apartment's lease, but maybe if Patrick had room... I knew my chances were slim. *I* wouldn't have had an extra room. The one-bedroom apartment I rented on the Upper West Side was nearly three thousand a month. That was for one bedroom, a living room, galley kitchen, and small bathroom. Square footage was extremely expensive in Manhattan. Not many people had extra bedrooms. Then again, in order to keep my dream alive, I'd sleep on a couch for three years.

Taking another drink of my California wine, I scrolled through my contacts. I hadn't seen Patrick since Christmas of my senior year at the academy. At that time he was a junior at Pratt. I thought I remembered hearing that he'd returned to Savannah for graduate school. That was why I was surprised when Mother mentioned he was back in Manhattan. I obviously hadn't done a very good job of keeping up on family happenings. Heck, he might not even have the same phone number.

I couldn't call my mother to get his contact information, and I wasn't sure Aunt Gwen would give it to me—not if she were in on Alton's plan.

I said a quick prayer and pushed his number.

Patrick answered on the second ring. "No way!" His excitement brought a ray of sunlight to my darkened spirit.

"You *are* still alive," I said.

"Oh little cousin, I'm alive and kicking. Did I hear you're going to Columbia soon?"

"You did." Aunt Gwen must do a better job of keeping him informed than my mother did me.

"And after all this time, I'm going to get to see all-grown-up Alexandria?"

"Alex."

"Oh, excuse me…Alex."

I shook my head. "Sorry. I just left the manor and I'm a little touchy."

"Yeah, that place can do that to people. It has Uncle Alton in a constant state of pissiness."

I laughed. "He's pissy even when he's out of town."

"No shit! What's going on with you?"

We talked about everything, except the reason I left Montague Manor and the reason I called. We talked about school and graduate school. He talked about interior design and how he was currently doing an internship with a well-known design firm in the business district. He said the name, but I didn't know much about interior design and had never heard of it.

It was when he said he lived on the Upper East Side that I perked up.

"Wow," I tried not to be too excited. "Pat, that's not far from Columbia."

"Other side of the park. I can probably see the buildings from my window. Great view."

"I can't imagine how much a place like that costs. I have a deposit on a one-bedroom on the Upper West Side, not far from the campus."

"Girl, we'll be close. I'm so glad you called."

I sucked in a breath. "God, Pat, I hate to ask this, but my apartment won't be ready for another week, and I was wondering…" I let my words trail away.

"Umm, when were you thinking?"

"Tomorrow."

Whatever Patrick was drinking must have sprayed the walls of his fancy-addressed apartment. From my end, I only heard him choking and sputtering. "That's not a lot of heads up. Let me… let me call you back."

The little bit of hope I'd had left evaporated. "No. That's all right."

"Little cousin, don't be all like that. Listen, I know you've been all big and grown up out in California, but New York's not Stanford. It's also *not* scary. You lived eighteen years in that house of horrors."

He had no idea.

"You can make it just fine here. Just like the song says, baby, *If you can make it…*" His impromptu rendition of *New York, New York* put the smile back on my face.

"Pat, it's fine. I'll come up with something—"

"No. I just have to check with my… roommate."

"What? No way. Is this a roommate or a *roommate?*" Patrick was always good looking. At the academy, even though he was older than me, I heard stories. He was well-known for his exploits: womanizer extraordinaire. Yet in private I never had that vibe. As a matter of fact, in private I had the opposite vibe.

"You mean you saw my mother and she didn't tell you all about it?"

I shook my head. "No, but you know the Fitzgerald code."

Patrick laughed. "Well, they haven't disowned me, but I don't think they're announcing it at parties either."

He was doing better than me. I had until the holidays and then I would be officially disowned. The hell with them. I'll disown them.

"Are you happy?" I asked.

"More than I ever thought possible."

I sighed. I knew that feeling, briefly. It was the best. "I don't want to cause any problems." I really didn't.

"No problems. Let me talk to Cy. I'm not sure if he'll be in or out of town. He travels a lot. I'll call you first thing in the morning. One way or another: We. Are. Getting. Together!"

"Thanks, Pat. Is this thing serious? I don't want to intrude."

"Love you, sweetie. I'll see you tomorrow."

"Tomorrow."

As I disconnected our call, the text message icon blinked wildly. I needed to text Chelsea and let her know that I'd reached Patrick.

I didn't recognize the number, and no name came up with it. My teeth clenched as I swiped the screen. Of course, I didn't know the number: it wasn't programmed into my phone. That didn't stop the message from popping up.

Unknown number: *"ALEX, THIS IS BRYCE. DON'T DO IT AGAIN. DON'T RUN AWAY. THIS WAS ALWAYS THE PLAN…"*

There were four messages.

Do I read or delete?

I hit the little icon of a trashcan.

Tomorrow.

Tomorrow I was leaving for New York. Tomorrow I was starting a new life. Neither the Montagues, Fitzgeralds, nor Spencers were going to dictate my life. They didn't own me. If they thought I'd simply give up my dreams because of money, they didn't know me.

They knew the girl they expected me to be. They knew Alexandria. Alexandria was gone. Alex was flying to New York *tomorrow*. She had a life to live.

There were millions of people in New York who had made it there. I would find a way.

CHAPTER 20

———•O•———

Present

WHAT THE HELL?

The taxi came to a stop at 1214 Fifth Avenue under a canopy, upon a private drive. "Are you sure this is the right place?"

"Yes, ma'am. Let me get your bags."

I trailed behind, my mouth agape as I backed onto the sidewalk, craned my neck up and up and up. The blue sky framed the glistening glass building. It was different than the traditional elegance I associated with New York and the Upper East Side. Most of the buildings were made of stone and brick with artistry and craftsmanship rarely seen anymore. This was the Museum Mile, Central Park, and all things refined.

This building, however, was different.

I passed through the opened door in utter awe; it was ultra-modern. As my eyes adjusted, I took in the large open lobby. The floor was bleached oak and there was a big desk in front of a lit ornately paneled wall.

How did Patrick live here? He was an intern. I knew the Fitzgeralds and Richardsons had money, old money, but I doubted either Uncle Preston or Aunt Gwen were willing to pay half of the rent on a place like this.

I paused with my suitcase near a large pillar and began to text Patrick.

Just as I hit send, the elevator doors opened and I was swallowed in a warm embrace.

"Alex!" He pushed me away by the shoulders and spun me around. "Look at my little cousin, all grown up." His brows moved up and down as his gaze settled on my breasts. "*All* grown up!"

I wiggled my brows back at him. Just like Bryce, Patrick had matured well. He wasn't overly broad, but definitely fit. At about five-foot-ten, I guessed he was about one hundred and eighty pounds of muscle. His light brown hair had receded more than most for his age, but all that did was make his light brown eyes showcase his handsome face. "Not too bad yourself," I said with another hug. He smelled divine.

He reached for my suitcase. "Well, come on up. It's not much… but we manage."

Once alone in the elevators, I asked, "Damn, Pat, this place is amazing. How—"

He nudged my side. "Wait until you see our place."

He was right. I couldn't do anything but hum and say things like wow, as he walked me around their three-bedroom apartment. We were on the forty-sixth floor, and the view from the windows in the living room as well as from Pat and Cy's room was breathtaking. We weren't next to the trees in Central Park—we were *above* them. From the window, I could see the park, multiple baseball fields, the lake… the view went on and on. "I bet you can see my apartment building from here."

"We can meet up in the park on Saturdays. Do you still run?"

I shrugged, still too stunned to speak. Finally, I answered, "Some." I had run at the academy. It gave me something to do and an excuse to get away from Montague Manor.

Patrick led me to a bedroom down the hallway from the open kitchen.

I'd seen pictures of the place I'd rented. My new kitchen was sufficient, but looked like it belonged in a shoebox or maybe a galley of a boat. It could fit into a corner of his.

I walked to the window in my room. The view was of roofs and buildings, not as amazing as the other direction, but still impressive. If I leaned to one side, I could catch a glimpse of the park. "So," I began with my arms crossed over my chest, "apparently they pay interns really, really well."

He put my bags on the bed. "Something like that. Do you want some lunch?"

I was starving. I'd taken one plane from Savannah to Charlotte and another from there to LaGuardia. It could have been worse, but it all began very early this morning.

I sat at the breakfast bar while Pat moved around the kitchen, cutting and dicing. By the time he was done, we each had one of the best-looking salads I'd ever seen.

"And you cook, too," I said with a wink.

"Oh little cousin, I *am* a man of many talents."

"Tell me about Cy."

Patrick shook his head. "You tell me what's going on. I called Mom last night after we got off the phone."

Just like that—*pop*. My balloon deflated.

My chin dropped to my chest and the tears I'd thought had dried turned back on. I brushed one from my cheek.

Patrick covered my hand and squeezed it. "What the fuck did they do?"

That was such a loaded question. Did I go back to when I was ten? Did I open closet doors that were better left locked? Did I dust off skeletons that didn't deserve to be brought back to life? Or did I concentrate on yesterday?

I took a deep breath and wiped my eyes with my napkin. "Recently?"

"Yes, sweetheart, otherwise we'd be here until tomorrow, and I only took one day off."

I hadn't even thought of that. "I'm sorry. I'm sorry you had to take a day off for me."

"I'm not. Look out there. It's a fantastic summer day in the most beautiful city in the world. Let's eat and go for a walk. If Central Park doesn't make you feel better..." He widened his eyes. "...there's a few little stores down on Fifth Avenue... oh, and some on Madison. I've got retail therapy down to a science."

"I don't think I'll be doing much in the way of retail therapy."

"Mom didn't know…" His voice trailed away.

I took a bite of my salad. "Transfer from Columbia to Savannah Law or drop out all together." My voice raised an octave, mimicking my mother's. "It is truly unnecessary for a Montague woman to work."

The light brown of Patrick's eyes clouded.

"Oh, and marry Bryce Spencer and carry on the bloodline. *Chop-chop…* make some babies."

"Are they fuck'n nuts?"

I laughed. "Don't we both know the answer to that question?"

His expression perked up. "But you're here." Then he added suspiciously, as if the thought just occurred to him, "You're not here to complete transfer papers or withdraw, are you?"

My lips pursed tight as my head swayed side to side.

"So you told them to fuck off?"

"I left after they told me my trust fund was being held hostage."

"Hostage? They can't do that. Can they?"

"Alton was citing clauses. Something about it covering undergraduate, but not graduate school and expenses. I didn't look at the paperwork. I couldn't stay in that place one minute more. All I know is that my trust fund is gone. I can access the account online and it's been closed."

He leaned back his chair, pushing off with his arms. The action caused his biceps to budge from the edge of his short-sleeved shirt. "Nothing? They left you with *nothing?*"

I just nodded as I took another bite. The salad was fantastic.

Patrick stood and paced, his hand going though his thinning hair. "Why would the powerful Fitzgeralds want everyone to know they'd let you go to New York with nothing?"

"I don't think they expected me to leave. I think this is what my mom meant when she said her father didn't want her going away. The way they see it, I had my chance—more of a chance than she did. I had four years in California. Now I owe them and the Montague name my life." I spoke louder. "My body and my soul."

He sat back down and gestured around the room. "This place… well, it's

Cy's. His name is Cyrus. You probably figured that out, that I didn't just win the lottery."

I grinned. "It's pretty high rent for an intern."

"He'll be home later tonight. I don't know about a three-year commitment, but I'm sure he won't mind you staying here for a little while. He knows people. He might be able to help."

A seed of hope burst in my chest. It was small and in need of tending, but it was there. "Thank you. If he'll do that for your cousin who you haven't seen in nearly five years, I'd say you did win the lottery."

Patrick smiled and it did my heart good. I'd seen that smile before. I'd worn it. Whoever this Cy was, he made Patrick happy.

"I hate that I need help," I went on. "The thing is that I'm willing to work, but I'm not willing to miss this chance at law school, at Columbia."

His gaze lightened. "Let me talk to him. In the meantime, let's go for a walk across the park and find your apartment building. I need to know how long it'll take me on Saturdays to get over there and wake your ass up. Cy hates to run and I love it. I need a running partner."

WE WERE BACK at Patrick's place and I was back on the barstool watching him cook something that smelled like heaven. He'd chopped and measured and never once used a recipe. There were three pans on the stovetop with sauces that made my mouth water. In the oven was a beef something or other. It even had little leaves stuck to it with little pin things. It looked like it belonged in a Martha Stewart cookbook.

"Where did you learn how to cook?" I asked, swirling the wine around my glass.

He scrunched his brow. "Are you saying you don't think it was from my mom?"

"Don't get me wrong, Aunt Gwen is more domestic than Adelaide, but that just means she knows where the kitchen is located without directions."

His laughter rumbled through the air. He really was handsome in a very non-rugged sort of way.

We'd spent most of the afternoon walking and talking. Central Park was beautiful. If I could make this work, I wanted to be Patrick's running partner. I wanted to get to know my way around the paths and roads. I'd been there before, but each time I was struck by the tranquility of nature that was surrounded by one of the biggest cities in the world. I don't think people who haven't actually walked the paths, or had only seen it in movies or TV, had any idea of the true splendor.

We found my apartment building. By going through the park or along the north edge, it was about a ten- to fifteen-minute walk from here. If only life were simple and I knew for certain I would be moving to that little one-bedroom in another week.

"So what did you think about your building?" Patrick asked as he refilled our glasses.

As I reached for mine, my eyes lit up. It wasn't the wine, but the location of my building. "Oh my gosh. I couldn't believe it when we turned that corner."

Patrick laughed. "Only you would sublet an apartment *online* that's right by Tom's Restaurant."

"I recognized it right away. I've seen it a thousand times in reruns. It's the one from Seinfeld."

"Well, that settles it. Saturday mornings, you and I go for a run, and then we eat breakfast with Jerry and the gang."

I shrugged and sipped the tart pinot grigio. It was a little better quality than what I'd had the night before. "If you're buying, I'm eating. At least then I'll have one meal a week."

He rolled his eyes. "Dramatic much?"

"Sometimes." I thought about the apartment. "When I did my search, I was looking for places close to the campus. I knew the park was close. I had no idea."

Just then the front door opened and we both turned that direction.

"Cy," Pat whispered.

"Really?" I asked with a smirk. "I thought maybe strangers come in your place without knocking."

The footsteps neared and a handsome, distinguished man walked in, wearing a suit. I'm not sure if he was what I expected, but that wasn't a bad thing. He had gray around his temples and peppered through his black hair. He was taller than Patrick, and his face held the lines of someone who spent his time thinking.

"Hello," he greeted. Walking up to Patrick he leaned over his shoulder and kissed his cheek. "This smells fantastic." He turned to me. "You must be Alexandria."

I smiled. "I am."

"She goes by Alex now," Patrick corrected.

"Alex, nice to meet you." He reached for my hand. His grip was firm and hands soft.

"It's very nice to meet you, Cyrus. Thank you for allowing me to stay here for a few nights."

"It's Cy, and any cousin of Pat's is a cousin of mine."

"Oh," I asked, ashamed I hadn't thought of it before. "Are you married?"

The two exchanged a grin that made my tummy flip, and then Cy poured himself a glass of wine and loosened his tie. "No, we aren't married, but if Patrick says you need a place to stay, I believe him.

"Excuse me for a minute while I get into something a little less stuffy. I can't wait to get to know you, Alex." He turned toward Patrick. "And I can't wait to eat whatever that is you have cooking. I didn't realize how hungry I was."

I looked away as they shared another look. It was as if I were the third wheel with two honeymooners. And while it made me happy for Patrick, it also made me a little sad for myself. After Cy walked away, Patrick looked at me with a *so-what-do-you-think?* look.

I lifted my glass. He did the same, as I professed, "To you. I approve."

"Whoa, I'm so glad. I'll be able to sleep tonight."

I'd forgotten how easy banter was between Patrick and me. We had always gotten along. That may be why the rumors of him at academy bothered me. The guy the girls described wasn't the cousin I knew.

A few minutes later, I asked, "How did you find Cy?"

It was apparently Cy's cue to return looking younger and even more handsome in jeans and a light blue button-down. The color made my breathing hitch. "Oh, I get this question," he said with a grin. "He didn't find me. I found him."

Patrick nodded. "It's true. Found me and saved me from a five-hundred-square-foot studio apartment with a tiny Pullman kitchen."

"Can you imagine?" Cy asked. "All this culinary talent going to waste like that?"

I sighed. "Gosh, Cy, you don't have any friends who are looking for someone to save, do you?"

When he only grinned, I stupidly added, "I'd prefer if they were gay."

Oh my God!

Although the apartment filled with the deep sound of Patrick and Cy's laughter, I was mortified. I needed to cut back on the wine. It must have been the salad at lunch and all the exercise. This was my second glass. I needed some food.

Cy leaned against the counter and dipped a spoon in the thick white sauce. Blowing on the contents, he asked, "Man or woman?"

My cheeks must have filled with pink. "I think I was kidding."

"If you weren't," Patrick asked.

I shrugged. "Well, I was thinking man. I mean, I can cook." Patrick raised his brows my direction. "I can. It may not be like this, but I make a mean spaghetti sauce. And..." I looked down at the shorts and top I'd worn on our walk. "...I actually clean up pretty well. I could make a stellar arm ornament for business functions." I thought of Nox's description of women he'd dated. "And if there's an illusion that's trying to be perpetrated, I could do that too. If not, I'd be a great friend."

"So you're saying no sex?" Cy asked.

I squared my shoulders. "Am I giving you a résumé?"

"You asked if I had friends."

"Well, I think maybe a blind date is the way to start that relationship, not,

'Here's my partner's cousin. She's down on her luck and needs a sugar daddy.'"

Shit!

"That's not…" I tried to pry my foot from my mouth.

Cy laughed again. "Stop, you're not telling me anything I don't know. Look at Pat."

I did and noticed the pink in his cheeks.

"He's talented, intelligent, well-spoken, and incredibly handsome. I'm lucky to have him in my life."

I took a deep breath and let it out. "Yes, I want what you have."

"He's also great in bed," Cy added as his eyebrows wiggled.

Patrick and I both laughed.

"In that case," I clarified, "your friend better be straight."

"Man or—"

"Man," I quickly replied.

After dinner as I helped Patrick with the dishes, Cy came into the kitchen.

"Alex, may I look at you?"

I took a step back. "Look at me?"

"Your hair. May I touch it?"

My eyes darted to Patrick, who nodded. "Um, all right."

He walked behind me and pulled the tie from my hair. Then he fluffed it and arranged the auburn waves on my shoulders and back. Cy took a few steps, walking around me, circling me. He never took his eyes from mine. Next, he gathered my hair and piled it high on my head. "Do you wear much makeup?"

"I can but not usually."

"Stanford?"

This was increasingly uncomfortable. "Yes."

"With honors?"

"Summa cum laude."

"Columbia Law?"

Patrick nodded.

"What are you two talking about?" I looked from one to the other. "You know I was joking, right?"

"Raised like me," Patrick said.

"What does that mean?" I asked.

"Well-bred, manners, can handle yourself well in most situations," Cy said.

I shook my head. "Most, but right now I'm feeling uncomfortable."

Cy handed me my hair tie and turned to Patrick. "If you trust her, give her the elevator pitch. If she's interested, call Andrew and get her an appointment for the morning. I'll arrange for an afternoon interview."

My eyes widened. "Pat, what the hell are you two talking about?"

Patrick threw the towel he'd been holding on the counter and reached for my hand. "I'd pour you more wine, but this isn't something you should consider when your faculties aren't intact."

Tugging my hand, he pulled me toward the couch in the living room. It faced toward the large floor-to-ceiling windows. As we sat, I saw beyond the darkness of the park to the glimmering Upper West Side.

"Little cousin, I can trust you, can't I? Like when we were kids, pinky-swear?"

"Y-Yes."

His smile grew. It was like we were kids and he was about to tell me some secret, maybe about a Christmas present. "Listen to me," he instructed. "When I'm all done you can ask questions or tell me I'm crazy, but promise you'll listen to everything first."

"I'll listen."

"I'm going to tell you about a company I work for."

"The design firm?"

"No, although I do work there too. I'm going to tell you about the other company I work for. It's very exclusive and privately run. People only learn about it by word of mouth. If you're ever questioned by anyone outside of the network, you've never heard of it."

"Pat, this—"

"No questions," he reminded me.

"Sorry."

"Alex, let me tell you about Infidelity."

CHAPTER 21

—•O•—

Present

I STARED AT Patrick in disbelief. Words weren't forming, not in a way where I could put them with others and string them into anything resembling a sentence. An elevator pitch, as in what Cy told Pat to give me, was by definition a succinct, persuasive summary, a sales tactic to be used when time was of the essence.

I didn't want short. I needed more.

Standing, I wrapped my arms around myself and silently walked to the windows. The spectacular view no longer registered. In the short time I'd been with Pat and Cy everything had seemed real. It was more than that—it felt real. I saw it. My life had been too much turmoil, too much emotion. Ever since Del Mar I'd been off kilter. I fought back the tears as I turned back to Patrick, still sitting silently on the couch, watching me with large eyes.

Is that the male version of doe in the headlights? Because, in the words of Nox, after what Pat had just told me, the innocent ship has sailed.

Sucking my lip between my teeth I worked to turn the chaos in my mind into coherent thoughts. "Are... are you saying this is all a sham?" My body trembled and I looked around for a vent or fan, something to cause my sudden chill. "This is no better than Savannah—smoke and mirrors. No, it's worse." My volume rose. "Worse! Oh God, Patrick. How could you?"

He wasn't angry. Instead, I sensed something between hurt and defiance.

"Little cousin, don't you dare judge me."

"B-But you sold…"

"What? My body, my soul, my heart? I didn't sell any of those. I simply agreed to rent them. Isn't that what dating is? Isn't that what happens when you meet someone and the two of you are mutually attracted to one another?" He stood and came closer. "Have you never…? Has no man ever had your heart?"

I squeezed my midsection tighter and nodded as tears now freely flowed down my cheeks. "Yes, but it wasn't a business agreement."

"It wasn't? Did he buy you dinner?"

"Dinner, not an apartment and spending money."

Patrick's voice lowered. "Is that all your heart's worth, a nice dinner?"

"No. No! That's not what I mean."

Pat turned me toward the window and hugged me from behind. His embrace was warm and comforting—nothing sexual—as he spoke near my shoulder. "Look out there. There are people in the park right now. There are people in Savannah. Those people would take what you have—your body, heart, and soul—for a lot less." He kissed my cheek and turned me toward him. "You asked if what Cy and I have is real. The answer is yes. You asked me on the phone if I was happy. The answer is yes. I'd take it even further and say that I love him. So what? We found one another through a service. It's like an online dating service, with perks."

"I don't think I understand. Cy said he found you. Did you have any say?"

"I filled out a profile and set my hard limits."

"Your *hard limits*?" I asked, the phrase prickling my skin.

"Yes. As the name insinuates, not all of the clients are single. I wasn't willing to be a third wheel or the reason a marriage or relationship failed. That was one of my hard limits."

"One?"

Patrick pursed his lips and furrowed his brow. "I restricted my profile to gay men. If you don't think I could get it up for some hot, wealthy woman, well, you're wrong, but if I did that, it would compromise who I am. Hard limits are important. Once those are set, Infidelity does its magic. The staff knows their clients. A profile isn't available to the entire world. First, only an exclusive number of people even know that this part of Infidelity exists."

We were sitting back where we started. "So Infidelity pairs *clients* with…"

"Employees," Patrick answered. "I work for Infidelity. I get a monthly check from them. When Cy joined, he agreed to provide housing and living expenses. Theoretically, my check from Infidelity covers my incidentals. Since I also work for the design firm, I have that check too, and…" He smiled with a shrug. "…Cy is very generous. My checks are mostly invested. Infidelity works on yearly agreements. During that anniversary month, Infidelity provides extensive interviews to determine if the agreement is renewed. There is even a buy-out clause if two people decide they want to stay together, without the company."

"What if you two hadn't gotten along? Could you quit?"

"At the end of one year."

I shook my head. "One year."

"The people at Infidelity can explain it better than I, but the year thing is there for a reason. The client is putting a lot of resources into this relationship. They don't want to do that to have it end in a week."

I took a deep breath. *A week is too short.*

"There's something psychologically reassuring about a year," Patrick explained. "Every day doesn't have to be wine and roses. I told you that what I have with Cy is real. We fight. We make up. Make-up sex is awesome!"

I couldn't believe I was smiling at him and really listening.

"Pat, what? How? How did you even learn about this?"

He shrugged. "I can't give specifics. Like for example, if you decide to look into this, you can't tell anyone it was me and Cy, other than Karen, the intake representative at Infidelity. I can tell you I learned about it while I was at Pratt. I didn't do it, not at first. Then, while I was working on my master's, I had offers for different internships and decided to take the one here. As I was cooking macaroni and cheese on my tiny stovetop, I made the decision to call the person I'd met while attending Pratt.

"It wasn't an easy decision. During the intake interview, Infidelity was extremely transparent. Although they put a lot of money and resources into this, not all matches work as well as ours. The thing that sold me was the exclusivity. Infidelity pairs its employees *once*. They don't serve as a pimp. If at the end of an agreement there's a mutual decision to end the relationship, the employee receives a severance package and he or she is done. Clients are given two chances.

"The network is small," he went on. "Confidentiality is paramount. To the world we are a couple. Cy has an important job. I'm his partner. He's met Mom and Dad. I've met his family. No one," he emphasized, "knows how we actually met."

I considered all he said. "You said some of the clients are married."

"Yes."

"Do they provide the same... housing and living expenses?"

"Yes."

I scrunched my nose. "Why?

"Why would an employee want to be paired with a married client?" Patrick asked, clarifying my one-word question.

"Yes? Why?"

"Commitments. The job still pays the same, but since this client is splitting his or her time with the employee and the spouse, well, the employee's services aren't required as frequently. Like, say the employee has another commitment... law school, perhaps."

I shook my head. "I-I can't believe I'm even considering this, but married men? That's my hard limit. What if Cy would've said no to the design firm?"

"It was in my profile. He knew I had a commitment to the firm. He came into this relationship understanding my priorities. Though I didn't know him, I agreed to enter being willing to support his."

"When is your one-year... anniversary... contract renegotiation?"

Patrick grinned. "It was last June. We're in our second year."

"You don't regret it?"

"Little cousin, do I look like I regret it?"

I tried to take it all in, but the more I thought about it, the more questions I had. As in most of my times of indecision, since Del Mar, my thoughts went briefly to Nox. "Pat, what if you met someone else?"

"I'm not looking."

"No, of course you're not looking, but what if?"

"He'd have to wait until next June. Monogamy is in the agreement. It was also on my list of hard limits."

A ridiculous thought occurred to me. "So if I agreed to this, I couldn't commit to Bryce until my contract was up."

"They call them *agreements*, not contracts." He shrugged. "It's a legal thing, and yes, but you couldn't tell Bryce, Aunt Adelaide, or Uncle Alton about the agreement. No one can know."

Patrick reached for my hand. "Little cousin, I know this is a lot to consider. Like I said, it took me almost two years before I decided to do it.

"Cy said he could get you an interview tomorrow. That doesn't mean you'll be accepted. Infidelity has a rigorous intake process. They wouldn't be as successful as they are and as exclusive, if everyone was granted employment." He tilted his head. "And they wouldn't be able to pay as well as they do."

"Can you tell me how much?" I asked, curious despite the fact that I was disgusted with myself that I was giving this company any consideration.

"No, but I can tell you that they'll pay you for the interview, for your time."

"If I go to the interview tomorrow, I'll be paid? No sex... just an interview?"

"Sex is down the line in this process," Patrick said. "They'll explain it better. Infidelity doesn't sell sex. They foster companionships. And yes."

"How much?"

"Five thousand dollars."

IT'S JUST AN interview.

I'd said it over and over to myself as well as to Patrick. He'd taken a second day off work to help me with this, and I didn't know if I was thankful that I had his hand to hold or if I should hate him forever for even suggesting this. More than once during the night I woke with near panic-attack-level doubts.

I was a Montague and I was entertaining the idea of selling myself, *my companionship*, as Patrick continued to remind me. But then, I'd think about my mother and Alton. Was what they wanted me to do any less degrading? They wanted me to forfeit my dreams and sell myself to Bryce, and for what? For the Montague name. In their deal, I lost everything. I lost my dreams and the future I'd planned. I lost my ability to choose my own husband. Their scenario was a lifelong sentence. In their plan, I wasn't only securing my own future unhappiness, but more than likely that of my children, future Montagues and Carmichaels.

With Infidelity, if—and that was a big *if*—I was accepted by the company and I agreed, I could continue law school. If I did this and became an Infidelity employee, I would agree to one year. After that time I was free. There was no lifelong sentence and no children.

That was part of my ongoing inner monologue as Patrick chatted away with Andrew, my first appointment of the day. Andrew was a stylist extraordinaire, apparently very high-priced, and sought-after. New clients rarely made it to Andrew's chair for hair and makeup, but with one call from Patrick, I was there at ten-thirty in the morning.

Patrick told me as we left the apartment that my attire didn't matter. Andrew would have clothes for my interview. I got the distinct impression that I was in over my head, and I hadn't done anything yet.

Every now and then I'd catch some of Andrew and Patrick's conversation. It was never about me, except to discuss colors of eye shadows or my blouse. Andrew shaded and perfected my complexion, painted my lips, and curled my hair. I was nothing more than a life-sized doll being made into something fit for display.

The dressing room didn't have a mirror as I shimmied out of my shorts and top and redressed, all the way from the lace underwear to a lace-accented, sleeveless sheath dress. I called Patrick to help me zip the back. When he did, the material came together hugging me in all the right places.

"Little cousin, you look amazing."

I didn't know. I hadn't seen myself. "Why the underwear? You said no sex."

"Because it makes you *feel* sexy. It's a package. You may not be selling sex, but in a classy way..." He helped me with the matching jacket, the one with matching lace cuffs. "...you need to ooze confidence. It's a persona and, Alex Collins, you're rocking it."

I sat on the bench and eased my freshly painted toes into black suede Prada platforms with an ankle strap. When I was done, Patrick reached for my hand.

"Come here, little one. Let me introduce you to Miss Alex Collins, Columbia law student, sexy and confident. Close those gorgeous golden eyes and when I say so, open them."

My heart beat erratically as I blindly followed Patrick's lead. With his hands on my shoulders he turned me to the side.

"Open."

I stood paralyzed as the woman in the mirror did the same. After the spa in Savannah with my mother, my hair was nice, but with the dresses she'd bought, I had the sensation of Alexandria, five years old and dressed for tea. That wasn't whom I saw today. Patrick was right. My hair was up, professional with more than a hint of sex appeal. The charcoal gray dress and jacket with the straight skirt flattered my curves. At the same time, there was nothing about what I saw that said I was selling my body or my soul. Even the shoes. They were sexy, but could easily be worn to court. My makeup was flawless, with just the right amount of bronze to highlight the red and blonde highlights in my hair.

Andrew and Patrick both stood behind me, waiting for my reaction.

Finally, I let the façade of indifference break away, and my entire countenance beamed with approval. "Wow! I don't know what else to say." I turned to Andrew. "Thank you. Obviously, you're a miracle worker."

"No. I'm an artist. All I did was highlight what you already have. You're stunning. You were before I began."

"Thank you."

When Patrick and I eased into the backseat of a taxi, he said, "I'm going to be dropped off at Kassee." When I looked at him as though I had no idea what he was saying, because I didn't, he went on, "the design firm. I can't miss this afternoon."

My pulse quickened. "B-But..."

Patrick squeezed my hand. "I would miss it for you. I would. But there's a big sales pitch this afternoon. I've put a lot of time into this and my boss wouldn't understand. Remember, Infidelity is an illusion so I couldn't exactly explain what I'd be doing with you today. Don't worry. You won't be alone. Cy's going to meet you in the lobby of 17 State Street. He'll escort you to Infidelity."

"All right. Pat?" I asked tentatively. "Is this a mistake? I had planned on looking for a job, like other people do."

"That's still an option. Go to the interview. See what Karen has to say. Then, if you decide waiting tables or maybe working the box office at the New Amsterdam Theater is what you'd prefer to do, do that. There's no obligation until you sign the agreement."

Five thousand dollars.

That would double the money in my checking account. That would give me another month's rent. I swallowed and nodded.

Before Patrick got out of the taxi, he kissed my cheek. "I can't wait to hear all about this tonight. Be ready to give me a full report."

I nodded, the blood draining from my cheeks. As the taxi driver maneuvered us back out into traffic, I straightened my shoulders and plastered my Montague smile in place. I told myself that this was better than what Adelaide had done. This was on *my* terms. This was one year. My mother and stepfather had forced my hand and I hadn't folded.

One interview.

I could do that.

CHAPTER 22

———— ●O● ————

Present

"YOU'RE STUNNING," CY whispered as he kissed my cheek.

He'd been waiting for me in the lobby as I entered the blue-glass building with the distinctive curved façade.

"Thank you. Andrew's a miracle worker."

"No. I may be gay, but I know a beautiful woman when I see one. So will Karen." He placed my hand on the crook of his arm and led me toward the elevators. "I wouldn't have made calls last night if I had any doubts. Tell me about yours."

"My doubts?" I repeated. "I'm nervous."

Our voices were low.

"Think of this like an admissions interview. That's what it is. Alex, you passed that interview for both Stanford and Columbia. I think you can wow Karen."

Since we'd entered the open elevator and were no longer alone, I didn't respond. Cy hit the button for the 37th floor. The elevator stopped at several other floors as busy people stepped on and off. With each movement upward, my anxiety increased. This wasn't like Stanford or Columbia. Those were accomplishments that I could one day list on my curriculum vitae. I was most certain that Infidelity would not be mentioned as *previous employment*.

When the doors opened, the large lobby with a glass desk and the beautifully scrolled lettering spelling *Infidelity* on the fifteen-foot wall surprised me.

"I thought this was a secret company?" I whispered.

"No, Infidelity is a website that caters to an exclusive crowd. It employs hundreds of people, everyone from writers and photographers, to janitorial personnel. It's a legitimate Fortune 500 company."

Cy walked us to the desk and spoke to the receptionist. "Mr. Perry and Miss Collins here to see Ms. Flores."

"Yes, Mr. Perry. Ms. Flores is expecting both of you. Let me tell her that you're here."

"Thank you."

I watched as women and men walked past. They all seemed to have important business down one hallway or another. If I hadn't heard Patrick's elevator pitch the night before, I would never have known what other activities happened behind the walls of Infidelity.

"Cyrus!" a gregarious middle-aged woman wearing a navy skirt and jacket said as she rushed towards us.

"Karen," Cyrus greeted her as they kissed one another on the cheeks. "Thank you for agreeing to meet our friend Alex."

"Why, of course. Any friend of Cyrus Perry's is a friend of mine." She turned her attention to me and offered her hand.

As we shook, I said, "Ms. Flores, very nice to meet you."

"Miss Collins, my name is Karen and I look forward to meeting you. Please..." She gestured toward the hallway. "...let's go to my office. We must talk."

Cyrus nodded as we began our trek toward Karen Flores's office. On our way, we passed multiple large office centers filled with cubicles and workers as well as private offices. Once we'd successfully wound around what I could accurately describe as a maze and I'd begun to wonder if in order to ever find my way out, I should have left a trail of breadcrumbs, we came to another elevator. Instead of one button, Karen pressed a badge against a sensor and turned to Cyrus. "How is Patrick?"

"He's well. Thank you for asking."

When the doors opened we stepped into the elevator. "I believe I heard he's doing very well at Kassee."

"Yes," Cyrus said, his shoulders broadening with pride. "He's a talented designer."

I stood attentive as they conversed about Patrick's attributes and promise of success. The entire scene was surreal. If only I didn't know the backstory, if only I didn't know that Cyrus had met Patrick with the help of this woman and Infidelity, I could take everything they said at face value. Now, however, with my knowledge, everything I heard was skewed.

When the elevator moved, I knew we were moving upward, but how far up or the number of floors. The control panel had only two buttons: *O* and *I*. Karen had hit I. When the doors opened, I had the distinct impression we were now at the real Infidelity, the reason for our visit.

We were again met with a large glass desk, a receptionist, and the word *Infidelity* in beautiful scroll upon the wall behind her. The difference here, versus the other lobby, was that there was only one door beyond this woman and to pass through that door, a security code was required.

Karen's office was lovely with a full wall of windows that looked out on the financial district and beyond to the Brooklyn Bridge. While Cyrus and I sat in the two chairs facing the desk, Karen asked, "Would you like anything to drink? Water, tea, coffee, perhaps something stronger?"

They both looked at me.

"I'm fine. Thank you."

Karen settled behind her desk and opened a screen on her computer. "Alex Collins, twenty-three years old, soon to be twenty-four, recent graduate of Stanford University, graduated with honors, and currently enrolled at Columbia Law." Her eyes widened. "Is that you?"

"Yes, ma'am."

"Alex, tell me why Infidelity should consider bringing you into our fold."

I sat straighter on the edge of my seat. "Ms. Flores, I'm not well versed enough with Infidelity to answer that question. I was given a brief synopsis of this company and what it does, but while it may be unusual, I'd prefer to learn more from you. While I'm intrigued, I have my future to consider. Besides the obvious financial benefit, I'd like to know what Infidelity can do for me."

Karen smiled and sat back against her chair. "Yes, indeed."

She continued to watch me as the silence grew. Finally, when I didn't speak, she leaned forward and began, "I'm sure from the brief description that you received you have questions. Miss Collins, let me make this clear, at Infidelity we do not sell sex. That is not what Infidelity is about. I'd like to get that misconception off the table right away. At Infidelity our clients buy class, poise, companionship, and compatibility. Our clients are exclusive and successful. Our employees are confidential and classified. Currently, we have over one hundred employees in extremely high-profile relationships. Whether the client is a CEO, politician, or in the arts, no one, not even their closest friends and family, know where they found their significant other. The beauty of our service is that relationships take time. If a client is high profile, every potential partner is under suspicion. Here at Infidelity, we guarantee that nothing will ever be disclosed. That is one of the reasons that we are very selective as to whom we employ.

"I'll be honest, Miss Collins. You are many things, but your life goal is what makes you a potential candidate for Infidelity. Yes, you're beautiful. You're also young. Youth spurs beauty. I can find beautiful women in every city or town in the country. You're intelligent. Your education speaks to that. However, we have intelligent employees who were never granted access to institutions such as Stanford. It's because of your dream for your future that you stand out.

"I'd venture to say that one day you'd like to be a successful attorney, perhaps even enter the judicial system. You obviously have the résumé, assuming you complete Columbia. Maybe your goal is politics... my point is that you will adhere to our strict code of ethics and confidentiality. If you don't, it's your closet that will be decorated for Halloween."

I nodded. That made sense. "Are your clients as well screened as your employees?"

"Yes."

"I apologize for repeating myself, but what can Infidelity do for me?"

Karen stood and walked to the front of her desk. Sitting on the edge, she leaned back. "Miss Collins, your background check has just begun. From what I could obtain, it appears you didn't have financial concerns while at Stanford. Your tuition, as well as monthly payments to your savings and checking accounts, was all paid by a trust fund brokered by the Savannah law firm of Hamilton and Porter. That trust fund is now gone."

I swallowed and looked from Karen to Cy and back to Karen.

"Miss Collins, that is my business—our business. I know about my clients and about my employees. I don't share that knowledge, but I make it my business to know."

"Everything you said is correct," I confirmed.

"The next natural conclusion is that you're in need of money. If we broker a mutually beneficial agreement, Infidelity reimburses its employees well. The average employee receives twenty thousand dollars a month for living expenses. You see, it's important for our employees to fit in with the clients and their world. While all of our clients agree to provide housing, their generosity beyond the basics—very high-end basics—is at their discretion.

"May I assume that twenty thousand dollars a month would be helpful in meeting your tuition expenses?" she asked.

No shit.

"Yes."

"Beyond that, Miss Collins, while it may not seem as if it would, Infidelity will open doors for you. You'll be seen with the best of the best. You'll brush elbows and interact with people who may one day consider you for their law firm or vote on your nomination."

"And they'll know that I was—"

"No. No one knows where you and your client met except you, him, and me." She looked to Cyrus. "Cyrus is officially your sponsor. No one comes to us without one. While he knows that you're here, no one will inform him of the client who purchases your agreement." She shrugged. "That said, Cyrus Perry is a smart man. He'll figure it out, but if he were ever to share that, he would be removed from the Infidelity network.

"That is why you'll never meet other employees, not in the capacity of colleagues. The few office staff and medical staff with whom you'll interact are restricted by rather strong do-not-disclose agreements. They're paid very well to keep secrets and forget who and what they see."

Just like the house staff at Montague Manor.

"I would venture to guess," Karen went on, "that you have met clients and employees alike without ever being the wiser. That is the beauty of Infidelity."

"I-I…" I leaned on the arms of the chair. "…can't… the man can't be married."

Karen smiled and walked back to the other side of the desk. "Cyrus, could you please give Alex and me a couple of hours. Let's say until three thirty?"

Cy stood and looked at me. "Alex?"

I took a deep breath and slowly released it. "I'm willing to continue this discussion. Thank you, Cy."

He smiled and turned back to Karen. "Take good care of her. She's important to Pat and to me."

The last part of his sentence sent an unexpected flow through me, bringing warmth to my chilled extremities.

For the next two hours Karen and I discussed everything that could be expected of me as well as things I deemed unacceptable. Our conversation wasn't limited to sex, though we did discuss that. We also talked about living conditions and my need to have time for classes and studying. We discussed travel and whether or not I had a passport. We discussed schedules and domestic responsibilities.

She even asked me about my preferences when dating. What I liked or looked for in a man. It often seemed as though I was completing a profile for an online dating service. I agreed to a photo session after our interview. Pictures were needed for my file.

"Each employee is given one client," Karen explained. "As you could assume, if a client is assigned to an agreement and it doesn't work out, if we then assigned that same employee to another client and the two clients know one another, it would be easy for the second client's confidentiality to be compromised. Therefore, we do our best to make compatible matches.

She straightened her shoulders. "I'm rarely wrong."

"I don't have any say in who…"

"No, Miss Collins. That would require your reviewing client's profiles. You'll be introduced to one client and one client only." She pulled a three-page agreement from a folder and laid it on her desk.

The agreement was already completed with my name and today's date.

"If you sign this agreement of intent, you'll be agreeing to a medical examination and psychological evaluation, to be completed today. Contingent upon the results of those evaluations, by signing this agreement you also agree to a one-year relationship with the client to whom you are assigned. One year from the date you are contacted with your assignment, you and the client must mutually agree to continue the relationship or the relationship will be discontinued.

"The only exception to this rule, the only way it could be voided, is physical abuse. To date that has never happened with Infidelity. As I've said, we research our clients. However, I'll give you a card with a number. If abuse is ever an issue, call the number on the card, not the local authorities. This exception makes null and void your length of contract, and removes you from our employment with financial compensation, but it does not remove you from the nondisclosure or confidentiality of Infidelity. Is that clear?"

"Yes."

She pointed to a clause on page two. "Then please initial here."

"During the agreed-upon one year," Karen went on, "you agree to keep yourself monogamous with your client. That means that you will not date or have relations with another man or woman. Doing so could create a media scandal for your client. We've never had bad press and we don't want to start. With some clients, the introduction of a significant other is best handled slowly. With others it is done on a faster schedule, like ripping off a Band-Aid. We have a public relations department that helps each client with his or her own unique situation."

"Her?" I asked.

"Yes, our clients are both men and women. Our employees are both men and women. Do you agree to being faithful to your client for one year?"

I began to wonder how many of the people I'd met or people I'd seen on television or in social media were in fact clients and employees of Infidelity.

"Miss Collins?"

"Yes, I agree."

"Are you currently in a relationship?"

While I should have thought of Bryce and the announcement Alton had planned to make at my party, my mind went to Nox.

"No, I'm not."

She pointed again. "Please initial here."

As I read through the agreement, the increased moisture of my palms made the pen in my grasp more difficult to hold. Nevertheless, I did hold it and I did initial. When we came to the final line, the one asking for my full legal signature, I took a deep breath and penned: *Alexandria Collins*. After all, if I were to own this decision, Alexandria would be coming along for the ride.

A few hours later, Karen escorted me down the secret elevator.

"Alex, I'll be in touch with you. I know that your classes will be beginning shortly. This process takes time. We won't have the results of your evaluations for at least a few days. After that, the pairing, while not rocket science, is an arduous procedure. Infidelity's success is contingent upon a successful coupling. It could take weeks or longer if the perfect client has yet to join our organization. Please do not contact me. I'll contact you. Once we learn the results of your evaluations, I'll inform you of your employment status. Other than your reimbursement for your time today, financial compensation begins then. The five thousand dollars for today will appear in your bank account in the next three to five business days. We thank you for your time."

"Thank you, Ms. Flores."

We shook hands as she left me alone to enter the main elevator. With each floor of my descent, I wavered in my resolve. Twenty-four hours ago I'd never heard of Infidelity. Forty-eight hours ago I was walking away from Montague Manor. I straightened my shoulders. Alton and Adelaide would never know how I'd ensured my education. They'd never know that I'd sold myself. All they'd know is that I went to Columbia and they were never burdened with the bill. In my mind, my defiance of their plan gave my decision credence.

Twenty thousand dollars per month for one year with no expense for rent. Even if I needed to purchase essentials, I could save money. I already had a decent wardrobe. After only one year, I could ensure my tuition at Columbia, not just for the rest of this year, but also for the entire three years of the program.

When I stepped into the lobby Patrick and Cy were both there. Their questioning gazes asked what they couldn't verbally.

Patrick wrapped me in a hug. "Hey, little cousin, how are you?"

I shrugged. "I think I'm all right."

Cy smiled at us. "I know a great little piano bar. Who'd like a drink?"

"Me," Patrick and I said in unison.

CHAPTER 23

◦○◦

Present

NOX

UNDER THE LIGHTS of my private gym, the small beads of perspiration glistened on my skin. Faster and faster I pushed as sweat coated my body, saturating my shirt and shorts. *Harder, quicker, one more mile...* the internal commands kept me moving, kept my feet in rhythm as I continued my workout. Sometimes I wondered who I punished the most—me or the treadmill. I knew the treadmill wasn't a person, yet sometimes I thought of it that way.

I'd assign it a name and beat it into submission: each slap of my foot was a mark, each pounding mile was the pushing of my designated person's limits. Allowing my mind to imagine while experiencing the physical exertion was socially more acceptable than the actual acts I envisioned. The law frowned upon bondage and corporal punishment. As CFO, senior vice president, and heir apparent of Demetri Enterprises, acting out my desires in real life would meet more than the law's disapproval. My father, Oren Demetri, CEO and president of Demetri Enterprises, would head the line to cast the first stone.

It didn't matter that I'd spent the last six years learning the ins and outs of every company in the Demetri Enterprises portfolio. I knew the CEOs, as well as their assistants, by name. I knew which ones made profits and which ones reported losses, quarterly as well as annually. I knew the extent of our investment and the margin on our returns.

My father would tell anyone who'd listen how he'd built Demetri Enterprises from nothing. He'd talk about his great ability, even at a young age, and how others had used it for their benefit. Then he'd bore the listener with his one-man rendition recounting his subjugated life of underappreciation, until the day he decided enough was enough and he deserved the benefits of his abilities—the day Demetri Enterprises was conceived.

In all of Oren's grand speech, he'd forget to mention how it all nearly came crashing down. He wouldn't admit that he was unprepared for the crash that brought Wall Street to its knees. Experts have argued that it hadn't been as bad as Black Monday in 1987; the difference was that the crash that almost ended Demetri Enterprises lasted longer.

Talking heads discussed the *loss of paper wealth* versus *real wealth*. That comparison was indistinguishable when margins were called and there was nothing to give. With financial institutions closing their doors and the unemployment rate soaring, panic became the norm.

Not long out of graduate school, it was my knowledge and understanding of the financial climate that kept Demetri from scrumming to the same fate as many other companies. My father may have birthed Demetri, he may have manhandled his way through board meetings and backroom agreements, but I had the education, knew the history, and worked my ass off to keep it solvent.

While Oren swam his way out of a bottle, I worked the new environment. It was a different terrain. Not unnavigable.

That's not to say I didn't take risks—I did. With me, Demetri Enterprises diversified. Every decision was calculated. It was a time when few businesses were investing. Therefore, even small investments were made with painstaking analysis. I didn't approach an opportunity because someone in a dark room of a private club told me I should. I scrutinized the data, the market, the climate, everything. Not only did Demetri survive, it was now stronger than ever.

That dedication to Demetri Enterprises cost me more than I ever imagined. I sold a part of my soul and lost her in the process. Would it have made it better if Oren had acknowledged my sacrifice? It wouldn't have brought Jocelyn back.

One more mile. Just one more.

The calves of my legs protested and my breathing labored, but the clock on the wall told me I had time. That's what waking before the sun will do. It provided more hours of productive time—hours that others wasted in bed. I will have accomplished a ten-mile run, cleared the demons from my head—the ones that gathered in the night—and still be in the office before half of our employees.

Since Jo, the name I called Jocelyn, I didn't waste time. I never slept late, never took my mind off the prize—with one exception. One week. My one true taste of what life could've been. I'd forgotten what happiness was, and now that I remembered, I wished I didn't.

Although I still checked my private cell phone daily for any sign of communication, in what remained of my heart I knew it wouldn't come. The first day and even the second after Del Mar, I'd hoped. Charli had shaken my world, made me forget who I was and what I believed. She'd also made me forget that hope was nothing but a vindictive bastard that took up residence inside and gave a false promise of something outside of your control.

In one short week, she'd made me forget that life was about control. Only I can control my own destiny. For a sliver of time I let myself have hope. With each passing day, I saw my error and worked to put that vindictive bastard back in the steel lined box it deserved.

In hindsight, I should never have allowed myself that luxury. I should have seen the signs. I knew them all too well. Shit, I carried them. They were banners written in a language that only those who share in it can read. There was a sadness and a drive in Charli's beautiful golden eyes, that I recognized and understood. We never said more, never shared our demons. We played by our rules.

That didn't mean I didn't see her ghosts lurking and watching. I saw hers because I knew mine. Just like the companies and Demetri Enterprise investments, I knew the names of my ghosts. My prize for surviving, when Jo didn't, would be that one day my ghosts would experience a punishment that only I could deliver. If Charli dreamt of the same fate for her ghosts, I understood how she was too focused to remember Del Mar.

Beep, beep, beep.

The treadmill's speed slowed and the incline decreased. A five-minute cooldown and I'd get ready for the office. As my steps slowed, I tried to think about the screen on the wall—the television broadcasting the latest financial news from the European markets. I willed myself to concentrate on the financial crisis in Greece. Hell, I even thought about what I'd eat for breakfast.

None of it stuck. They were but fleeting thoughts as the scent of Charli's auburn hair filled my senses—the sweet aroma as she slept, her back against my chest, my chin on her head, her soft curves wrapped in my arms, and her firm ass rubbing against me. Instead of running and pushing my legs for that last half-mile, when I closed my eyes, I was easing into her tight pussy, feeling her warmth as her body hugged me, contracting in warm waves.

Beep, beep, beep.

Fuck!

Not only would my shower be cold again this morning, but my legs wouldn't be the only part of me getting a workout. Jacking off just got moved to the top of my morning schedule. I should have known. Since Del Mar it had become a permanent staple in my routine.

I'D TEXTED ISAAC, my driver, to be outside of the building at seven o'clock. Traffic was beginning to build and leaving early could save me as much as twenty minutes on the nearly eight-mile drive. It all depended upon the backup on the FDR.

I hadn't looked at Isaac's response until I was in the elevator. Every morning it was the same: *YES, SIR, MR. DEMETRI, I WILL BE WAITING.* That was why I was surprised when I read today's.

Isaac: *"MR. DEMETRI, MRS. WITT INSISTED ON ACCOMPANYING YOU TO THE OFFICE TODAY. SHE IS WAITING IN THE CAR."*

What the fuck?

Mrs. Witt wasn't my housekeeper as Charli had surmised. Even Deloris laughed when I told her that. Deloris Witt was the head of my security. She wasn't the muscle. Those were the people she hired. She was the brains. With a CIA background and computer skills that rivaled some of the best hackers in the world, she was the one who kept me informed on all things Demetri Enterprises. Hell, she kept me informed on all things Lennox Demetri.

We had a regularly scheduled appointment every Monday morning. During that time she briefed me on everything I would need to know during the upcoming week. Today wasn't Monday. It was Wednesday.

Deloris was more than the brains behind my security, she was one of the few people I considered a friend. Jocelyn introduced us, and after I lost my wife, Deloris was the only one who understood. Although there wasn't enough of an age difference, Deloris had thought of Jocelyn as a daughter. Since Jo's family shut me out, and my family didn't care, Deloris Witt was the one who acknowledged my loss—our loss. Sometimes I wondered if her current devotion was because of me or because of Jo. Either way, it was there.

Deloris had been with me in Del Mar because of the sensitive meetings scheduled during that trip and because she had family in the area. As the head of my security, she'd kept my detail intact and out of sight. As my friend, she'd been elated that I was interested in someone. It was impossible for her two roles not to meet.

From the time I met Charli at the pool in Del Mar, until hours before she entered the presidential suite, I had no doubt that Mrs. Witt knew everything about her. I didn't need to ask. If she hadn't known or had learned anything that she felt would be detrimental, she would have suggested I cancel the first dinner. Instead she made menu suggestions and helped.

Although I was curious when I asked the front desk to deliver flowers to Charli's room and learned there was no one by that name listed in their reservation, I never asked Deloris for more information. Even after Charli ran off, I sought out Chelsea myself. I wanted to learn about Charli with an *i* from the fascinating golden-eyed beauty herself.

After the first night, after I found Charli in her suite, I specifically told

Deloris that I didn't want to know any more. The mystery of Charli was part of her allure.

"Good morning, Mr. Demetri. It's going to be another warm one." The doorman greeted me as he opened the door to the street. I didn't need the weather app on my phone. I had Hudson.

Instead of replying, I simply nodded, letting Hudson know that I'd heard. I was too preoccupied with the reason Deloris was in the backseat of my car.

Hudson was right, as usual. Humid air blanketed me as I exited the cool building, instantly plastering my starched shirt to my skin beneath my suit jacket. The semi-circular drive only held a few cars at once. That limitation often required drivers or taxis to idle out on the street and be called when the riders were ready for pick-up. Isaac was never on the street. If I said I'd be present at seven o'clock, I meant six fifty-five. I never wondered as I stepped onto the brick walkway if Isaac would be there. He always was.

When I saw the large car, I knew it was Isaac, even though he wasn't driving my usual Mercedes. Instead, he had one of the Demetri Enterprises limousines. The change in vehicle set my nerves on alert. Something was going down and whatever it was Deloris wanted to discuss it privately.

Stepping from the driver's seat, Isaac met me at the backseat door. "Sir, good morning. Did you receive my text?"

"Good morning, Isaac. I did. I see Mrs. Witt wasn't comfortable in the sedan."

"No, sir," he answered as he opened my door.

I tried to read Deloris's expression as I sat, but with her experience she was a master of non-disclosure.

Once the door was closed and we began to move, she began, "Mr. Demetri, I considered calling you last night, and then I decided this information was best shared in person."

"You have my curiosity piqued. Is it Oren? Did he do something?"

"No, sir." She uncharacteristically took a moment to consider her words.

"Mrs. Witt…" When she addressed me as *Mr. Demetri*, it meant the matter was strictly business. "…out with it."

"It's about Infidelity."

I clenched my teeth. I hated that company. Demetri Enterprises was one of its biggest investors. I wished I could blame my father for that one, say that he got involved one late night in a high-stakes poker game and ended up with a company that sold *companionship*, but I couldn't. It was all me. It had nothing to do with the business itself. What I saw was a financial opportunity and took it. Demetri Enterprises was involved from the ground level of Infidelity and that partnership had netted us millions. My biggest fear was that one day the companionship side of Infidelity would be made public. The name, Infidelity, was bad enough. The exclusive website portion was a great cover and actually profitable. It was the companionship side that bothered me. Ashley Madison had been hacked. Infidelity could be too.

On more than one occasion, I voiced my concerns to Deloris. She agreed that while anything was possible, she personally worked with Infidelity techs to ensure that the latest firewalls and preventive measures were constantly in place.

"Was it compromised?" I asked, my question coming out more as a growl while I forced my shallow breaths to enter and exit from my nose.

"No, sir. The information is secure. It's something else. Something that I found yesterday."

She handed me a large manila envelope.

Releasing the clasp, I pulled out a picture, one printed on standard white paper. The medium made the photo grainy but that didn't stop me from recognizing the woman. I knew her immediately, every inch of her.

"What the fuck?" I asked as I checked the envelope for more information. "What does Charli have to do with Infidelity? How the fuck...?" I couldn't make the necessary mental connections to form articulate questions.

"I have more," Mrs. Witt said. "I have her profile. But I thought maybe you might not want... well, you'd said you didn't."

"She has a *profile*?" I asked in disbelief.

"Yes, it was just created yesterday. From what I've seen, she was interviewed yesterday by Karen Flores. Ms. Flores's comments were favorable. Her recommendation was to accept... umm... *Charli's* application for employment, contingent upon the results of her medical and psychological evaluations. Miss Charli signed the agreement of intent."

I turned my head to the window, trying to tether the rage flowing rapidly through my system. If this were a man delivering this news, I might very well have punched him, but it wasn't.

"Lennox," Mrs. Witt said in a more placating tone. "I found this before it was forwarded to anyone. No clients have been considered. Besides the customary employees—doctor, psychologist, Karen, photographer, and assistants—no one knows about this. All of those people are bound by confidentiality."

"How? Why?"

"I'm not sure of how, other than that a gentleman named Cyrus Perry is her sponsor."

"Cyrus Perry, that name sounds vaguely familiar."

"He's not employed by Demetri or any of its subsidiaries. I'll look further into him," she said as she scribbled a note in the margin of her notebook.

"Why?"

"From the profile, it appears as though she has had a recent loss of financial stability. She had a trust fund that's now gone. She's recently been accepted..." Deloris's voice trailed away. "I'm sorry. I've probably already said more than you wanted to know."

"She's been accepted...?"

"To Columbia Law."

Columbia Law School is here. Charli's here in Manhattan.

"This profile was completed yesterday?" I asked. "Blocks from my office?" Infidelity had expanded to numerous locations throughout the country, yet Charli had been blocks from me.

"Yes, sir."

If she had financial problems she should have called me. Why the fuck didn't she call me? Did she delete my number? My jaw clenched and unclenched. Silence prevailed as my thoughts swirled. They were a tornado, a violent cyclone capable of massive destruction. Clenching my teeth, I tried to calm them, at least a little.

Finally, Mrs. Witt asked, "Would you like me to call Ms. Flores?"

And what? Tell her to reject Charli? If she'd been willing to do this for money, what would she do if this didn't work? As much as I hated Infidelity, the people there did a good job of insuring the health and wealth of their employees as well as the anonymity of their clients.

"No, Deloris. Give me Ms. Flores's direct number. I'll call her."

"Sir, I don't need to remind you that using your office or home phone…"

"No, you don't."

Deloris reached into her purse and pulled out a flip phone. "This is a burner."

I nodded. "Thank you. Thank you for bringing this directly to me."

"Her profile?"

I sighed. "I would assume that if I asked Ms. Flores about *Charli* she wouldn't know who I was speaking about?"

"That's correct. The name on the profile is Alexandria Collins."

Alexandria Collins?

Where the hell did *Charli* come from?

As memories of Del Mar and 101 settled the storm in my head, I began to form a plan. "This conversation never occurred, and after I speak to Ms. Flores, Alexandria Collins's profile will be deleted permanently. Can you take care of that for me?"

"Yes, sir."

CHAPTER 24

———•○•———

Present

ALEX

As I LAY in bed, the quiet apartment did nothing to ease my laziness that minute by minute was augmented by self-pity. It was after eleven in the morning and the one thing I wanted to do was call Chelsea. I kept thinking about the time difference and knew she'd be awake now. I wanted to talk to her and confess what I'd done. Patrick and Cy had been supportive and encouraging throughout last night, but they weren't Chelsea, weren't my best friend. They didn't know me like she did. No one did.

I couldn't call. Speaking to her about Infidelity would be a breach of the agreement.

I couldn't even discuss the specifics last night with Cy and Patrick, and they knew about Infidelity. Even without my saying much, it was clear they both understood my ongoing inner turmoil. One minute, I was happy that I'd found a solution and law school was secure. During those moments, I wanted to hug Patrick and Cy. Then, five minutes later, I was mortified at the solution I'd accepted. I questioned my decision: maybe I should have looked around more for another job or I could have spoken to the bursar's office at Columbia about student loans.

It was as I lay in bed that I began to worry about my *client*. What if I didn't like him? What if he didn't like me? What if I ended up being the first exception to Infidelity's abuse clause? What if he wasn't my type? Though I'd answered a very intense and extensive list of questions, was that really enough to accurately pair me with someone I'd never met?

I also wondered about my apartment. I didn't know if I should keep it or call and break the lease. Housing was mandatory for Infidelity. My client would provide it, and more than likely it would be with him. Then again, just because I was required to live with this unknown man, having a place of my own sounded nice. After all, my apartment was near campus. I could use it as a place to study. With a monthly salary of twenty thousand dollars, the apartment's rent of three thousand was no longer an issue.

I stared at the ceiling. As tears dripped like a leaky faucet from the corners of my eyes, I wondered if I could do this. At this moment, getting out of bed seemed a monumental effort. How could I follow through? My pillow was damp, but I made no attempt to hold back my tears. I contemplated curling into a ball and never moving. I'd tried that before, but no matter where I hid, Jane always found me.

With each passing minute my sense of loathing grew. Every ounce of the repugnant emotion was directed at myself. *I'd* done this. I'd betrayed everything I'd ever stood for. I lied to myself, thinking that Alex was an improvement over Alexandria. She wasn't. She was worse. I'd made this decision. It wasn't done to me.

Adelaide and Alton had been right about one thing: they knew Alexandria would sell herself given the right incentive. They just didn't realize I would sell myself to a stranger.

Would I be better off back at Montague Manor with Bryce?

The ringing of my phone shattered the silent air, stilled my interior monologue, and pulled me from my funk. The number flashing on the screen was unknown. I suddenly worried that it was Bryce. Why hadn't I programmed his name in my phone before I deleted his text messages?

Wiping my eyes, I made the decision that I was done hiding. It never worked when I was young; it wouldn't work now. I sat up and steeled my shoulders. Exhaling a deep breath, I answered on the fourth ring, barely saving the caller from my voicemail. "Hello."

"Miss Collins?"

The voice wasn't Bryce's. It was a woman. "Yes, this is she," I replied as my mind came to life with the possible identity of the caller: someone from Columbia—Alton had withdrawn my tuition, someone about my apartment—they needed to see me. I hadn't had the chance to reach the correct possibility before the woman spoke.

"Miss Collins, this is Karen Flores from Infidelity. We spoke yesterday."

Did she really think I'd forgotten?

"Yes, Ms. Flores, I remember." Maybe I failed the exam? Probably the psychological one. They thought I was too crazy to be someone's companion. If I had failed, I wondered if I'd be relieved or upset.

"Miss Collins, this is highly unusual. However, I need you to come to the office immediately."

"Immediately?"

"As soon as you can get here. How soon could that be?"

I hadn't moved since last night. After the piano bar, Cy, Patrick, and I went to dinner. By that time, I'd consumed a few too many martinis. It wasn't my drink of choice, mostly because I wasn't used to them. After dinner, we came back to the apartment and Patrick poured me more than one glass of wine. The alcohol had undoubtedly been my coping mechanism, helping me come to terms with the decisions I'd made. I was getting closer to becoming Adelaide day by day.

Considering the circumstances, I decided I had the right to overindulge. That was fine then. Now I reeked of stale booze and needed a shower. "I'm afraid it will take me a few hours."

"This is extremely important. Be here by one."

Shit! That is in two hours.

"Yes, I can do that. Ms. Flores?"

"Yes?"

"Is there a problem with my application?"

"We'll discuss it in person." The line went dead.

Reflexively, I tapped the first four numbers of Chelsea's cell number.

That was all it took to have her full number, name, and smiling face on my screen. Before I hit the green icon, I remembered that I couldn't tell her about Infidelity or ask her what to do. The sense of loneliness surrounded me as I deleted the numbers and called Patrick.

"I don't know," he said. "That didn't happen to me. I told you it was about three weeks before I was introduced..."

I sighed. "Well, I'd better get cleaned up and go."

"Yes," he confirmed. "Don't be late and let me know what happens."

"I will," I said, disconnecting the call. Talking to Patrick didn't ease my nerves. If anything, it made them worse. My stomach twisted as I worked to make myself less of a hungover, depressed excuse for a human and more of the confident put-together woman who'd been at Infidelity yesterday.

I had no idea what to wear. I wished I could wear the suit I'd worn the day before, but that wouldn't do. My clothing choices were limited. The movers weren't going to get my things from California until tomorrow. All that I had with me were the clothes I'd taken to Savannah.

With my clean hair—smelling like shampoo instead of old alcohol—pulled back into a low ponytail and my best attempt at reproducing Andrew's makeup, I decided to wear a simple sleeveless navy sheath dress and navy pumps. If the dress had a jacket it would be very Jackie O. Luckily, I'd packed it with Montague Manor dining protocol in mind.

That made me laugh.

Well, thank you, Mother, for your ridiculous dress code. If you weren't of that disposition, I wouldn't have the proper attire to meet with my new pimp.

That sounded brash, even inside my own head, but I couldn't think of a good argument to refute any of it.

As the taxi approached 17 State Street, I rubbed my moist palms over my dress for the hundredth time and looked at my watch. The traffic was worse than it'd been yesterday, or maybe it was just my imagination. Either way, I was pushing my deadline when I raced into the lobby and pushed the up button in need of an elevator.

There were so many elevators in New York. I wondered if anyone knew the exact number. There was the elevator in Patrick's building and the one here. I could go an entire week in Palo Alto and never ride one elevator. I didn't mind steps. That said, steps to a third floor and steps to the thirty-seventh were two different things.

"Miss Collins—" I began to say to the receptionist sitting behind the large desk for Infidelity when she lifted her hand and stopped my words.

She pushed a button near her ear and spoke into a Bluetooth, "Ms. Flores, Miss Collins has arrived." She lifted her eyes to me. "She'll be right out."

I was certain that I was paranoid, but Karen's greeting was less friendly than it seemed yesterday. I didn't say anything until we were behind her closed office door. When we were, I asked, "Is there a problem? Have I done something wrong?"

Maybe someone heard me talking to Cy and Patrick. I worried about my five thousand dollars. I needed that money. Even if I was going to be told that I didn't meet the criteria for Infidelity, I'd already made mental plans for the interview money.

Karen sat and adjusted her shoulders. "No, Miss Collins. You haven't done anything wrong. Your pairing has moved with record speed."

My heart stopped beating as the blood drained from my face and settled in my stomach. "M-My pairing?"

She had a black pen in her hand and twisted it as she spoke. "Yes. Today is the first day of your one-year commitment, the first day of your agreement."

"I-I thought maybe you called me here to reject me."

"No, Miss Collins. You are officially an Infidelity employee, and I have strict instructions for you." She took a deep breath, stood, and walked to my side of the desk. Looking down, she continued, "Your agreement has been sold. The client paid not only the first and last month's fee, but in order to expedite the process, he paid a rather large bonus. A percentage of that will be added to your first month's salary."

The butterflies in my stomach turned into full-grown bats.

Oh my God, this is happening.

"H-He's not married, is he?" It was the first question that popped into my mind.

"No. Your hard limits were taken into consideration."

"Is he… is he nice?"

Karen's upper lip disappeared momentarily between her teeth before she answered. "Your client's name is Mr. Demetri. He asked that I not say any more. Mr. Demetri is a very decisive man who knows what he wants. Alex, he wants you, and now he has you, for one year. Granted, I do not know him the way you will get to know him, but *nice* isn't an adjective I've often heard associated with Mr. Demetri. I've only spoken to him on the telephone, but I've seen his picture. He's handsome, refined, and well-mannered. He's also high profile. He knows what's at stake." She reached back on her desk and picked up a card. "This is the card I promised you yesterday. I don't believe it will be necessary, and, as I told you, it has never been needed in the history of Infidelity; however, you should keep it. It's your safety net."

My eyes widened as I reached for the card. Gripping was increasingly difficult with my trembling fingers. As I dropped the card in my purse, I asked, "Is he in New York? I can't be somewhere else. Maybe I should withdraw my application?"

"Miss Collins, Mr. Demetri is aware of your law-school obligations. He's an important man and has set his sights on you. From today until this date a year from now, for lack of a better phrase, Mr. Demetri *owns* you. When you signed the agreement yesterday afternoon, you forfeited the ability to withdraw."

"W-What do I do?"

"Whatever he tells you to do."

The thundering of my heart threatened to drown out her words.

Whatever he tells you to do.

I fought to breathe, to take in deep breaths. "Will he contact me?"

She handed me a piece of paper, a Post-it note. *Really?* On the small yellow square was a telephone number. I recognized the Manhattan area code of 646. It was the same as Patrick's. "You are to call him."

"H-He wants me to call him?"

"Now."

"Now?" I asked, staring at the ten numbers.

"Miss Collins, I didn't take the order as a request when I was given the instructions. Neither should you."

My mouth dried as perspiration coated my skin. "You want me to call him right now, here... in front of you?"

She nodded.

Shit!

"May I please have a drink of water?"

Karen stepped to a sideboard and poured a glass of water. The silver metal pitcher was covered in droplets of condensation. Next she opened a cabinet, removed a crystal decanter with amber liquid, and poured a finger into another tumbler.

"Here," she said, handing me both glasses.

"Thank you." I placed the strong-smelling liquid on a nearby table and took a long drink of the water. Placing the empty glass next to what I assumed was whiskey, I removed my phone from my purse and began to dial.

6- My fingers shook. 4- Patrick's name came to the screen. 6- I took a deep breath. 5- My screen read: *NOX- PRIVATE NUMBER.*

My eyes widened as they simultaneously blurred with tears.

"No." My head moved from side to side as the barely audible word hung in the air.

I looked at the yellow Post-it and back to my screen. It was the same number.

My phone fell to my lap as I sucked in a breath and held tightly to my lower lip. "I-I can't. I can't call this number." If I did I was breaking our rule. If I did I'd have to face *him*. It wouldn't be like it was at Del Mar. This would be different. I would need him and he'd know it. "Please, Ms. Flores, please let me back out of my agreement. You don't even need to pay me for yesterday. We'll just call it a mistake, and I promise I won't tell a soul."

"Miss Collins, Mr. Demetri is waiting for your call."

The words she'd said earlier rang through my mind. *He set his sights on you. For the next year, he owns you.*

I didn't need to dial any more numbers; all I needed to do was touch the little green icon next to his name.

Oh fuck. I'm going to open the door.

I pushed it.

"Charli." The deep, velvety voice came through my phone, sending shivers down my spine.

I reached for the whiskey and swallowed.

"Nox," I replied, trying my best to sound confident.

"Mr. Demetri." His tone held no emotion. "The rules have changed."

The end of *Betrayal*...

CUNNING

CHARLI & NOX

Coming January 19, 2016, the continuing story of Charli and Nox.

As old rules are broken and new rules are set,
who will prove the most CUNNING?

Book #2 of the Infidelity series, *Cunning*, by Aleatha Romig.

SNEAK PEEK:

CUNNING

●○●

ALEATHA ROMIG

"MR. DEMETRI?" I couldn't process, couldn't do much more than to repeat his words. In only a matter of minutes I'd become a parrot, not the strong, confident woman I wanted to project.

"Yes, *Miss Collins*. New rules... *my* rules. You should say thank you."

I squeezed the phone tighter. The whiskey running through my veins had worked to still my trembling but had done little to slow my rapid heartbeat. I closed my eyes, trying to remember the man at Del Mar. His tone didn't match.

"Miss Collins, I told you to say *thank you*."

I wasn't sure if it was hearing his deep voice again or the difference in his demeanor, but my tattered nerves were ping-ponging between an emotional breakdown and a hysterical fit of laughter. I looked up at Karen, unsure if she could hear. When she nodded, I knew she did.

He owns you. Whatever he tells you to do.

"Thank you," I whispered.

"By calling my number you broke our rule. I told you once before how I'd respond if you ever again broke one of my rules. Do you remember?"

I remembered. I also remembered he hadn't been specific. Now didn't

213

seem like the time to mention that. My chin dropped to my chest.

"Nox, please."

"*Mr. Demetri.* Don't make me repeat myself. Listen closely. This is exactly what you will do."

I swallowed. The rush of blood coursing through my ears, my injured pride, and the multiple rebuttals forming in my head and gathering at the tip of my tongue, all worked together to dim the volume of his words. Nevertheless, as the Infidelity employee I now was, I did as my client said and listened.

"Go down to the street. My driver is waiting. His name is Isaac, and he'll recognize you."

"I-I—"

"Miss Collins, your opportunity for negotiation has passed. It's time for our reunion. I paid handsomely for it."

I might have thought it before, but now it was official: Nox owned me.

I might have sold my soul, but by the way my insides clenched at the velvet voice, I knew that my soul wasn't the only commodity Nox had purchased.

After he finished speaking, I sat statuesque, holding the phone, waiting for anything, a goodbye, something. Instead, silence prevailed. When I turned the screen toward me I saw only his name and knew he'd hung up.

Oh shit! Now what do I do?

As if reading my mind, Karen handed me the glass with the remaining whiskey, nodded, and said, "*Whatever* he tells you to do."

CUNNING
Coming… January 19, 2016.

WHAT TO DO NOW...

LEND IT: Did you enjoy *Betrayal?* Do you have a friend who'd enjoy *Betrayal?* *Betrayal* may be lent one time. Sharing is caring!

RECOMMEND IT: Do you have multiple friends who'd enjoy *Betrayal?* Tell them about it! Call, text, post, tweet... your recommendation is the nicest gift you can give to an author!

REVIEW IT: Tell the world. Please go to the retailer where you purchased this book, as well as Goodreads, and write a review.

STAY CONNECTED
WITH ALEATHA

Do you love Aleatha's writing? Do you want to know the latest about INFIDELITY? CONSEQUENCES? TALES FROM THE DARK SIDE? and Aleatha's new series coming in 2016 from Thomas and Mercer?

Do you like EXCLUSIVE content (never released scenes, never released excerpts, and more)? Would you like the monthly chance to win prizes (signed books and gift cards)? Then sign up today for Aleatha's monthly newsletter and stay informed on all things Aleatha Romig.

Sign up for Aleatha's NEWSLETTER: (recipients receive exclusive material and offers) http://aleatharomig.blogspot.com/

You can also find Aleatha@

Check out her blog: http://aleatharomig.blogspot.com
Facebook: http://www.Facebook.com/AleathaRomig
Twitter: https://twitter.com/AleathaRomig
Goodreads: www.goodreads.com/author/show/5131072.Aleatha_Romig
Instagram: http://instagram.com/aleatharomig
Email Aleatha: aleatharomig@gmail.com

You may also listen Aleatha Romig books on Audible.

BOOKS BY NEW YORK TIMES BESTSELLING AUTHOR ALEATHA ROMIG

INFIDELITY SERIES:

BETRAYAL

Book #1

(October 2015)

CUNNING

Book #2

(January 2016)

DECEPTION

Book #3

(TBA)

ENTRAPMENT

Book #4

(TBA)

FIDELITY

Book #5

(TBA)

THE CONSEQUENCES SERIES:

CONSEQUENCES
(Book #1)
Released August 2011

TRUTH
(Book #2)
Released October 2012

CONVICTED
(Book #3)
Released October 2013

REVEALED
(Book #4)
Previously titled: Behind His Eyes Convicted: The Missing Years
Re-released June 2014

BEYOND THE CONSEQUENCES
(Book #5)
Released January 2015

COMPANION READS:

BEHIND HIS EYES—CONSEQUENCES
(Book #1.5)
Released January 2014

BEHIND HIS EYES—TRUTH
(Book #2.5)
Released March 2014

TALES FROM THE DARK SIDE SERIES:

INSIDIOUS

(All books in this series are stand-alone erotic thrillers)

Released October 2014

DUPLICITY

(Completely unrelated to book #1)

Release TBA

ALEATHA ROMIG

Aleatha Romig is a New York Times and USA Today bestselling author who lives in Indiana. She grew up in Mishawaka, graduated from Indiana University, and is currently living south of Indianapolis. Aleatha has raised three children with her high school sweetheart and husband of nearly thirty years. Before she became a full-time author, she worked days as a dental hygienist and spent her nights writing. Now, when she's not imagining mind-blowing twists and turns, she likes to spend her time with her family and friends. Her other pastimes include reading and creating heroes/anti-heroes who haunt your dreams!

Aleatha released her first novel, CONSEQUENCES, in August of 2011. CONSEQUENCES became a bestselling series with five novels and two companions released from 2011 through 2015. The compelling and epic story of Anthony and Claire Rawlings has graced more than half a million e-readers. Aleatha released the first of her series TALES FROM THE DARK SIDE, INSIDIOUS, in the fall of 2014. These stand-alone thrillers continue Aleatha's twisted style with an increase in heat. In the fall of 2015, Aleatha will move headfirst into the world of dark romance with the release of BETRAYAL, the first of her five-novel INFIDELITY series. Aleatha has entered the traditional world of publishing with Thomas and Mercer with her SAVED series. The first of that series, INTO THE LIGHT, will be published in 2016.

Aleatha is a "Published Author's Network" member of the Romance Writers of America and represented by Danielle Egan-Miller of Browne & Miller Literary Associates.

Made in the USA
San Bernardino, CA
12 December 2017